I0760741

The Sword and The Savage

By Elexis Bell

This is a work of fiction. Resemblance to actual persons, living or dead, is purely coincidental.

ISBN: 978-1-951335-21-2

And if you're eager to stay up to date on the latest dark fiction by Elexis Bell, sign up for her newsletter here:

http://eepurl.com/gnTZwf

Contents

The Sword and The Savage
Valkaihlen Village
Lessiyara's Cabin
Ronan's Cottage
Soorahk Mine
Cemetary
Soorahk Village

Pronunciation Guide

Of course, you're free to pronounce things as you wish inside this book, but for those who wish to have a pronunciation guide, here's how I pronounce the names in my head.

Main Characters:

Lessiyara- Less-ee-YAH-rah

Ronan- RO-nan

Other Characters:

Berinasten- Bear-i-NAHS-ten

Brahtek- BRAH-tek

Coren- CORE-in

Reti- REH-ty (like tea)

Selto- SELL-toh

Sihetva- See-HET-vuh

Skarsi- SCAR-see

Sureenassa- Soor-ee-NAHS-uh

Tivasta- Ti (as in tick)-VAHS-tuh

Vahken- VAH-kin

Vasret- VAHS-ret

Vilashi- Vil (like in village)-AH-she

Races:

Soorahk- Soo-ROCK

Vaikahlen- Vai (silent a, long i)-CALL-in

Named Plants:

Bastevi- Buh-STEV (like the first e in 'ever')-ee

Slanta- SLAHN (like the a in 'call')-tuh

Velsta- VEL (like in Velcro)-stuh

Named Animals:

Maurubeast- MAHR-oo-beast

Sivets- SIV-its

Chapter One
Lessiyara

If a child's heart is strong enough, Sihetva's mark will appear within days of birth.
- The ways of Sihetva

I grit my teeth as the cane slams down on my back, and a small whimper escapes me. My breath comes in harsh gasps, and I try to hold back the tears. They swim in my eyes, blurring my snow-white wrists, my coal-black fingers on the stone floor.

"Another, then?" Father asks, voice cool, controlled.

He brings the cane down once more, and this time, I make no sound. My jaw aches, and I worry my teeth may break apart with the force of my clenched jaw.

But I'm quiet.

A single tear splashes onto the stone, and I shift my hand to cover it, even as I brace for the next hit.

But it doesn't come.

"Good," Father says. "Maybe if you can learn to control your emotions, one of my men might consider taking you off my hands."

A foul prize that would be.

"As it were," he continues, voice as even as ever, "your weakness means you are still my problem."

Not for long. Not if I can help it.

The thought of my little home in the woods, my home in progress, eases some of the tension. I take a few deep breaths, regaining some level of control.

"Go, you little savage. Into the woods with you. Commune with our mountain, our cold winds. Maybe this time you can learn from them."

I sit back on my haunches, staring up at him with my face as expressionless as I can manage. He meets my gaze, features unblemished by the wild emotions that rule me far too often. His long white tail rests in the air behind him, the black tip still. The furred tips of his ears perch steadily. They don't flick to the sides, tracing the sounds of the wind, looking out for threats.

Because he's safe here.

Our village lives according to his rule.

And so do I. For now.

With a sage nod, I climb to my feet and move toward my room to pack. Silently, I hope he'll be gone before I return, chiding myself all the while for what his trip away means for the Soorahk people in the valley.

***

Just get out of here.

Shouldering my pack, I keep my footsteps light on the stone floor. Father should be asleep now, resting for his coming journey and likely exhausted from the caning he gave me earlier. Bruises already discolor my back, but it's nothing new.

My heart spasms in my chest, but I draw a deep breath, schooling my features, hiding the fear and loneliness that slither through me.

After all, my stupid heart got me into this in the first place.

I slip through the door, relishing the cold wind on my face. My pack sits heavily on my back, comforting me despite the agony of its weight on fresh bruises. I'll need everything it holds in the coming weeks.

Repressing a sigh, a sign of emotion, I step out into the snow and ice of our mountaintop village. The other residents move about, unconcerned. These people should be kindred spirits, but they barely offer me a glance. They keep their gazes cool and controlled, their faces unwrinkled by smiles, laughter, or sadness.

Placid.

Strong.

Better than me.

Again, my heart twists, and a frown tugs at my lips.

A nearby woman stares at me, blinking slowly. She doesn't show her disapproval, but I feel it in her gaze, heavy and hard to bear. I buckle before her, dropping my eyes to the snow at my feet.

"You'll learn eventually," she says, her voice completely even, bordering on monotone.

I draw a deep breath and regain my control. Meeting her gaze without expression, I say, "I must venture out to commune with the mountain for a few weeks."

Silently, I congratulate myself for my smooth tone. No hint of emotion leaked out, despite the shambling pace of my heart after yet another beating, yet another cold lecture of the dangers of my untamed emotions.

I measure my breaths, count my heartbeats, trying to even them out.

"The cold will do you good," the woman answers. The white and black fur at the tips of her motionless ears blows in a gentle breeze. She holds her long white tail perfectly still, one with the mountain and the ice. Its black tip doesn't move, doesn't flick back and forth.

But mine does.

Breathing slowly, evenly, I still my body.

I nod, agreeing with her assessment, Father's assessment. Then, I turn and trek out into the trees to commune with the cold mountain we Vaikahlen are meant to embody. I feel the magic of our home in the ruthless wind, in the stoic mountain.

My feet send showers of snow ahead of me, kicking the soft powder loose with every step, disturbing the pristine beauty of this place. Just like I always do.

The wind whips my braids in front of my face, and I resist the urge to touch the taller bump of hair pinned atop my head, to check that it hasn't blown astray and exposed me. But I can't risk drawing attention to what it conceals.

My mind drifts to my mother, sending bursts of pain through me.

Did she know what her choices would mean for me?

Tears prick at my eyes, and I clench my jaw. Swiping them away angrily, I curse myself.

Stop being so weak.

Control yourself.

I breathe deeply, pushing the emotions away. I smooth my features, moving my jaw to loosen it.

After all, she's been dead far too long for this to affect me so.

Never mind that her actions still shape my days, still keep me on the outskirts of this village. She made me weak. She made me pitiful.

She birthed the emotions that cripple my magic, the emotions Father tries so hard to beat out of me.

I sigh, knowing I can't blame her for long, not with all she suffered to give me a few good years.

A little voice inside tries to remind me that she tried to give me more than just a few good years, but I shove that voice aside with all the pain that accompanies thoughts of Ma.

Stepping carefully through snow drifts, I duck beneath low-hanging branches, bowed by the weight of winter. Trudging along, I seek my camp, my secondary home, silently thankful for the time away from Father.

Chapter Two
Ronan

"In the face of a battle worth fighting, I'd rather fail than never try."
- The wise words of Tivasta

My fingers curl around the handle of my war axe. It slides into the loop at my belt easily, waiting, craving the blood it will soon spill. I stare up the mountain at the snowy pines that hide a village of monsters, and my blood boils.

My mind fills with the faces of those we lost last spring when the Vaikahlen people attacked. My friends. My father. I see them, bloody and broken in the soft grass.

The stories of those lost in prior attacks, when I was still too young for battle, haunt me. Children in meadows culled like cattle. Parents speared on pikes of ice.

The mountain looms over us, its pines holding shadows, the white peaks concealing monsters as cold as the snow itself. Every shadow, every gust of wind, every icy gale, might be the one to bring them down the mountain after us again.

But no more.

Berinasten and his Enlightened have taken too many of our people, spilled too much of our blood. Even just the name makes my nails dig into my palms.

I take a deep breath, but the late winter air makes my lungs seize. The piercing cold of the mountain seeps into me, biting harder than the chill in the valley below. I cast my gaze back toward my home, filled with waves of longing for the life I may never return to, the simple future I may never have.

Smoke swirls upward from chimneys, so idyllic, so pretty. My mother and sister, Coren, must be curled up in their beds still, and I can't help but wonder Coren's baby will come while I'm away.

My heart swells at the prospect of a better life for my future niece or nephew, a life unspoiled by ambushes under the cover of blizzards. Every bit of me cries out for a world I could raise a family in, without fear of losing them to such cruelty.

And though battle isn't something I relish, I'll do it.

For them.

For the family I have.

For the family I may never get.

My gaze falls to the tree line at the base of the mountain, the new growth springing up under charred older trees. The scars of my attempt to push back the assault mar the pines, but finally, after nearly a full year, I'm ready to finish this. My body has recovered, and Sihetva swirls around me on a light breeze, warm and reassuring.

I take a deep breath.

"We'll end this," I whisper, letting Sihetva see my determination and bitterness and fury.

I roll my shoulders, stretch my arms, curl my fingers. I test my body once again, making sure I'm fit for the trek and the battle to come. Months of bedrest after the attack left me weakened, but I've built my strength up now.

Vilashi worked wonders.

I send out a silent thanks to the older woman for her treatments and vigilant care.

Sihetva curls a breeze against my face, brushing the hair back from my cheek. Waves of remorse sift through me.

I sigh, shaking my head. "I offered myself," I say. Again, I show Sihetva that day, filling my head with it to remind Sihetva just how desperately I wanted those flames. "It isn't your fault. I knew the risk."

And now that I'm healed, I'll do it again if I must. I'll exhaust myself, run myself ragged.

One way or another, Berinasten will die.

And though I feel Sihetva's regret still, feel the shy touch of the wind, the softening of the light around me, the gentle warmth in the leather armor I wear, I also feel the same desperation for revenge, for an end to the man who killed so many of my family and friends.

The man who has oppressed Sihetva for years, forced it to kill.

And I know, even if it exhausts me, if I offer the chance again, Sihetva will take it.

My shoulders fall with a sigh of relief.

***

My Sword Siblings bustle about, packing up their gear, tucking everything into their packs in preparation for another day's trek up the mountain. A low whistle rolls through camp, and I rise to my feet, prepared for the steep climb ahead.

Reti approaches, dark skin and hair dotted with snow. Her sharp horns pierce the air, warning winter itself not to defy her. "Ready to go?" she asks, toeing the end of my boot.

I nod, offering her a weak smile and trying not to encourage her attention. After all, there's no use getting attached if we don't come back from this.

Or if we fail to kill Berinasten.

She bats her hazel eyes, then struts away, casting a glance back over her shoulder.

Widening my eyes, I shake my head. I adjust my boots, securing spikes on the toes. Pulling on my pack, I join my Sword Siblings at the foot of the cliff.

One form moves, unafraid. Skarsi. She doesn't hesitate, driving a climbing axe into the cliff face. She slams another in, reaching higher, hauling herself up. One move at a time, she scales the rocky precipice, heedless of ice and winds. Her strong form moves effortlessly, up and up and up. At the top, she turns, black hair flying about her face.

Is she smiling?

I squint against the glare on the snow, peering up at her, but she's too far, too high. I can't tell.

With a wave, she turns and trudges away from the edge. We wait patiently, bundled in wool and shivering anyway. She shouts a warning, then tosses a rope over the edge. The end hurdles down toward us, burying itself in a snow drift.

One by one, my Sword Siblings take up the rope, making the climb. But the winds grow stronger, defending the Vaikahlen mages. I feel Sihetva seething within the gusts that slam into us, trying to resist their control.

Each climber clings tighter to the rope, hangs closer to the wall. They move cautiously, drawing the process out, but they make it to the top.

I send Reti ahead. The winds grow stronger by the second, and her climbing skills might not be a match for this if she waits much longer. She begins, bracing her legs wide.

But she sways.

A sudden gust of wind knocks her feet out from under her, and she drops. My heart lurches. Her firm grip spares her a fall, but she slams into the rock wall with a muffled grunt.

Relief and concern sweep through me in alternating waves. Slowly, the wind abates, and she rights herself, moving higher.

I let out a long breath, picking out footholds for her as she climbs. When she moves too far for me to see where she might step, I look instead to the crowd awaiting her at the top.

Several of them lie on their stomachs, gloved hands ready to reach for her. Black horns stick out from every head, gleaming in the sunlight.

She reaches them, and they haul her upward.

I take up the rope.

Grip firm, I begin my ascent. With knees bent and feet wide, I fight the winds that threaten to knock me down. Every step propels me into colder air. It nips at my nose, doubtless lending a rosy hue to my tan cheeks.

But hand over hand, step after step, I climb, spiting the windy defenses the Vaikahlen people forced upon Sihetva.

Strands of black hair slip free of their ties to whip about my face. One stings my eye, sending tears trickling over my cheek. My breath puffs out on little clouds, and I take another step.

The wind picks up, howling and screeching through the mountains, desperate to push us back down. But we're here for a reason. We're here to keep our next generation safe, to make sure they have parents to raise them.

So, I keep moving.

A gust of wind catches me, knocking me off balance and swinging me out away from the cliff. I slam into the rock with a thud, and my pack rips open against the jagged edge, spilling its contents. They fall for what feels like an eternity, and the wind screams, obscuring the sounds of their landing.

My bedroll hangs free, flapping and catching the wind. It sends me spinning. I catch an arm, a leg, on the rocks. I grit my teeth, tucking my head between my arms to try to protect myself.

But my hands slip.

Scrambling for purchase, I squeeze tight, palms growing warm as the rope flies through my grip and burns through my gloves. My shoulders jerk as I catch myself on the rope, just in time to stop my palms from burning. I slow, stop spinning, stop falling.

But the rope catches on a rock high above me.

My Sword Siblings shout their pleas, begging me to try again, to be careful. They tug at the rope, joining together to try to pull me up.

But the rope is stuck.

And the wind has other orders.

It sends me spinning again, catching the bedroll hanging from my pack like a sail and leaving me no choice. With a glance below, I assess my chances.

My heartbeat quickens.

It's a long fall.

But I should make it.

"GO!" I shout. "I'll find another way up."

They scream down at me, but the wind carries their words away.

I suck in a breath and reach for my axe. The loop on my belt hangs limp, broken open by jagged stone. Trying not to search the snowy ground below for it, knowing it's too far to truly see it, I pull my dagger from its sheath.

Above, they scream, tugging on the rope with all their considerable might. But it doesn't budge. Caught in a crack, pinned by rock high above my head, it resists them. It creaks painfully in my hands.

How long will it hold?

Not long enough for me to climb down.

"GO!" I shout again, insisting that they leave me.

I reach up to cut the rope, but it spares me the effort, snapping in the crook of the rocks. My stomach jumps into my throat as I fall. Tossing the dagger as far as I can, I hope to land far away from it, far away from the axe that lies somewhere below.

The wind whirls past me, screaming as the level ground we camped on rushes to meet me. I close my eyes, gritting my teeth, and prepare for impact.

Snow wraps around me, cushioning the landing, but pain still explodes through me. The air rushes from my lungs, and I stare up at the cliff, the black rock, blinding white snow, the dark shapes of my Sword Siblings somewhere at the top.

They blur together in smears of color and screams.

I take a slow, ragged breath, and darkness wraps around me.

***

Blinking awake, I rub a hand over my face. The scratchy glove, burned through as I tried to grip the rope, grates against my cold skin.

But my palms are only red, barely saved by the thick fabric.

I stare into the blinding white world, utterly disoriented. My head aches, and my back protests beneath my weight.

I need to get warm.

I need a fire.

I lurch onto my side, force myself to my hands and knees. Snow greets my palms through the holes in my gloves, and I push myself up to standing to spare my poor, aching hands.

They'll freeze soon enough if I don't get a fire. No need to hasten the process.

Already, my teeth chatter, and the chill air settles into my bones.

My head spins as I rise to my full height. The valley spreads out before me, still unblemished by this newest winter storm. Brown and grey in the winter light, it stares up at me, wondering what I'll do.

If only I knew.

My thoughts roil, full of the vengeance I can't seek, the future I can't shape from this cliff. My heart twists at the injustice of it all.

They force Sihetva to harm us, to batter its allies.

And I can do nothing.

My teeth grind together, and the chattering stops. I force myself to calm down, to remember that I have more pressing needs. I can find a way to go after Berinasten later.

For now, fire.

I lurch into the woods, gathering pine needles and small branches off dead trees. Taking shelter beneath a tall pine, I arrange the kindling.

Calling out to Sihetva for some of its power, I feel it build within my heart. I tap into the well of emotions within me, letting the luxurious memory of an evening with friends warm my chest. Sihetva takes that feeling, amplifies it, carrying heat surging out through my veins. I close my eyes, relishing the sensation of warmth in this violently cold place.

I reach out to the kindling, body sated with the magical warmth. The small bundle of pine needles rests in my palm, and I let the memory grow sharper in my mind, recalling the laughter we shared, the stories we recounted, the glow of the fire in the hearth nearby.

My palm grows warm as the pine needles catch, and I settle them in with the sticks I've arranged. It takes off quickly, fed by Sihetva, and I pull my gloves off, holding shaking hands out to warm by the flames.

Slowly, I arrange my thoughts as the sluggishness of cold falls away. I pull off the remnants of my pack and take stock of what remains within it.

A small pouch of jerky. The tattered remnants of my bedroll. A small length of rope.

Nothing else.

Swallowing, I stave off the hopelessness that threatens to overwhelm me. Retrieving a piece of jerky, I chew it methodically, extracting every bit of flavor and letting my stomach settle.

I'll search the area where I fell once I've warmed up.

Silently, I hope that my dagger or axe will be nearby, but a morbid laugh rises within me at the likelihood. Casting a glance at the trees around me, I look for anything that might be of use, vowing to search for game trails soon.

Then, I can make my decision.

Abandon my quest for justice and return home. Or find a different, hopefully less treacherous, path up the mountain.

***

What's left of the morning passes quickly, and I make my choice. I tuck the remnants of my food into my pack alongside the shredded bedroll, then tie it off with my rope. My reclaimed dagger slides back into my sheath, and I kick snow into my fire, abandoning the rest of my scattered equipment as a lost cause. The snow has claimed it and searching blindly will do no good.

My eyes trace the shapes of houses in the valley, follow the smoke up toward the cloudy sky. I glance at the mine on the opposing mountain where Sihetva guides our people safely to the best veins, aiding us by choice.

Then, I turn and move along the cliff, searching for a path, a game trail, anything to lead me to food or a way up.

Chapter Three
Lessiyara

On cold days, Sihetva has been known to
blaze brighter in the hearths of the weary.
- The ways of Sihetva

The pines greet me, welcoming me back to my favorite campsite, my future home. I breathe in their tangy scent, relishing the way the crisp air fills my lungs. With every step I've taken away from Father over the last three days, it's gotten easier to breathe. The wind moves around me, sighing through the branches as if it's as relieved as I am.

I settle in upon a bed of pine needles while the shadows lengthen, staring up at the swaying greenery. Beyond the trees, the sun droops toward the horizon, ready to tuck itself in for the night.

Stop being so sentimental.

Berating myself, I rise and set up camp. My tent goes up easily, and I spread additional layers of pine needles within it to further cushion my makeshift bed. I layer blankets and furs atop them, then settle my bag of food into the little cellar I carved into the hillside on prior trips.

Turning my attention to a fire, I gather kindling and harness the magic of the mountains. My mind fixates on the process of destruction, the all-consuming nature of fire. I reach out, feeling the shape of the wood. I trace the fibers with a gloved finger, feel their edges, their contents, their makeup.

And slowly, it grows warm.

A soft glow illuminates the sticks, and elation sweeps through me. But I lose my concentration.

It flickers out, and rage boils in my veins, reforming my attempts. The fire bursts to life, consuming the sticks before me in a heartbeat, and I scramble to throw more upon the pyre.

But I feel no joy at this success, this savage magic I shouldn't be able to use.

It calls to mind my mother and the man we shared those few good years with, and my heart spasms in my chest.

With the fire blazing, I sit upon the pine needles, resting my hands on my knees with palms up and coal-black fingers open to begin my communion. I listen to the world around me, feel the solidity of the mountain, focus on the cold, relentless wind.

I just have to embody this.

Control. Ruthlessness.

I have to harness it, subdue it

Then, maybe I can spare my back.

But my stomach turns. Control may be the way of the Vaikahlen people, but the world around us doesn't seem to like that. It slips from my grasp.

The wind howls through the mountains, whipping snow off the branches. The thick powder lands with soft thuds all around, and I close my eyes, feeling the way the mountain breathes.

But today, it doesn't just breathe. It groans.

My eyes snap open, peering along the ridge I traversed mere hours ago. A Soorahk man walks the edge, eyes downcast to survey the ground at his feet. My heart stops.

Torn between hiding or fleeing, my mind fills with all the terrible things he might do if he catches me.

Surely not all Soorahk people are as kind as…

I shake my head, unwilling to entertain further thoughts of him or Ma. I force my attention to the man before me.

He must have seen my fire, already. That must be what drew him in this direction.

My heart hammers in my chest, pounding behind my ears. But the mountain groans again, louder than the blood rushing through my veins.

Panic grips me, winding my nerves tight as I watch realization dawn on him. He stills for half a heartbeat. Snow drifts around him, speckling his dark hair, his black horns, as he gazes up the ridge.

And then, he takes off, sprinting toward me. His huge frame unsettles the already shifting ridge, and it crumbles behind him.

I bite back a scream, launching myself to my feet without a thought and running toward him. The mountainside falls away, nipping at his heels, but he stays one step ahead.

Until he doesn't.

With one final push, he launches himself forward, leaping to grab the ledge, to hold onto anything. But he disappears from view.

I push farther, run faster. The edge looms, closer and closer with every step, and I slide to a stop, lowering myself to my stomach. Crawling closer, I peer over, afraid that he'll be there and afraid that he won't.

A gloved hand clings to the rocky edge, just within reach. He stares down at the sheer drop, swinging madly.

"Take my hand!" I shout, drawing his attention as I reach for him.

His nostrils flare, and fear shines in his dark eyes. With a quick nod, he swings his free arm up, and our hands lock together. His grip tightens on mine, and I use every bit of my strength to haul him higher. Every scrap of distance is hard-won, but one of his feet finds a hold on the cliff face.

His breaths come in gasps, clouding the air around us. With a look of desperation, he lets go of the wall and throws his arm higher, seeking a new handhold.

My shoulders burn beneath his weight, but I hold fast. Briefly, I consider summoning my magic, but my fragile concentration would splinter it.

"Hold on," I say, heaving the man upward.

He grasps the ledge for a moment, casting a wary glance at the ground far below.

Rising onto my knees, I take a deep breath, then draw one foot up under me. Suddenly, every climb, every hike, every load of firewood I've carried seems to have strengthened my legs specifically for this moment.

I grasp his arm with both hands as he clutches mine. My muscles scream in protest, marveling at the sheer weight of this man, but I can't let up. He hops his other hand up the side of the ridge, helping to heft himself upward.

Finally, his arm lands on the top of the ridge, and he scrambles upward. Kneeling once more, I pull on his coat, his pack, his pants, grabbing any scrap of clothing I can to pull him up and over the edge.

Huffing, we scramble away from the ridge. My heart races, lodges in my throat.

But he's safe.

Dropping into the snow, I let out a sharp bark of laughter.

For better or worse, he's safe.

Beside me, the stranger laughs, but it sounds hysterical. I push myself to my feet, aiming to put some distance between us.

Just in case.

He rolls onto his stomach, then sits back on his haunches. He looks back at the ridge with a shake of his head. A dazzling smile lands upon me, and I stare at him in shock. He rises, and before I can move away, he reaches out, drawing me up against him.

My heart beats frantically, desperate to get away, to escape the dangerous embrace of the savage I just saved.

But he merely wraps me in a hug, chuckling. His breath warms my skin, gusts through my hair.

And I go still.

"Thank you," he whispers, lips perilously close to my ear.

Warmth flows through me, and some desperate ache within me cries out. Of their own volition, my arms rise, and my hands land on his sides. I wrap my arms around his waist, hugging him back, shocked by my boldness, my lack of control.

And by how nice it feels.

How much I needed this gentle touch.

Tight knots inside my chest begin to loosen. Brittle walls fracture, and my already tenuous control over my emotions, over my magic, slips.

He tightens his embrace, crushing me to his chest, and I try to bite back a whimper as his arms dig into the bruises on my back. He pulls away, and cold air rushes between us. Waves of disappointment wash over me, despite all my better judgment.

Gripping my shoulders, he stares into my eyes. "Are you hurt?" His brows furrow, and he looks me over. "Did your shoulder dislocate when you pulled me up? I know a bit of field healing. If it's that or a cut or something, I can help you."

A small part of me wants to wave it away, to hide my weakness. But the warmth of his embrace, the hearty, sultry sound of his laugh moments ago, his voice so close to my ear… It all has me off balance.

So, I say, "It's only bruises."

With a devilish smile, he asks, "Did you fall off a couple of cliffs too?"

My mind fills with my most recent beating, and I drop my gaze. Tears prick at the corners of my eyes, but I blink them away. I shake my head to answer his question, unwilling to trust my voice.

Schooling my features into a mask of perfect placidity, I meet his gaze. The concern in those warm eyes almost breaks me, but I hold it together.

With an even tone, I say, "Come. As long as you mean me no harm, you can warm yourself by my fire."

Chapter Four
Ronan

"Smile more oft than I, Darling of mine.
Cry better than I, Prodigy mine."
- The half-remembered songs of Ma

The little Vaikahlen woman leads me to her camp, and I trail along after her, stunned. Her tail swishes from side to side, black tip brushing the snow. The furred tips of her ears flick restlessly in all directions, assessing her surroundings, which isn't so far-fetched given the circumstances.

Except that Vaikahlen are heartless.

The cold, unfeeling people show no emotion in battle or bed.

But she cared enough to save me. Me! A Soorahk! She laughed with me after the fact.

She sank into that hug.

And her bruises...

My mind fills with the frown that marred her marble features when I asked if she fell off a cliff. Her eyes nearly welled up. Her brows furrowed.

They furrowed!

But where did her bruises come from?

What happened to make a Vaikahlen woman cry?

Staring openly, I lumber through snow drifts that she plows through easily, clearly adept at winter travel. Her strong legs make quick work of the short climb up a steep incline, tail flowing seamlessly in whatever direction she needs for balance.

I slip once, twice, barely staying upright with arms thrown wide as counterweights.

She has me off balance in too many ways.

The fire at the center of her camp burns hot, licking a little too close to the branches above.

But it shouldn't.

She should hold it lower, should have more control over it. That's what the Vaikahlen people are good at.

Control.

Bitterness moves through me at the thought, but her fire softens me. It burns wildly, uncontained.

She stands near the flames, casting glances at me. Something in her ice-blue eyes seems off, strained, as they sweep over me. I swallow, uneasy before this person who bears no semblance to the Vaikahlen I've encountered in the past.

Chewing at the inside of her lip like any normal Soorahk would when anxious, she seems to come to a decision. Taking a deep breath, she relaxes her features, sliding back into the mask I know too well, the mask she wore for an instant as she invited me into her camp. Blank eyes stare at me, framed by a face devoid of emotion.

I take a step back, suddenly wary.

She brings her hands up to shoulder height, then joins them together before her stomach, wrapping them, interweaving them to form an upside-down bowl. I tip my head, considering her, as she rotates them as if spinning a bowl in one direction, then the reverse. The air around us shimmers for half a breath, and I realize what she's done.

A ward.

No attack or violent offensive, just protection.

I relax with a soft chuckle.

"We'll be safe in here," she says, voice so toneless that the hairs stand on the back of my neck. "My wards are strong. Nothing and no one that wishes harm on those within can pass through."

I furrow my brows. "That's a peculiar ward."

She tips her head to the side, an odd gesture of curiosity for such an expressionless face. "I assume yours keeps everything out?"

I nod, taking a cautious step toward the fire with my head full of stories of Soorahk people able to build wards like hers, wards to check hearts. But she built it with control and gestures, like Vaikahlen people. My eyes never leave her, never stop watching for something, anything, that might give away her next move.

But nothing slips through her mask.

She settles in upon a small log near the fire, holding her hands out for warmth. Her white palms seem to glow, but her black fingers drink in the light. Her tail drapes, lifeless, on the pine needles behind her.

I pull a small log from a stack of firewood and set it on the ground, careful not to let the roaring fire obscure the sight of her but keeping distance. Taking a seat upon it, I let the heat of the fire seep into me, chasing away the chill of the mountain.

"My name is Lessiyara," the woman says, eyes fixed on the flames.

"Ronan," I answer, wondering where I've heard her name before.

I cast a glance around her camp, noting the little lean-to that holds more firewood, clearly stocked ahead of time in a sign of semi-permanence. The tent is nothing more than a temporary structure, but poles stand not far from the wood pile as if waiting for another structure to be completed.

I've never heard of lone Vaikahlen living away from the villages that dot the mountainsides.

But I know her name from… somewhere.

"Do you have food?" she asks, pulling my attention outward.

I consider her, still uneasy beneath her emotionless eyes. But she's given me no reason to mistrust her so far.

She could've just let me fall…

The strain in her eyes then, the panic that pushed her to the edge of a collapsing ridge to haul me up, flashes before my eyes, and I decide to trust her, revealing just how little I have.

I shake my head. "Not much. A few pieces of jerky." I recount my earlier fall, the rocks tearing my pack open and shredding my bedroll.

She fights it, but a smile tugs at the corners of her lips. It even tries to sparkle in her eyes. "You seem to fall off a lot of cliffs," she says, suppressing most of the amusement in her voice.

But it's there.

A little bit shines through.

I pull in a deep breath, shoulders easing. "It's an unfortunate hobby of mine," I say, smiling broadly, hoping to tease some sort of emotion from her.

"I wonder why you'd ever take up such a hobby," she says, eyes dancing, either with the reflection of the fire or with laughter.

Chuckling, I say, "I didn't get much choice."

With a breath, she pushes herself up to her feet and retreats to the wood pile. Her figure draws my eye as she walks away, clearly strong despite the layers she wears, but I force my gaze upward.

Sweeping snow out of the way, she reveals a small wooden board. Lifting it, she digs a jar out of a hole in the ground before returning to the fire. She offers it to me, face carefully neutral. "Eat."

Our fingers brush as I take the jar, and I consider her, marveling at the strange warmth that moves through me at her touch. My mind races with questions, desperate to understand what she's doing here, why she saved me, why she's so different from the other Vaikahlen.

Raising one eyebrow, I watch her as I fill my stomach with the cold, dried fruits.

"Where were you headed?" Lessiyara asks, tone flat once more.

I nearly choke on a bite of food.

Can I tell her that I was on my way to kill the Vaikahlen leader?

I eye her carefully. My gaze roams over the campsite that seems to be edging toward permanence.

Would she live here if she liked her leader? Why not reside in a village?

"I was looking for my Sword Siblings," I answer simply. "We were traveling and… got separated." I watch her, gauging her reaction to having us on her mountainside.

Unperturbed, she teases, "I assume that by 'got separated' you mean the first cliff you fell off?"

Smiling, I nod.

Maybe she isn't with Berinasten or his Enlightened. Maybe she doesn't like his leadership.

Her face falls, and she stares out at the pine woods around us. Her ears twitch. She stills, brows furrowed in concentration.

With a sigh, she whispers, "It's just wolves."

But I don't share her relief.

Just *wolves?*

What else is out here?

I cast a glance over my shoulder, and my eyes pick out an entire wolf pack slinking through the shadows between the trees. My nerves wind tight, and my heart races.

The wolves move into the open, snarling and spreading out to flank us. I rise to my feet, and my hand instantly goes to my side, to the broken loop and the vacancy where my axe should be. I raise my hands instead, ready to commune with Sihetva, to fight with whatever power it will give me, instead.

But Lessiyara doesn't even look up, doesn't care at all.

She stares into the fire, face impassive. She catches me staring at her, and a hint of amusement dances in her eyes.

My mouth falls open.

Before I can turn back to face the wolves, one lunges for her.

I leap forward, grabbing her and pushing her to the ground. I roll, turning her away from the wolf, startled that she wouldn't even move.

But the wolf smashes into her ward with a thud.

The pack snarls and sniffs at the edges of camp, testing the magical boundary. My heart races, but slowly, they give up, filtering back out into the shadows of the trees.

I drop into the pine needles, sprawling on my back next to Lessiyara with a laugh.

"Did you not trust my ward?" she asks, turning her head to look at me. Eyes as cold and emotionless as ice peer into mine, framed by alabaster skin and braids.

I prop myself up on an elbow and look down at her. My eyes trace her dark lashes, the contour of her neck. I force my gaze to rise, to hold hers.

"I forgot about the ward, to be honest," I whisper, voice huskier than intended.

She stills, cheeks flushing a soft pink.

A few strands of crisp white hair lay across her forehead, and I reach up to smooth them away. Heat rushes through me, and my breaths come quick. My heart hammers, and a longing I've stifled for the better part of a year sweeps through me. My fingers brush over her skin, and I push the strands back. "They came loose from your… little bump of hair."

I smile, moving to tuck the strands into the pins atop her head meant to hold her long hair from her face.

But panic lights in her eyes, and she rolls away from me, springing to her hands and knees just beyond arm's reach.

"I can do it," she says hastily.

And I stare at her, stunned.

Chapter Five
Lessiyara

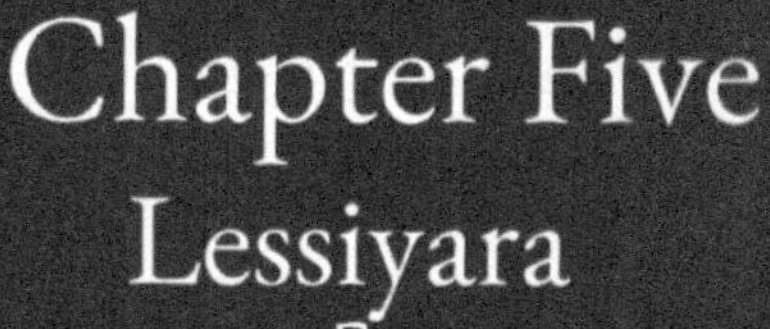

Sihetva knows all hearts and only willingly
grants power to those it trusts.
- The ways of Sihetva

My heart races, and I struggle to get control of myself.

He was too close.

He almost... He touched my head. He almost touched my hair. He almost touched... them.

I suppress a shudder, terrified of offending him. And something tells me that shuddering at his touch would offend.

But he almost saw.

He almost found out.

I grapple with my heart, clearing the panic from my face, from my eyes, and hating how easily my emotions overtake me. I drop my gaze from him, blinking to reassert control. My eyes land on his pack, just beyond the shimmering barrier.

"Your pack," I say. "It's outside the ward."

Ronan shakes his head, looking to the pack, then back at me. "I'm sorry," he says. "I really shouldn't have... I don't know what came over me. I just thought..." His mouth opens and closes, but no more words come out.

"Can you get your pack?" I ask, sitting back.

Taking a deep breath, Ronan rises. He stares at me all the while, listening for the wolves as he ventures beyond the ward to grab the shredded pack. I try not to watch the way his breeches draw tighter as he bends, try to keep my cheeks from flushing.

But I fail.

My eyes drop to the pine needles as he comes back, not quite sure if I want the answer to the question I'm using as a distraction.

But he comes back through the ward, dark eyes still locked on me.

I breathe a sigh of relief, head collapsing into my hands.

A soft chuckle rumbles through the air, and I look up.

He nods slowly, a smile playing at the corners of his lips. "Sorry," he says. "That ward is handy, isn't it?"

"More than you know," I whisper, head filling with all the nights I've used my wards to keep Father at bay.

Ronan comes forward, settling onto the log by the fire once more. He drops the pack next to him, and it lands too softly.

How little does he have?

"Do you have a tent?" I ask, ignoring the emotions on his face, the things he doesn't even try to hide.

He startles out of his sympathetic reverie and shakes his head. "The first cliff tore my pack open. I lost nearly everything."

I turn to look over my shoulder, hiding a blush as I consider my tent. Clouds peek in through the trees, promising another snowstorm.

"We'll share, then."

He did pass the ward. He doesn't mean to hurt me.

He looks at me, dark eyes shining in the low light. Slowly, his eyes move over the tent, likely assessing how small it is.

It'll be a tight fit, but it'll be warmer that way.

He glances at the posts sticking up from the earth, the beginnings of my future home. My escape from Father.

Silence descends on us. I try to piece together what to do next, how quickly I should move to the fire. How close to, or far away from, him I should sit.

The cold snow melts beneath my knees, soaking into my pants. Pushing up to a crouch, I wipe all traces of emotion from my face.

He flinches.

Slowly, I rise, watching him carefully as I walk past, keeping my gait even, measured. I settle in upon the log, staring into the fire.

"I'm sorry," Ronan says. "I didn't consider how my actions might have worried you. I'm glad you have this ward though."

I nod, struggling to keep my face neutral despite all the memories flooding me. I can still see Father staring into my room, commanding me to remove the ward so that I might receive punishment. I still feel the tears that rolled down my face each time, worsening the punishment that I knew would come.

Shaking my head, I call myself back to the present, to Ronan's fidgeting hands. I watch his long fingers, watch them move together. I trace the furrow between his brows, letting my gaze linger on the frown lines around his mouth.

He wears his emotions so openly, so bravely.

Are all Soorahk people like this?

Is Father telling the truth?

A spark of hope burns in my chest, despite the feelings of revulsion Father meant to inspire in me.

Would they accept me? Could I go there?

My lips part as if to ask the questions, but I don't let the words pass.

They'd just think me an abomination.

Just as the Vaikahlen people would if they knew why I am the way I am.

I sigh, blinking to clear my head. My eyes refocus, centering on his face, his lips. The lips I've been staring at this whole time as my mind moved away from here.

I snap my gaze up to meet his eyes, blushing scarlet, only to find him watching me. The heat in my cheeks burns hotter, and I turn away.

He'll think I was thinking of kissing him…

I stare into the flames, mind suddenly drifting, wondering what it might've been like if I hadn't panicked, if I hadn't rolled away from him…

If I'd let him kiss me.

No. Stop that.

Rising to my feet, I busy myself with construction efforts, dragging logs across camp. After only an instant, Ronan lifts the opposite end of the log, helping me carry it. I fetch my lashings after we place it near the posts, then begin securing it in place.

"You don't want to live in a village?" Ronan asks, free of any preamble.

I shake my head. Keeping my voice as even as possible, I say, "I don't quite belong in the villages. I'm too…"

Weak.

Soft.

Savage.

I sigh and finally say, "It's better this way."

The beatings, the flat words that bite like slaps, the empty stares somehow full of judgment… They all wash over me in waves.

"I may be biased since you saved my life," he begins with a smile, "but I think you deserve better than to live alone out here."

I glance at him, wanting to read everything he offers, every line on his face, every glint in his eyes. I want to drink in the expression and soak in every possible meaning.

But I tear my eyes away. I glance over my shoulder reflexively, waiting for Father to catch my slip, to bring the next beating down upon me for the hope that no doubt shone in my eyes.

***

The light falls behind the mountain, and the fire casts flickering shadows over us. But several logs now adorn the posts, stacked two high on all sides and lashed into place. The boards I carefully cut and planed last time I was here rest beneath stacks of stones to undo the warping of moist days. The straightest ones have been placed within the structure that will be my home one day, providing a partial floor.

It's more progress than I could have made in three days alone.

I glance at Ronan, sipping from a cup of melted snow near the fire. His strong figure draws my eye, as it did many times during our work.

He turns to me, catches me staring, and smiles.

Heat blossoms within me, and I smile back before I can think better of it, before I can even look over my shoulder to see if Father has materialized.

But Father should be preparing for his trip down the mountain, too busy to chase after me.

With a sigh, I let my smile widen.

Ronan's eyes twinkle, or maybe that's the flames flickering over that devilish grin. "You're getting the hang of that," he says, deep voice resonating in my chest.

I swallow hard, stomach a mass of nerves and heat.

Looking away, I stare out at the darkened valley. The light of our fire doesn't reach far, and the sun has long since bid us farewell.

I fetch rations from my pack and split them with Ronan. Silence rules our camp as we eat, broken only by the crackling of the fire. Every so often, my eyes dart to the tent. Each time, dread and curiosity flow through me in warring waves of ice and fire.

I take the last bite of my food having noticed none of the bites that came before. I chew it slowly, keeping my gaze carefully trained on the fire.

"How many rations do you keep here?" Ronan asks.

I stare at him, confused, but answer honestly. "It hasn't been long since my last visit," I say, mind slipping back to my last temporary exile. "My rations are lower than I'd usually like them to be at this time of year, but I have enough to last until I… have to go back."

"You really don't want to go back to your village, do you?"

I take a deep breath, nearly a huff, and pull my mask back on. My features go slack.

He's making me lax. I'm supposed to be communing with the mountain, learning how to survive Father until I can get this place done.

"Not particularly," I say. "Why do you ask about the rations?"

One corner of his mouth lifts, dark eyes sparkling, and he gives a slow nod.

Does he know I'm trying to distract him? Does he know how much I hate my village? Does he know how weak I am?

How much can he tell from my face?

What's wrong with my face?

But he says nothing more about my upcoming return. Instead, he forces the smile from his lips, letting it play in his eyes only. "I've been eating your food all day. For tomorrow, I'd like something fresh, something to repay you. I'll set some traps before we go to bed."

Before we go to bed…

The words hang in the air, heavy and palpable. They cut off any argument that he need not bother, that I have enough to sustain us both for a few weeks.

He watches me carefully, but my mask is firmly in place, holding everything in. Or… at least, I think it is.

"I'll go set the traps," he whispers.

And though I wonder why his voice is so soft, so low, I know it should be. Somehow, it just *felt* right.

He retrieves the rope from his pack and saunters off. A glint of light catches on his horns, sparkling in his eyes as he casts a glance back at me before disappearing into the shadows.

Chapter Six
Ronan

"My heart, my darling, Love better than I.
My heart, my darling, Do more than survive.
For Sihetva sees you, and lives in your heart.
My heart, my darling, Love better than I."
- The half-remembered songs of Ma

Filling myself with the warmth of Lessiyara's smile, the one she let slip as we made progress on her house, I share that small part of my heart with Sihetva and ask for a small flame to hover over my palm. I carry it through the woods, picking out game trails with ease and setting snares accordingly.

My ears strain for signs of the wolves that assaulted us earlier but find nothing more than the hoot of an owl. I move faster, hoping to reach a stable cliffside before my extended absence arouses suspicion.

Lessiyara doesn't seem to be fond of the Vaikahlen people or their ways. But that doesn't necessarily mean she'd like the mission my Sword Siblings and I were on. Killing her leader might take it too far for her liking.

The trees grow sparse as I move closer, and the stars peek in at me through the canopy. They watch my progress, battling with my flame to light the safest path.

Once clear of the trees, I stare out at the valley, but no fires burn bright enough to show my sister's home, or even my mother's home, so much closer to the edge of the village. Turning, I look up the mountain. A full day's travel separates me from my Sword Siblings, and the faint light of their fire is every bit as distant as I expected it to be.

For half a breath, I regret staying here all day.

But she saved my life, she fed me.

I couldn't just walk away without doing something to repay her.

Smiling, I shake my head, knowing full well that isn't the only reason I stayed.

There's something different about her.

She's... Well, for a Vaikahlen, she's positively unstable, but... in a good way.

I laugh, chiding myself. After all, my plans haven't changed. I'll take Berinasten out, whether she approves or not, whether I survive the battle or not.

And I don't need to be getting attached to someone in the meantime.

The admission sobers me. Rubbing a hand over my face, I stare up at the faint light in the distance.

But an idea forms in the back of my mind.

If she's like this... Are the other Vaikahlen people so emotional?

Is it just Berinasten's Enlightened that come down to cleanse us? Are they forcing this ludicrous restraint on their people?

Or is she an exception?

My original plan to set out tomorrow to find my Sword Siblings shifts, and I find myself justifying it, telling myself that I owe it to the potential innocents in the mountain villages to find out for sure.

But I can't deny the curiosity building within me, much as I want to pretend it doesn't exist.

Turning, I make my way back through the woods, guided by the light of Lessiyara's fire. My heart beats faster with every step, pulled by the promise of spending just a bit more time with her, of figuring out just how different she might be.

Because I need to find out. I need to know if there are others like her, other innocent people that mean no harm to us or Sihetva.

I swallow hard, casting a glance up the mountain.

That's all it is.

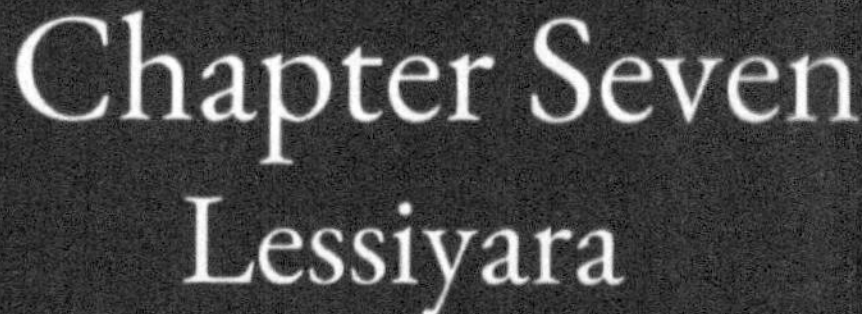

Chapter Seven
Lessiyara

"Come back to me, Darling. You're not on the mountain anymore."
- Da's half-remembered words to Ma

Forcing myself to my feet, I focus on the cold wind brewing above us, whispering across my skin with the promise of more to come. I pull it into me, letting my magic wrap me in a chilly numbness.

Heaving a great sigh, I stow the jars of food in the little root cellar and feed more wood to the fire. Sparks spiral into the air, threatening to catch the branches above.

Harnessing my magic, I pull the flames back with a quick jerk of my hands. Sweeping my hands outward, I set a barrier in place above the fire to keep us safe through the night.

Footsteps crunch through the snow behind me, and my heart lurches. I spin on my heels, ready to run if Father appears, ready to call out to see if Ronan is safe from him.

The smile slips from Ronan's face as he appraises me. "I won't hurt you," he says, voice exceedingly gentle. He holds his hands up, palms toward me. "Nothing changed while I was out there. I promise."

Something in his tone makes me feel guilty, and I rush to say, "It isn't you that I'm worried about."

I snap my mouth shut, eyes darting around, searching the shadows. The flames paint them all a shade too bright, as if someone made of alabaster stood there, staring in at me.

But my ears find no trace of movement, no shifting fabric, no crunching snow.

With slow steps and a few glances over his shoulder, Ronan crosses through my ward into camp, reaffirming his statement that he won't hurt me. I close my eyes, exhaling my relief.

"Let's go to bed," I say, barely sparing a glance for him.

I pull the chill inward, forcing myself to be calm, to be even.

To be civilized.

Moving forward, I keep my eyes trained on the tent. I sit inside the mouth of it, pulling my boots off and setting them near the opening. Turning, eyes carefully lowered, I crawl into the tent, maintaining my hold on the cold winter air. I pull it deeper inside me, cooling my heart, my mind. My body.

Folding back my blankets, I don't look when Ronan settles in the mouth of the tent. My ears catch every movement, every rustle of fabric. His boots drop to the ground, just beside mine.

But I busy myself with the removal of my coat. I fold it and lay it atop my pack in the corner. Only then do I turn to face Ronan. He kneels in the mouth of the tent, facing me. Our eyes meet, and I struggle to hold the chill.

His eyes dip to my lips just a moment, and a spike of heat surges through me.

I quickly reassert my control, grasping for every bit of wind, every drift of snow beyond this tent. Breathing them in, I crawl beneath my blankets, turning on my side and pulling them up to my neck.

Ronan removes his coat, and I block it out as best I can, trying not to imagine the shape of him without that bulky fabric.

"Do you want this with yours?" he asks.

I nod, turning to take it from him.

"No need," he says, planting one arm on the blankets beside me. "I can get it."

Reaching over me, he drapes his coat over mine.

I grit my teeth, losing my grip on the cold winter air. Warmth blossoms within me.

He crawls under the blankets. His leg brushes mine as he stretches out, and I draw my knees up, pulling myself away from him.

"Sorry," he whispers.

My heart races in my chest, despite all my efforts at control.

He shifts, moving just a bit closer. "It's a little cold outside the blankets," he says, voice low and husky.

Guilt smacks me, and I scoot back, maneuvering the blankets to allow him more cover. My backside presses against his side, and I stiffen.

Is this normal?

Having never been so close to a man for sleep, having no certainty that *my* reactions would be a good way to measure normal, I can't be sure.

For half a breath, I fear that he'll find out why I'm so broken, that our proximity will give me away.

But it's dark. And he isn't touching my head.

It's fine.

I'm fine.

Ronan raises an arm and slides it beneath his head. I feel every move, every ripple of the blanket, every shift of his frame. A small voice tells me he's too close. He'll find out.

But another voice says he isn't close enough.

Desperate for a distraction, I say the first thing that comes to mind. "I should warn you. I talk in my sleep. I hope you sleep deeply."

"I should warn *you*," he counters, voice shaking with a laugh. "I cuddle in *my* sleep." The laugh fades, and he adds, "I don't want to be on the receiving end of your magic or any other attack you might launch, as strong as you are. I don't want you to think I'd try to… force… anything."

I roll to face him, laying my shoulder onto his as I do. The shadow of his face is close, too close.

"If it's too… uncomfortable for you," he says, "I can sleep by the fire. I don't mind."

"You must truly think me heartless if you think I'd risk your life in a snowstorm to avoid having you near," I say, trying for levity, trying to communicate with him in the tones he understands.

But I can't be sure it works, can't see any smile he might offer.

Turning serious, I give up and drop the tone from my voice.

I shouldn't be trying to convey emotion. All that'll do is get me hurt when he leaves, when I have to go home.

"I don't know you, don't know if I can trust you yet," I say. "But I trust my ward. It checked your heart. It wouldn't have let you pass if you were that sort of man." I roll away, desperate to break the contact, to reassert some semblance of balance within. "You won't hurt me."

And though I mean to leave it at that, the warmth of him breaks my fragile control.

"I think I'd know that without the ward, though I'm not sure why. Or how."

Silence falls, and I regret my words, regret the lull they forced upon us. I rack my brain, trying to figure out what I could have said wrong.

The pillow shifts as he turns his head to look at me, and my heart shrivels.

I thought he'd like that last part.

And though it scares me that I'm trying to impress him already, it hurts that my attempt to get into his good graces may have pushed him away.

He knows.

He must.

He has to know I'm just an abomination now.

I fight the urge to touch the tiny bumps hidden within my hair, the little horns that mark me as half, less than.

But when Ronan finally speaks, his voice isn't cold, it isn't biting. His words come out light. "Do you always face away from those you lie next to?" he teases.

"You ask as though I have a lot of experience," I say, trying to match his tone and hating myself for it all the while.

"Someone had to tell you that you talk in your sleep," he says.

I don't tell him that it was my mother.

"I was the one to break it to my sister," he says with a laugh. "Back when I was a child, I think I'd only seen 10 summers, my cousin pushed me out of the way of a Maurubeast, got hurt pretty bad. I was so worried. I cried for days while the healers worked on him."

I turn back, laying on his shoulder again to stare at him in disbelief. "You cried?"

And you admit it now? To a stranger?

Chuckling, he says, "Of course, I cried. Tears are natural."

I turn away from him once more, staring at my fingers clasped before my face. Taking solace in the darkness, I allow my brows to furrow as I consider his words.

"Well, eventually, my sister got tired of listening to me cry, especially since the healers were doing so well with him. She started dreaming about it. One night, she was talking so loudly she woke me up, almost yelling. She said, 'I'll carve out your tears with a shining purple laugh,' and I just had to tell her the next day." He laughs, and the sound fills my belly with warmth. "Of course, I was completely serious, very calm, when I told her."

"Really?" I ask, finding that hard to imagine.

He laughs harder. "No. Not even close."

He sighs, but there's no disappointment, no exhaustion, in it. It sounds… pleasant.

Heat builds within me, yet again, electrifying the night air.

"I'll have to teach you about sarcasm," he says.

I nod but say nothing, not sure I can trust my voice.

He wants to teach me things?

He wants to bother?

I don't let myself wonder how long he'll stick around. Given what he was likely here for, I'm sure he'll go to his Sword Siblings soon.

Maybe they'll be the group that finally takes out Father.

I don't dare get my hopes up, don't dare try to wade through the guilt that threatens to strike me down if I entertain those hopes. Gritting my teeth, I push the thoughts away.

Ronan's breathing evens out, slowing as sleep overtakes him. Given his earlier warning, I brace myself for him to reach out for me. My heart beats madly, and I pull the cold air inward, trying to calm myself.

Don't be stupid.

It means nothing.

It's just something he does in his sleep.

My mind fills with his unnecessary attempt to save my life earlier and the kiss that almost followed. His eyes so close… His hands on me…

But I panicked.

I ruined it.

Suddenly, all I can feel is the heat of his fingers brushing my face, sliding up toward my hair. And again, panic grips my heart.

What would he do if he knew?

I reach up to touch the horns concealed within my hair, so small but so terrible. The filed points press into my fingertips, but I pull my hand away quickly.

Ronan turns, rolling toward me, and my heart stops. His arm slides around my waist, and he pulls me against his chest. Scooting in close, he presses his face into my hair and inhales deeply. He sighs, breath hot on the back of my neck, and the sound sends shivers down my spine. My lungs struggle in the sweltering heat that blossoms in the tent.

Paralyzed, I wonder how long he'll stay like this. A few heartbeats? Until the storm reaches us and wakes him?

For the rest of the night?

Could I be that lucky?

The thought catches me off guard. The warmth of him soaks into me, and my hands move of their own accord, gripping his arm.

Because I don't want him to let go.

I don't want to be alone again.

Because isn't that what I am?

Alone.

Isn't that what I'll always be?

His words from earlier come back to me, telling me that I deserve better than to be alone out here.

The arm beneath his head moves, slipping beneath my neck. He reaches around, gripping my shoulder and pulling me closer.

And something inside me breaks.

Tears spill forth, dripping onto his arm. Sobs rack my body, all at once, and all I can do is hope that he doesn't wake, doesn't pull away.

Doesn't desert me.

Chapter Eight
Ronan

"Trust in Sihetva. It sees everything, while we see so little."
- The half-remembered teachings of Da

Soft sounds pull me from sleep, tugging at my heart. I open my eyes, blinking in the darkness. My tired mind struggles with what my heart knows.

Lessiyara is... crying.

Her body shakes in my arms, and tears soak into my sleeve. Her nails dig into the fabric, gripping my arms tight. Whimpering quietly, she crumbles in my embrace.

I open my mouth to ask what's wrong but think better of it.

She won't tell me.

She'd just pull away and stuff it all down again.

And something tells me she needs to get this out.

Nestling against her, I tighten my embrace and sigh, a drowsily comfortable sound. The tears come faster, and she bows her head forward, burying her face in my arms.

My heart twists in my chest, and I ache to offer more comfort than this small embrace. Every fiber of my being begs me to speak up, to find out who hurt her.

Tension builds within me, impotent in the face of this crying woman who I can't help, who I know wouldn't *let* me help.

"Stop it," she whispers.

My heart obeys her command, stilling in my chest for a moment.

She can't know I'm awake…

Surely not.

"Stop crying," she demands of herself, voice thick with the emotions she tries so hard to subdue. "Stop being pitiful. This doesn't mean anything. You're still…"

A hoarse whimper cuts her words off, and she shakes her head. "You're still alone," she finally says, voice so small I barely hear it.

My mouth goes dry.

She sobs harder, and something inside me breaks.

I pull her closer.

Lessiyara grips my arms tighter, holding on for dear life. But she goes still.

Pulling in a deep breath, I press my lips to the top of her head.

Her breaths come slower, too slow, and I recognize that pace. I remember trying to stop tears when I needed to do something, when I needed to focus.

Her chest expands, but she doesn't exhale for a long time. I sit, waiting, hoping she exhales, hoping I don't have to check to make sure she's okay, only to embarrass her.

Finally, she lets out a shaky breath, then holds. I try to count my heartbeats before she takes another breath, but it races. One beat clamors over another, and I lose track.

But finally, she inhales again.

She repeats this process a few times, and I lie awake, mind a whirlwind.

When she lets herself breathe normally, her lungs only hitch a little. She releases my arm to wipe the tears away, and blood returns to my hand, pricking with pins and needles.

My brows furrow, and I marvel at how quickly she's regained control of herself. Shocked and dismayed, I fight the urge to pull her closer, to speak up. My mouth opens once more, but I clamp it shut, gritting my teeth.

It won't help.

Just let her have her privacy.

But my heart won't let it lie.

She touches my wrist, slides her hand over mine. I barely suppress a gasp as she laces our fingers together and buries her face in the crook of my arm.

Her breathing evens out as she drifts off to sleep, but I'm left awake. A riot breaks out in my mind, in my heart.

Never, in all my years, did I expect to feel sympathy for a Vaikahlen.

But I do.

Never did I think I'd want to comfort one, but I do.

Swallowing hard, I marvel at the heart buried deep beneath the marble façade and wonder just how broken it is.

***

I wake from dreams of my Sword Siblings to find near darkness on all sides. Lessiyara's warmth still presses against me, and a drowsy smile spreads over my face. Her slender waist fits nicely in my embrace, and her firm backside presses against me. I scoot closer with a sigh, ready to fall back into slumber.

"You make that sound a lot in your sleep," Lessiyara whispers, and I wonder if she even wanted me to hear her.

"What sound?" I ask, voice pulled low by the weight of sleep.

"It's half sigh, half… moan."

I open my eyes, scrunching them to try and see her in the darkness. She's so still, so tense. But she still grips my arms.

After that comment, I wonder if she's blushing.

Chuckling, I pull one hand free to brush a strand of her hair from my face and say, "It's contentment. Comfortable happiness."

She nods but says nothing more. Hesitant, I put my arm around her again, and her hand finds mine instantly. Silence stretches out, and for a moment, I think she's fallen asleep again.

"It isn't quite dawn," she offers up.

"Okay…"

"I don't know when you wanted to set out. I'm sure that's why you're awake now. I assume you don't want to stay here for long… You probably want to get back to your Sword Siblings."

I pull in a deep breath, ready to speak, but she rushes on.

"It just seems like a bad idea to set out while it's still dark."

I smile. "I'm not setting off in the dark. Do you want to sleep longer?"

She nods, and I curl around her, tucking her head beneath my chin. But she stills.

Only then do I remember the bruises she said she had on her back.

Are there more?

Panicked, I ask, "Are you injured? Did I hurt you?"

Her answer comes quickly, nearly cutting me off. "No, I'm fine."

But I remember the way she flinched as I hugged her before, and guilt seeps into me.

"Do you want me to release you?"

She shakes her head, and words tumble from her lips. "No, you're fine."

Taking a deep breath, I pull her close, careful not to squeeze too tight. But my mind spirals, wondering what life must be like for someone like her, a Vaikahlen who clearly struggles to contain emotions, living under Berinasten's reign.

Did he put those bruises there?

Did he beat her?

Or was it one of his Enlightened?

My insides twist.

No wonder she wants to live in a little cabin by herself.

Chapter Nine
Lessiyara

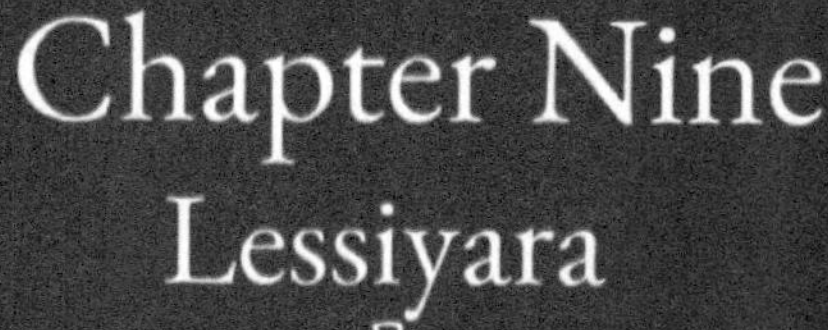

"We know so little of a stranger's heart. Be kind, whenever you can."
- The wise words of Tivasta

Light reaches in through the flap of the tent, and my eyes snap open. The apex of the tent looms overhead, and the bruises on my back protest the rocks and dirt beneath me.

But Ronan's arm drapes over my stomach, having slipped beneath the hem of my tunic in the night. His head rests on my shoulder, and his leg twines between mine, sending heat flaring through me.

My hair tangles around his horns, and I marvel at them. I've never been so close to another's horns, not since...

I swallow, stuffing those years down, refusing to think of my mom, my real dad. I can't. Not right now.

I'm too unstable, too fragile, to handle thoughts of them without crumbling completely. Ronan's warmth, the feel of his hand on my bare torso, the smile he gives so readily...

He's knocking me off balance.

Gritting my teeth, I extricate myself from his embrace, hating every move I make. But I can't be close to him. Everything in me cries out to hold on, to soak up every second that he'll allow me.

But if he knew…

I shudder, slipping his hand from my waist and laying it gently in the warmth left in my wake.

If he knew who I am, what I am…

I slide my leg out from under him, slip my tail free. Kneeling, I grab my coat and pull it on, casting cautious glances at him. He doesn't move, so I crawl to the mouth of the tent and pull my boots on.

He hasn't said, but there's only one reason for him to have come up the mountain with his Sword Siblings.

He must be after Father.

And though I wouldn't mind being free of Father, I can't expect leniency from someone born across enemy lines.

I cast one last glance at Ronan's sleeping form. He doesn't feel like my enemy. But if he knew Berinasten thinks I'm his daughter, if he knew I'm a halfling abomination…

I shudder, imagining the disgust that would surely cross his features, then I crawl out of the tent.

***

"Lessiyara?" Ronan calls softly. His deep voice echoes through camp. Even the needles on the pines seem to tremble.

I pretend my heart didn't skip a beat, pretend I'm not touched by the note of concern in his voice. Taking a deep breath, I let the lines of my face go smooth. Closing my eyes for just a moment, I feel the cold around me, pull it inward, letting the magic of the mountain lend me strength.

"I'm over here," I answer, voice as flat as can be.

I listen for him, barely able to discern his deceptively nimble footsteps. But I don't turn when he reaches me. I keep my hands busy with the lashings, tying them around the log I drug over mere moments ago.

"Are you…" he begins but trails off. "I wish you would've woken me. I could have helped."

"You needed rest," I say.

And I needed time to think.

Time to remind myself that I'm not meant to have someone close, that I'm only tormenting myself.

Ronan circles around me, comes into view. He reaches over the log, passing the lashing underneath, and handing it off to me. Stepping around, he puts a hand on the small of my back.

I close my eyes, hands still moving, tying the lashing.

"Are you okay?" he asks, voice so soft and gentle that I almost believe he wants to know.

It almost breaks me.

Almost.

I nod, not quite trusting my voice.

"You know… It's okay if you're not." He steps closer. "Lessiyara?"

And despite myself, I look at him.

His brows reach for each other, and something shines deep in his eyes. My throat grows tight.

But it's not real.

I know it isn't.

He'll go to his Sword Siblings soon. Maybe they'll take Father down. And then, he'll go back to the valley and forget all about me.

I'll be some oddity, some weird creature in the woods, but better a weird creature than a halfling abomination.

I stare up at him, features cool, calm, perhaps a testament to my control. Or my fear.

His lips purse, and he nods slowly. Something about it feels like he's… giving up. He abandons his line of questioning, drops his hand from my back.

"Which log are you bringing over next?" he asks instead.

My heart twists, but I lead him toward the stack. We bring the next one over, tying it off, then another. And one more.

As the light moves higher, chasing most of the shadows from the deeper parts of the woods, I ask, "When did you plan to set off?"

Ronan startles, staring at me. He rubs a gloved hand over his face. "I don't know. I suppose I should go soon. They likely think me dead," he says with a chuckle. "But I'm not sure of any other ways up to…"

He stops, swallowing. His eyes assess me.

"To Berinasten?" I ask.

With a great, heaving breath, he nods.

"I can show you a way," I offer, surprising both of us. I blink several times, trying to figure out why I've just offered this, why I'm torturing myself with more time around him.

Why I'm willingly heading back toward Father.

"Really?" he asks.

Slowly, I nod, chewing at my bottom lip. As soon as I realize I'm doing it, I stop, smoothing my features once more. "I'll help you get back to your Sword Siblings."

I'll help you reach Father.

Maybe you can rid me of him.

Ronan's dark eyes roam over my face, searching for something. But I don't know what he's asking of me, let alone what answer he expects.

"Thank you," he finally says.

Shaking my head, I whisper, "Thank *you*," so quietly that maybe he doesn't hear me.

I *hope* he doesn't hear me.

But the subtle drop of his jaw, his sudden intake of breath, tells me that he did.

Chapter Ten
Ronan

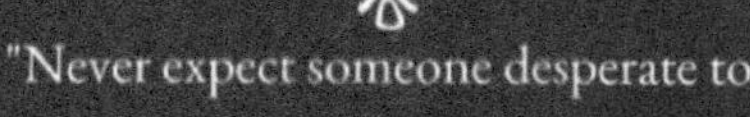

"Never expect someone desperate to back down."
- The wise words of Tivasta

Using Lessiyara's knife, I kill and clean the rabbit that triggered my snare in the night. She busies herself packing her rations and supplies to lead me through the mazelike woods around us. Yet, I can't help but wonder why she offered.

Why she thanked me.

Securing my catch to the spit, I place it over the fire. But I move without thought. My mind ruminates on her, on what she could possibly stand to gain from the fall of Berinasten. Casting a glance at her little campsite, I wonder if she'd prefer a village if under different leadership.

But that doesn't seem like enough.

She doesn't seem to mind it here, and the weight of her words was far too great when she thanked me for it to be something so simple.

It has to be the bruises...

They must come from him.

I take a deep breath.

But why?

Why would he be so concerned with one person?

Pursing my lips, I stare into the flames, listening to the hiss of the meager drippings of fat from the lean animal as they bubble on the embers. I hold my hands out, rubbing them together near the flames for warmth. Thoughts swirl in useless circles within my mind, finding no answers.

Lessiyara comes to sit beside me, setting a pack on the ground between the logs we sit upon. She leans a sword against it, gently stroking the pommel before tucking her hands in her lap.

I glance over at her, tempted to just ask. But would she answer? Or would she withdraw again?

"What is it?" she asks, voice flat and eyes barren.

I won't get an answer right now…

"When do you want to set out?" I ask.

"After we eat? We'll still have most of the day to travel."

I nod, watching her for a slip, a glimpse of something deeper. But I see no sign of the woman this morning. No sign of the woman who wept in my arms last night.

A stranger sits before me, pretending to be a statue.

***

I kick snow into the fire, stopping when Lessiyara moves to grab the pack. "I'll carry it," I offer.

She startles, pausing with the pack swinging in her grip. "What?"

"I can carry it." I reach out, taking the pack gently.

Something in her gaze softens, and a hint of the woman from last night, from this morning, peeks out at me. "Why?"

"Your back," I say.

"You… You don't have to. I'll be fine. I carried it all the way here like this," she says with a shrug. "And I'm sure your back feels terrible. You fell off a cliff. I just got—"

She stops, mouth hanging open. She stares up at me, and I can see her retreating, see the panic in her eyes.

"Well, my back is fine. I guess I didn't fall as far as I thought I did." I slide my arms through the straps, shouldering the pack easily. "And I promise not to fall off another cliff. I won't lose all your stuff."

I smile, hoping my joke pulls her back out, keeps her here with me.

She smiles, dropping her gaze to the snowy pine needles at our feet. "You'd better not. I'd hate to have to save you again."

Laughter bubbles out of me, drawing her eyes upward.

"I'll do my best."

She nods, still smiling, eyes sparkling and full of life. In a few quick motions, she straps her sword to her belt. Another oddity among Vaikahlen people. Without a backward glance, she sets off into the woods, tail swaying behind her.

I follow, chuckling as I trip through snow drifts she fords easily.

***

The sun perches overhead, casting rays of light through branches to dapple the snow. We stop in a small clearing, letting it warm us as we build a fire and take our midday rations. The cold seeps out of me, and the muscles in my back slowly release.

I lower myself to sit near the flames, savoring the taste of the jerky Lessiyara provides. She considers me, eyes impassive.

But her gaze lingers, betraying the distance she paints across her features.

I smile at her, hoping to ease the tension, to loosen her tongue. Her head tips to the side, and I wonder if my attempt will be successful.

But her voice is flat when she asks, "What sent you and your Sword Siblings up the mountain?"

I swallow, assessing her.

Her smooth features belie nothing. But the tension in her shoulders, the soft flick of her tail… They give her away.

The answer to this question matters.

But which answer will bring her out from behind the mask? And which will push her further beneath it?

Either way, I give her the only answer I can. The truth.

"We sought Berinasten and his Enlightened. To end his purification madness." My eyes fall to the flames, and my voice softens as I add, "To avenge our fallen."

"Did he…" her voice trails off, quiet and gentle. Breathing deeply, she tries again, "Did he kill anyone you care for?"

My chest rises with a deep breath. I close my eyes as the ambush of last spring washes over me, as fresh as if it happened yesterday.

They step free of the tree line with arms raised, white cloaks billowing about them in the wind, a sign of *purity*. My father and my friends, run to meet them with swords raised.

Grabbing an axe from a wood pile, I sprint toward them. Chaos erupts as some of my Sword Siblings crash into the front line. I see my father barrel through two enemies, taking them down with the brutality of his charge and a single sweep of his blade to finish them off.

But the Enlightened raise their arms, push them forward, abusing Sihetva, forcing it to hurt us.

And the stones of the mountain do their bidding. They rise, rushing toward me, toward so many of us, separating us from the fight.

I dash to the side, dodging the boulders careening my way. My heart hammers in my chest, blood roaring in my ears. I spare a glance over my shoulder for our village, for the innocent, the old, and the young staring on in fear.

And I run faster, leaping atop the stones which lie useless, trying not to see the bodies beneath them, the limbs sticking out at odd angles. I run atop the boulders, leaping from one to the next, desperate to meet the front line, to protect my people.

I push myself to meet the vile creatures who attack a village full of unarmed people, the vile creatures who force Sihetva to bend to their will and yet dare to think *us* savage. Rage fills me, and I offer it up, asking for power.

All around me, Sihetva burns with the same violent fury, and it eagerly grants my request. I feel the magic it lends me, guiding it into my legs, my feet, surging forward, cracking the stones beneath my feet.

A righteous need for justice courses through every heartbeat, and I use that too. Drawing my axe back, I guide the power Sihetva offers into my arm, into the axe itself. Launching it forward, I send it straight into the nearest Enlightened.

It buries itself up to the handle in his chest despite the metal beneath his white covers, knocking him back into the robed man behind him. Crimson spreads over the pristine white robe. It soaks into the pale blue trim.

Fury begs me to unleash it, to set fire to the whole tree line, to burn the whole mountainside. My hands curl into fists, and flames erupt over my skin. My chest heaves with deep breaths, but I restrain myself, unwilling to abuse Sihetva's trust in me.

My anger burns for the Enlightened.

Not the trees. Not the animals residing within the woods.

I stare at the group before me, struggling to pick one from the group. Their heights vary. The cut of their hair, the shapes of their builds differ, but they look so much the same.

Cold and unyielding. White faces slack and blue eyes blank. A shiver runs over my spine.

But I know how to warm them.

Sihetva gives me fire, and I shape it into a whip. I snap it across their ranks, letting it jump to their hair, their clothes, their skin.

My face contorts into a snarl as I rush toward them, shaping the flame, even now, guiding my rage to consume them quickly, to burn them away. The fires grow hotter, slipping from orange to red to purple. They scream when their infernos turn blue.

But their voices fade quickly.

Five of Berinasten's Enlightened fall by my hand, ashes drifting in the wind, metal armor falling in droplets and heaps.

Lifting my arm, I prepare to let loose my whip one more time, careful to guide it beyond my Sword Siblings in the front line. But the power Sihetva offered me fizzles out, stolen by an Enlightened, leaving me weaponless atop a boulder.

My eyes search the battlefield for a weapon, but instead, I find one man standing apart. He watches the battle impassively, hands making small movements. He stands behind the rest, eyes raking slowly over the scene in robes of perfect white. No blue trim.

Berinasten.

I grind my teeth, offering my emotions to Sihetva. It obliges, giving me power once more, and my flames burn bright, swirling about me like a serpent.

One man breaks through the fold, barreling toward Berinasten, and my breath catches. For half a heartbeat, I dare to hope that the one-man battering ram has gone unnoticed. I watch my father lean into his charge, dropping a shoulder to drive it into Berinasten's gut, running too close for me to chance an attack with flames that might be stolen and used against him.

Berinasten twitches one finger, and a ball of ice slams into my father's chest, knocking him back. Another move of Berinasten's hand, and a spear of ice drives upward, piercing my father's chest.

The world falls away beneath me. I crumble to my knees as his blood drips down the shining spear.

Berinasten twitches his hand once, twice, and a new set of spikes claims another of our warriors. Over and over, such deft little moves break my world into pieces, claiming everyone close enough to suffer such a fate.

A violent fury rumbles through me, and it resonates with Sihetva. I feel it seething around me, crying out for revenge, for freedom from Vaikahlen clutches and abuse.

We damn them all.

Sihetva seethes at my fingertips, leaping to move as I bid. But a memory floats through my mind, an old story used to caution children first learning to work with Sihetva. A method of funneling it into the world, letting it move as it needs to with more force than normal, too wild even for Vaikahlen control.

At a cost.

All around me, my people fall. They bleed on the ground. They scream as they fight to their last breath. Blood spills over the earth, and bodies collapse.

Gritting my teeth, I offer myself up as a vessel to concentrate Sihetva's power. And Sihetva accepts. It burns through my veins in shocks and sparks, in waves of pain and righteous fury. It courses through me, potent and oh so sweet.

Lightning arcs over my skin, leaping from me to strike the nearest Enlightened. She falls with a scream, flailing on the ground, but I keep moving. I leap from the final boulder, and the earth shakes beneath me, beneath the weight of Sihetva moving within me. It rips its way up my throat, and I scream, letting it pour outward.

Dropping to my knees, I slam my hands on the earth, and it splits beneath me. Cracks race toward the Enlightened, and they flinch.

All but Berinasten.

Sihetva begs for more, begs to break them into pieces, begs to burn them all to ash. I let it move through me as it wishes, giving myself over to the destruction of the savages who killed my people.

My arms rise beside me, and a wall of fire reaches up into the air. Sihetva funnels through me, lacing the flames with lightning, pushing the elemental wall forward, sending it chasing after the beasts from the mountainside. It parts around my Sword Siblings, sparing them as it consumes the Enlightened.

Screams erupt as the flames catch the closest ones and the lightning jumps to those beyond.

But my lungs burn. My heart stutters, and my arms grow weak. I fall forward, catching myself to kneel on hands and knees.

And my wall falls.

I lift my head to see ten Enlightened escape into the woods, led by Berinasten. The bottom of his robe has burnt away, and bits of his metal armor are deformed and scorched.

But he limps away.

My teeth grind together, but darkness moves in on me. My head falls, lolling between my arms, and I topple onto my side. I roll, staring up at the pale blue sky.

My eyes flutter closed as Sihetva recedes from me, fluttering anxiously in the air, in the grass. Every bone, every muscle, grows heavy and sluggish. I try to move, but my body betrays me, letting a deep sleep claim me.

Returning to the present, I run a hand through my hair, wondering how much to tell Lessiyara. She waits patiently for me to speak, and I can't even meet her gaze for more than a heartbeat.

Blowing out a breath, I decide to just let it out. I relay the events of last spring to her, unable to watch her blank face as I speak. I stare into the flames, watching them shift and consume.

"I woke three days later in our healer's cottage. I vowed that day to go up with my Sword Siblings as soon as I thought myself strong enough for the trek. We buried our fallen. We rebuilt. *I* rebuilt…" My voice grows strained. "There's a reason we aren't supposed to give ourselves over to Sihetva so entirely. It can wreak havoc on the body. Its power has no limits, but mortal bodies do. It nearly burned me up."

"But I've grown stronger now. I learned my limits that day, felt the moment when it became too much. And I never forgot the cold emptiness of Berinasten's eyes when he…" I grit my teeth, swallowing back the words. I shake my head. "I vowed to be the one to go up after him."

"The Burning Wall… It was you?" Lessiyara asks, and the quiet awe in her voice draws my gaze upward. She stares at me, openmouthed and eyes sparkling.

A small spark of pride ignites within me at the notion that my deeds carried, that my actions were spoken of, that they were *named*, within their village.

I nod.

"Well, take heart," she says. One corner of her lips turns up in a hint of a smile. "Your wall reached him. It didn't kill him…"

Her eyes darken. The smile slips away as she adds, "But he did have to get a cane after that day."

Waves of warm satisfaction roll through me, but the tightness around her eyes tempers it.

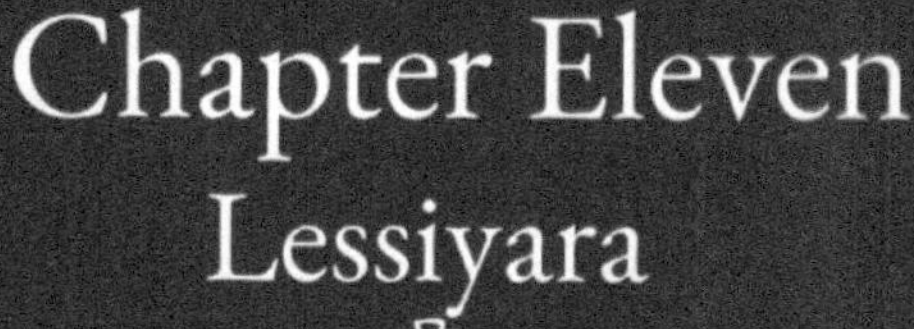

Chapter Eleven
Lessiyara

"Sometimes you must accept things as they are.
And sometimes you must fight to change them."
- The half-remembered teachings of Da

Snow falls around me, and the wind whips at the branches overhead. But my mind drifts to Father and the change worked in him by the Burning Wall.

His Enlightened performed their best magic on him in the field, but they fell short. He walked with a limp, forever after.

And they walked no more.

He came home with a cane of solid ice, infused with the magic of the mountain. Blood stained his clothes, his hands. He spoke of his Enlightened and their failure.

But he said nothing of the Burning Wall.

He didn't have to. We saw it from our mountainside perch.

And that cane...

My back aches, the bruises remembering the cursed thing. From that day on, he never used his hands or his magic to beat me.

Only his cane.

Until it broke, and he made a new one.

Even now, even so far away, I want to snap it in half. My hands ball into fists, and my teeth grind together.

But I'm fooling no one.

I'll never be strong enough, never be brave enough to stand up to him.

Sighing, I listen to the woods around me, ears turning to trace the world. Ronan's footsteps grow distant again.

I stop, turning to face him. He trudges along, moving within the track I cut through the snow. And though I move easily, he stumbles and slips.

Smiling, I say, "You haven't spent much time in the mountains, have you?"

He offers me a laugh, but it belies the struggle his lungs face. Breathing hard, he says, "Not quite."

It won't be long now though. I know the path he said his Sword Siblings would take, and despite everything, we're making good progress toward it.

If they trip through the snow as he does, we'll catch them this afternoon.

I look forward once more, plotting the best course through the snow and the tree trunks.

Ronan comes up behind me, huffing. "How much longer?"

"Not long."

We move forward, and soon, I pick up their trail. Excitement builds within Ronan, but I grow tense.

I didn't think this through.

I'm walking into a Soorahk camp.

Will they give me a chance as Ronan did? Or will they just kill me?

And yet, some small part of me isn't truly worried about the prospect of dying here. I pull my coat tighter around myself, unwilling to consider the implications of that.

Tucking my head down, I brace myself against a particularly shrill wind. I expect to hear Ronan's Sword Siblings shrieking or complaining about it, but when the wind fades, I hear nothing.

No Soorahk swears.

No footsteps.

Not even a bird.

I go still, listening to the mountainside. My ears twitch, searching for something, anything. But the world is silent. A sick feeling settles deep within me.

There should be something.

A gentle winter wind blows through, and I reach out to it, feeling the way it bends around the trees, the way it shapes the snowy grounds.

But nothing shapes the wind in turn. No one moves within it.

I pick up my pace, content to let Ronan catch up. Pushing forward, I follow the trail they left in their wake, the snow violently disturbed by so many feet.

But no voices reach out to me.

No fire crackles at their camp.

I run faster, trees rushing past.

Ronan calls out, "Lessiyara! What is it? What's wrong?"

A clearing appears, and the trees part around me. Skidding to a stop, I look on in horror. My hand rises to cover my mouth, and my heart sinks.

I turn to face Ronan, flinching at the panic in his eyes, as a carrion bird squawks overhead.

Chapter Twelve
Ronan

"Only a fool goes up the mountain
confident that they'll return."
- The wise words of Tivasta

Lessiyara takes off, leaving me to trail after her. "Lessiyara! What is it? What's wrong?"

I chase her, stumbling through snow drifts and the dead undergrowth buried beneath. A clearing appears ahead of her, and she slides to a stop on its edge.

Thank the valleys...

But when she turns to face me, one hand over her mouth, my heart sinks. I slow, then halt, not quite close enough to see what lies ahead. Panic surges through my veins, and suddenly, I don't know if I want to see what, or who, lies in the clearing.

A large bird squawks overhead, circling us, circling the clearing. My head jerks up, staring at the massive scavenger bird, a black mark in the white sky.

Swallowing roughly, mouth dry, I step forward. Snow crunches underfoot, and the wind swirls around me, whipping my hair into my face. My eyes lock with Lessiyara's, brows scrunched together.

Sihetva hangs low around us, drooping in the branches, heavy in the clouds.

I breathe deeply, trying to prepare myself.

Lessiyara stares up at me as I approach, holding my gaze. Streaks of red blur behind her, swimming in the glaze of tears that coat my eyes. Her blue eyes blur before me, but her words come through, all too clear.

"I'm so sorry, Ronan," she whispers. Soft as they may be, her words batter my heart.

A great shuddering breath rattles through me. I swallow, nodding. My eyes flutter, pushing the tears free to freeze upon my cheeks.

Lessiyara reaches up but thinks better of it before her hand finds my cheek. She pulls back, closes her eyes. Stepping aside, she lets me pass.

And my heart falters.

Bodies fill the clearing, bloody and broken. I take two steps forward, and then one more. Everywhere I look, carnage awaits me. My Sword Siblings lie discarded in snow drifts dyed red with their lives.

A few Enlightened lie with them, cold faces looking no different than they did in life. Blank and expressionless, they stare into space.

But my people… Their faces once held such life, such vibrant exuberance. They laughed and cried, they loved and hated.

They *lived.*

And now, they're dead.

I fall to my knees at Skarsi's side, letting a hand rest on her forehead. Gently, I close her eyes. She was so vivid, so fearless. I can almost see how she would've rushed her foes, just as she forged ahead through every mountain pass, every cliff.

But her face is slack in death, empty and broken.

Snow and blood matt her long black hair, tangling it over her neck.

But it doesn't hide the gash that nearly severed her head, doesn't hide the muscle and bone peeking out at me.

I gag but hold my gorge back.

Taking small, shallow breaths, I try to keep the scent of their deaths from permeating every fiber of my being, but it sinks into me all the same.

Rising, I look for Reti. I find her, bloody torso splayed open despite her leather armor. I kneel beside her, closing her eyes and pulling her cloak over the exposed skin and bone and organs.

Tears flow freely, and I choke back a sob. The snow melts beneath me, soaking the knees of my trousers with snowmelt and blood gone cold.

Revulsion and hatred flow through my veins, filling me with a violent heat.

I grind my teeth together, going from one of my Sword Siblings to the next. Everyone I left home with lies dead at my feet, and a black chasm opens up within me, threatening to swallow me whole.

I find Vlaseen with his arm severed and a puncture in his gut. Sprays of blood, long since cooled, reach out from his shoulder, and the rest of his arm lies within reach.

But I can't touch it, can't bring it back to him.

The corners of my eyes prick, and tears flow, crystallizing in the scruff on my jaw.

His family…

Tosva appears in my head, long dark braid swinging as she leans over the crops, belly bulging with their newest babe.

How can I tell her?

How can I tell her this *is how it ended?*

And their children… What will I tell them?

I picture their faces, hear their cries, and I crumple into a heap, weeping into my hands. My body shakes, and my throat grows tight.

A hand on my back startles me, and I turn to find Lessiyara, the sole source of life in this field of death. She kneels beside me, reaching out.

Sympathy shines in her blue eyes, warm behind glittering tears. She opens her mouth to speak but shakes her head. The wind whispers through her long white hair.

Swallowing, she tries again. "I'm sorry…" And though I know it can't be easy for her, she opens her arms for me.

I fall into her embrace, grateful not to be here alone. My heart twists in my chest, and my fingers curl, gripping the fabric of her coat.

She tightens her arms, her soft cries buried beneath the hoarse sobs ripping me apart. Her hair swirls around us, mingling with mine in the cold breeze, and I bury my head in her shoulder to keep it from stinging my eyes.

She leans into me, resting her head against me. Her hand wraps in my hair, and I grip her tighter, my anchor in a sea of despair.

The scavenger bird overhead screeches, and I hate it, hate that it will prey upon these beautiful people. I pull back, intending to scream at the vile thing, but Lessiyara goes rigid.

Her ears twitch from side to side, and she shoots to her feet. "We have to move," she whispers. "They're still close."

Her chest rises and falls quickly, too quickly. Her eyes dart around, searching the shadows beneath the trees for any sign of movement.

I glance around, trying to figure out what she's heard, what could have alerted her to danger, but she grabs my hand. Hauling me up, she drags me along in her wake as she plunges into the undergrowth, going back the way we came.

I spare a glance over my shoulder for the bodies we leave behind, the people whose families I'll have to comfort, and then, I stumble along after her.

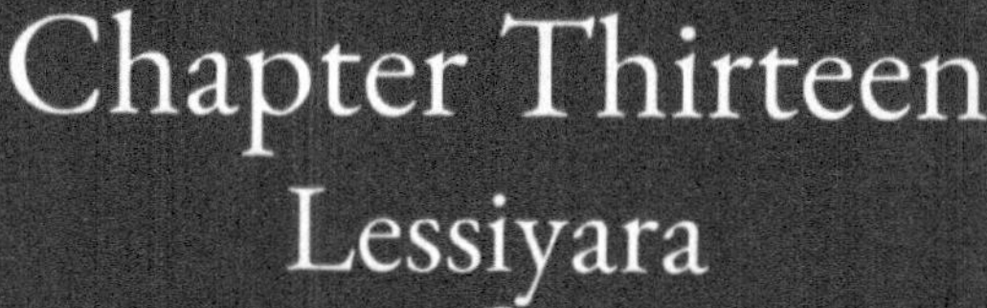

Chapter Thirteen
Lessiyara

"The mountain looms, Too close to breathe.
I feel his eyes, Still watching me."
- The half-remembered songs of Ma

I sprint through the snow, dragging Ronan along. He grips my hand, struggling to keep up. The wind shifts around us, around our pursuers, and I pick up my pace. Trees slip by in a blur, and twigs whip against my face as I duck beneath low-hanging branches.

The wind bends strangely, and I turn to find Ronan's horns have snagged a few twigs. Releasing his hand, I say, "Free yourself," and move my hands to form the wind into the barrier my mother taught me years ago.

My heart races, but the barrier falls into place just as swiftly and securely as ever. I wipe my sweaty palms on my pants, waiting, heart in my throat as I hope no one followed us.

But I know better.

I feel them.

Ronan steps up to me, hands gripping my shoulders. His eyes dart over me, reading things in the features I've never quite mastered. "Lessiyara, what is it?" he asks. "What's wrong?"

Footsteps crunch through the snow, but they're still relatively distant. I close my eyes, desperate to compose myself.

But my heart rattles in my chest. My lungs convulse, gathering shallow, broken breaths.

I press my fists to my temples. "Stop it. Stop, stop, stop, stop, stop!"

He's going to see me.

He'll see how weak I am.

I wince, already feeling the impact of the cane as my bruises throb, waiting for their brethren to bleed through me. I thread my fingers into my hair, dragging them over the sides of my scalp. Stilling, I drop my hands to my side.

Slow breaths…

Desperate, I try to quell the panic, try to wrestle these emotions back into their prison. Locking my gaze on Ronan, I ask, "What's wrong with my face? Why can you see what I'm feeling?"

He flinches, stunned. His mouth falls open, and he stares at me.

"What's wrong with my face?" I whisper-shout. "What gives me away?"

His mouth opens and closes, then he says, "*Nothing* is wrong with your face." The ferocity of his voice shakes me.

"But I see your emotions here," he whispers, touching my jaw. "You're clenching your jaw. And I see it here, in your furrowed brows."

His thumb slides over one of my eyebrows, and I can almost feel the muscles smoothing out beneath his touch.

Almost.

He touches the skin beneath my eyes, his thumb moving slowly across my cheek. "Your eyes are tight, narrowed." Touching my neck, he says, "You're breathing hard, quick. Your pupils are… wide."

"I can't fix that!" My voice rises as I say it, and I cringe at my tone, hearing the fear.

"Do you need to fix it?"

"Yes!" I shake my head, stunned that he still doesn't get it.

"Lessiyara," Ronan says, eyes softening. "It's okay to feel things. You know that, right?"

A derisive laugh bursts from me as Father's footsteps grow closer, shaking the brush around him. The wind bends over his form, around the sticks that crack beneath his feet.

"No. No, it isn't," I say, words muffled by my gritted teeth. "Maybe for you. Not for me."

"Why not for you?" Ronan asks, staring into my face.

I'm supposed to be stronger. I'm supposed to hide it, so no one uses it against me…

But my throat tightens, and I can't say the words.

The wind bends around Father as he approaches our ward, all his Enlightened waiting in the thick woods behind him. My heart stops, and I close my eyes.

Ronan tenses, and I know he's seen him. He tucks me behind him, stepping up, somehow knowing that I'm not up to a fight.

I'm so obvious, so weak.

I grind my teeth together, stopping abruptly when I remember that that's one of the things that show my feelings.

"Oh, daughter," Father says, voice as flat and cold as ice. "If this is the company you keep, it's no wonder you're such a savage. Go ahead and tell him. Tell him what I do when you're too weak to contain your feelings, what I will do soon, as it seems your weakness has not abated."

"This is your father?" Ronan asks, voice tight. But he doesn't turn to face me, doesn't tear his eyes away. His voice drops to a sinister whisper as he says, "He killed my people."

I crumple in on myself, shoulders slumping.

I should've told him…

He'll want nothing to do with me now.

"I'm cleansing the world," Father says.

"You're *murdering* innocent people. My father. My friends," Ronan hisses.

"Ridding ourselves of savages does not equate to murder."

The wind shifts, rushing between us as Ronan takes a step forward. My heart pounds, frantic and fragile, and I grab his arm. His muscles are tense in my grip.

"Ronan, please. Stay in the ward," I beg. "He can't get in."

"That's right," Ronan spits. "Because he'd kill me, just to be rid of another *savage*."

"And because he'd hurt me," I whisper. "There's a reason my mother taught me to make these wards."

Ronan's teeth grind as he pieces things together, jaw working furiously. His hands ball into fists.

"And you want me to let him live?" he hisses.

"He's not alone," I say. Words tumble out in a rush as I add, "There are others. I don't know how many. Far too many for one man to fight. Please, stay. I don't want to lose you."

The words slip out, unintended.

But they're true.

I can't lose the only person that hasn't beaten or berated me for my lack of control. I can't lose the only person that's helped me, that's cared about me, since my mother and my true father died.

With a visible effort, Ronan unclenches his fists. The air shifts as he calls magic, but I warn him off.

"It'll only reflect back at us."

Standing straight, chin up, he stares Father down. Ronan's chest rises and falls with quick, staccato breaths.

"No matter," Father says, expressionless. "Hide in your ward like the weakling you are. I'll punish you later. The cleansing awaits."

Ronan's eyes never leave Father, but he pulls me in, tucking me against his chest. His arms wrap around me, but the tension is still there, coiled in every muscle.

I listen to the wind, feeling the way it shifts as Father turns and marches his Enlightened away. Tears prick at the corners of my eyes, and I bury my face in Ronan's coat.

Chapter Fourteen
Ronan

"The hearts of our youth sometimes know
more than the minds of our elders."
- The wise words of Tivasta

Lessiyara's shoulders shake, and I wrap my arms tighter. But my eyes never leave Berinasten. Her father. My jaw clenches as I watch him walk away to kill more of my people.

I have to do something. I have to stop him.

But she's right.

As he moves away, his Enlightened filter through the snowy shadows behind him, far too many for me to fight without my Sword Siblings. I pull in a deep breath, swallow hard. Impotent rage simmers within me, surging through my veins.

When the last of them have disappeared from view, I close my eyes.

Lessiyara's hands release my coat, and she pulls away. My arms fall from around her, sliding down, and I take her hands in mine. She stares at the ground, motionless. Broken and bruised, she stands silent.

Bruised...

The bruises on her back...

Berinasten's promises of punishment come back to me, and suddenly, it makes sense. The way she cries in the night. The way she hides her emotions, pulling a mask into place as quickly as possible whenever one breaks through.

He beats her.

A sickening rage coils in my gut, winding tight and begging for release. My eyes dart to the path he took, the footsteps he left in his wake. My body aches to call fire down upon him, to burn the whole mountainside to get to him. Damn the consequences and damn the exhaustion that would claim me.

But Lessiyara lifts her head, drawing my gaze.

Eyes closed, she still doesn't look at me. Sihetva moves in the wind. It slips through her hair, lifting it, teasing it. Telling her secrets.

"There was an avalanche on the other path, the quicker path. That's why they came this way," she says.

Her voice is cold and flat. Only the crystallized tear tracks show her heart.

My brows furrow, and I shake my head. I touch her face, thumb moving over the icy tracks. "Stay with me," I whisper. "He's gone. He isn't going to hurt you."

Her eyes snap open, and she sucks in a breath. Fear shines in crisp blue, but it isn't the only thing hiding in the shadows of her gaze. She opens her mouth to speak but stops herself.

Taking a deep breath, I say, "Has it always been… Has he always…"

I can't bring myself to speak the horror of her life.

She nods. "Since I was a child. My mother taught me the ward before she…"

Her voice trails off, and I know I can't leave her here.

"I need to warn my people," I say. "Come with me. The two of us can surely travel faster than them, and I could use the help finding my way down the mountain."

"You'd probably get there faster without me. Falling is faster than climbing down, after all." Her eyes glitter, and a tiny laugh emerges.

My heart soars, even as she catches herself, as she freezes.

I force some levity into my voice, trying to show her that it's okay to open up, at least around me. "Believe me, I'd rather walk."

A smile tugs at the corners of her lips, but only for an instant. It falls, and her eyes drop to the ground. She shakes her head. "I can't. Your people… They'll think I'm an abomination. They'll kill me."

A burst of pain shoots through me, and I touch her neck, tip her head back with my thumb. "They won't. If they see the side of you that you've shown me, they'll accept you."

I stare into her eyes, willing her to see it, to know that my words are true.

She swallows, neck moving against my palm. "I…" Her eyes close, robbing me of their brilliant blue. "I'll go," she finally says, voice a bare whisper.

My heart leaps. "Thank you," I say, voice low and deep.

Blue eyes open, dark as they seek me out. My gaze drops to her lips for just a moment, and color rises on her cheeks.

Don't do this…

I remind myself of every bedridden day spent vowing revenge. I tell myself over and again that I need to hold myself apart, that I can't afford to get close to her. That I have too much at stake to go into a battle afraid of not coming back.

But my heart races, and my blood roars through me. My stomach flips, waiting, aching.

And I give in.

I lean forward, watching her carefully, stopping just a hairsbreadth from her lips. Heat builds between us, and I wait, searching her gaze.

Finally, she brushes her lips over mine, soft and hesitant. I kiss her gently, heart thudding against my ribs.

She steps into me, hands grasping my waist, sending waves of heat through me.

A deep ache settles within me, and I slide my hand to the back of her neck, pulling her in. Our mouths move together, and she tastes like springtime. Fresh and clean and pure.

Breathing hard, I pull back, forcing myself to stop. I lean my forehead against hers, trying to slow my hammering heart, trying to cool the fire burning within.

I smile at her, letting my hands slide down her arms, taking her hands in mine. She stares at me with flushed cheeks and a fire burning in her gaze, and my smile widens.

Clearing my throat, I ask, "Which way should we go?"

Chapter Fifteen
Lessiyara

It moves in every breath, feels the beat of every heart.
It mourns every death, treasures every new start.
- The ways of Sihetva

I owe him. I owe his people.

That's all this is.

But I look at him over my shoulder too often, struggle too hard to hide the smile that wants to peek out at him.

And he doesn't look like he blames me. He meets my every gaze with soft, warm eyes. My heart dances in my chest at the sight, and a blush spreads over my cheeks.

I turn forward, hiding my reaction as I lead him through snow drifts, below tree branches heavy with winter. My mind busies itself, trying to place that expression.

It reminds me of...

It hits me, stealing my breath, and I shove it away.

I shut the thought down, refusing to think of my mother and my true father and the way he looked at her. I refuse to think of our years in the valley, far from any villages where I might have been treated like an abomination. I refuse to think of the life I could've had if Father hadn't found us.

My feet send clouds of soft snow flying with every step, and I focus on that, on the chill soaking through my coat and the wind slipping through the trees.

***

The fire crackles as the sun slips away. Beside me, Ronan tucks his gloves into his pocket and holds his hands out toward the flames. Strong, nimble fingers stretch out, then curl inward. I watch the shadows tracing them, playing over them.

Ronan bumps my shoulder with his. "Why are you staring at my hands?"

I tear my gaze away, looking up at him. He stares at me with one eyebrow raised.

I turn away, staring into the flames to hide the blush that creeps over my skin. I shake my head. “Nothing.”

I shut my eyes.

That didn't make sense.

Why did I say that?

Needing something to busy myself, I say, “I’ll be right back.”

I rise to my feet, schooling my features and focusing on the wind to chase the color from my cheeks. But I don’t miss the smile tugging at Ronan’s lips as he watches me.

When he turns his gaze back to the flames, I gather a few rocks, flat and large enough to make themselves awkward to carry. I haul them over to the fire, then let them tumble from my grasp. Taking a stick in hand, I push them to the edge of the blaze.

“What are you doing?” Ronan asks.

“The wind holds a chill. Tonight will be especially cold,” I say.

"So, of course, we put rocks in the fire." His deep voice holds a teasing tone, sending little thrills tickling through me.

I don't look up, but his smile sparkles in my periphery.

"I'll bury them under the tent tonight. They'll keep us warm."

His expression changes, and finally, I look at him. Raised brows and slightly pursed lips. A light shining in his eyes.

"What?" I ask.

"It's just… I never would've thought of that. It's a good idea."

I stare at him, unaccustomed to such open praise. "Thank you," I mumble, unsure what else to say.

Tossing the stick aside, I wipe dirt from my hands. My eyes drift over the mountainside below us, covered in trees and snow. The sky above darkens, dotted with countless stars.

A ribbon of vivid green curls through the air, just barely visible above the next mountain. My heart skips a beat, and I don't even think about my actions. I sit beside Ronan without hesitation. I don't fight the blush that creeps over me when he laces our fingers together.

"It's so close…" he whispers, voice hushed by the awe it holds. "We can barely see the aurora from the valley, but here…"

"It's beautiful, isn't it?" I say, marveling at the strands of yellow and green that dance on the horizon.

The light catches on snowy treetops, reflects on a frozen lake on a faraway mountain peak.

Fire burns within me as Ronan's thumb moves back and forth over my hand. My skin tingles beneath his touch, and I wonder for a moment if the stars feel this when the aurora brushes past them.

The wind slows, drifting just beyond my reach, and the heat within me grows. Ronan shifts closer, releases my hand. My breath catches as his arm slides around my shoulders, pulling me close.

I hold myself still, staring at the dancing sky and the twinkling stars. A warm sense of peace floods me, and I let myself lean into him. I rest my head on his shoulder, watching ribbons unfurl in the moon's absence. My hands rest in my lap, and I hate how limp they feel.

But what can I do with them?

A deep blush warms my cheeks. There are many things I could do with my hands, things I've done a few times. But it was different.

Those men were cold, unfeeling, and so was I. A bodily need was sated, nothing more.

But this…

I glance up at him, at the light in his eyes and the soft smile on his lips. My heart stutters as the memory of our kiss drifts through me, tender and achingly perfect.

This is different.

Butterflies move in my stomach as his arm tightens around my shoulder. Heat pools within me, and I take a chance.

I turn my gaze to the sky again and slip my arm around his waist. My body burns with the added contact, and I lose focus on the aurora for a moment.

A trickle of fear slips through me, but he isn't Vaikahlen. He won't punish me for feeling, for wanting comfort and closeness.

But a new fear follows in the wake of the old.

Please, don't pull away.

The ferocity of my need surprises me.

But he leans into me, presses a kiss to the top of my head. My heart thrills at the contact, shudders at the proximity of his lips to my little stubby horns. He almost kissed one, almost found out.

But my secret is still safe.

I look at him, lit up by the fire and the aurora. His dark eyes hold mine, and I find little flecks of gold hidden in their depths.

My lips part, and I try to speak. But no words come out.

He leans closer, eyes flicking back and forth between mine. His nose brushes mine, and heat flows through me. His eyes fall to my lips, then rise to meet my gaze once more.

And I can't hold back.

Something in me shudders, snaps, and I lean in. Our lips brush. I swallow, heart in my throat.

He pulls back, touches my cheek, my neck, sliding his thumb over my jaw, and tension builds, deep within me. Fire races through my veins, and my breaths grow shallow. Finally, he presses soft, warm lips to mine, and I melt into him.

My hands grip his hair, tangling in dark locks. His heart pounds in his neck, pulsing against my touch as I slide a hand down, coming to rest on his strong chest.

His mouth moves on mine, hungry but somehow tender. Our lips part, and some wild part of me begs to be unleashed.

I want to push him back, to climb atop him, to move with him. I want to feel him on top of me, moving within me.

But the firelight…

He'd see the marks on my ribs, the marks that would give away what I am.

I glance at the tent and the darkness within that promises to hide me as the darkness of my bedroom has done in the past. My breath comes in gasps, and he reads me, so easily. He sees what I mean, what I want.

And for once, I don't mind that my feelings show so clearly on my face. It means I don't have to say it.

He eyes the tent, hands knotted in my braids, in the fabric of my coat. He nips at my lips, stealing one last kiss, then pulls back. "Are you…" His eyes move between mine. "Are you sure?"

I nod, and he kisses me again, lips burning me alive.

I rise to my feet, pulling him along after me as I walk to the tent. Ducking inside, I marvel at myself, finally doing something, finally giving myself what I want.

Determined not to hide, at least not for the night, I tug my coat off. Ronan enters, casting his coat aside, but I see only a silhouette, a shadow of him. My heart pounds, and I breathe a sigh of relief and disappointment.

I won't see him.

But he won't see me.

He pulls me against him, presses his lips to mine. My blood boils, and my body aches for more.

My mind drifts to the other men I've been with, so cold, so hesitant to kiss. But Ronan seems to delight in the taste of me, savoring every touch of my lips. The men in the past stared into nothing in the darkness, but Ronan drinks me in, despite the blindness of the night. They barely touched me, but his hands roam, pulling clothes away in a flurry of movement as if he can't get to bare skin fast enough.

I jerk his shirt upward, every bit as desperate, and my hands fall upon his bare chest, his stomach, his back. I trail my fingers over his spine, delighting in the shudder, the groan, that my touch elicits.

He lowers me to my back, kisses my neck. A shiver rolls through me as he moves lower, kissing my breasts, treating my body in ways no one else has. I arch my back, pressing against his questing mouth.

Desperation strips our pants away, and I almost wonder if they've burned off in the heat between us. My hands stray, moving over his ribs, tracing the marks I know he bears on his back, his ribs. The valley magic marks those it chooses, and I know these marks, know them because I bear them too.

He shudders at my touch, light as a feather, and his mouth finds my neck, ravaging and savoring. His hand dips low, testing, teasing.

My toes curl, and I gasp.

My tail slides up the inside of his leg, tickling delicate flesh, tugging a moan from his lips. He moves his fingers, pushing me toward the edge, and I arch against him.

His mouth finds mine in the darkness as he works me to a fever pitch. He stares into my eyes, and suddenly, I wish I could see him, wish he could see the fire that must burn in my eyes.

His hand retreats, moving to grasp my hip, and he takes the plunge. I gasp, eyes closing as I press against him, hands digging into his back. Our lips meet, breaths coming hot and fast. We move together, burning the world to ash.

My heart shudders in my chest, and my hips move in time with his. I tangle my hands in his hair, pull him in. Our lips crush together with a violent need, and he grasps my thigh, hoisting it up as he drives deeper, moves just a little bit faster.

And my world shatters.

I fall to pieces, breaking apart around him. I cry out, mouth moving against his. His lips curl upward, smiling against mine, and he pushes me further, finding one more collapse before tumbling down after me.

His body quakes, and his voice rumbles through me as he growls my name. My heart flutters at the sound.

***

Ronan's arm slides over my waist as he rolls toward me. His breathing evens out, slow and easy in sleep, as if trying to lull me along with him.

But I lie awake.

I count the moments, waiting until I know he's deeply asleep. I fight my body's attempts to tug me down into sleep after him, to stay in his arms.

His thumb trails over my skin, and heat pools within me. The echoes of our time together rock through me as he nestles in close. He buries his face in my hair and takes a deep breath.

A shiver rolls down my spine.

He settles in, bare chest pressed against my back. His legs lie tangled with mine, and he holds me tight.

But the moment can't go on forever. Sleep washes over him, tugging him along in currents of exhaustion.

He won't wake up.

Just go.

I have to. But how I wish I could sleep like this, just lie here naked in his arms. I wish I could let him wake to see me, see the marks. I wish I could know he wouldn't run, wouldn't hate me.

But fear coils in my belly.

I take a breath, then slowly extricate myself from his embrace. His arm falls to the blanket as I slide out from under it, and the sound makes me flinch, almost like I'm betraying him by hiding this.

Like I'm betraying myself.

Funny how it never seemed like that before. Hiding just made sense. It kept me safe.

But I'm not the person he thinks I am.

I glance over my shoulder, tracing his shadowed form. The wind whips at the tent flap, and a sliver of firelight reaches in, illuminating his dark lashes fanned out over his cheeks.

My heart thrills at the sight of him, but it also sinks. Because if he wakes, if the wind betrays me, he'll know what I really am. He'll know I'm some half-blood thing, some abomination.

Swallowing, I snatch up my clothes and tug undergarments on in a hurry. I reach for my pants and stick my legs into them, shivering at the chill that crept into the fabric in my absence. I crouch to pull them up, tying the knot above my tail, then sit and shove my arms into my shirt.

The wind slips through camp again, and the tent flap flutters. I freeze, listening, trying to pick his breath from the wind.

Please, still be asleep.

I pull my shirt down, letting out a breath. I reach up to touch my hair, only to find the pins half fallen and one stubbed horn fully revealed. My heart skips a beat, and I refasten it quickly.

A soft touch finds my back, drifting down my spine before slipping around my side, fingers sprawling over my ribs, almost as if tracing the mark of the valley magic.

The mark I shouldn't have.

My breath catches, for far too many reasons.

Ronan kisses my neck as the tent flaps again, but I'm hidden, now.

Surely, he didn't see.

"You're beautiful," he whispers against my skin.

My chest tightens, and my heart leaps into my throat. I look at him over my shoulder, dumbstruck. For a moment, I wish he *had* seen, wish that compliment was meant for the whole of me, not just the half I show.

His arm wraps around my waist, pulling me back against him.

"You're not running into the woods, are you? Did you take what you wanted from me and now you plan to leave?" He chuckles, hot breath blowing through the fur at the tip of my ear. His mouth descends to my neck once more, and I melt in his arms.

"Why would I run into the woods?" I ask with a laugh, spirits buoyed by his lips on my neck, just below my jaw.

"Why else would you have dressed in the night?"

I freeze, struggling to come up with something, anything, to say to him. "I told you it was going to be a cold night. I forgot to bury the hot rocks beneath our bedroll."

The words cut me. A lie and a slip.

This isn't our *bedroll.*

We *don't actually have anything.*

But even that feels false after what we just shared.

"You need only wake me. I'll keep our bed plenty warm," he says against my neck.

Butterflies erupt within me, rioting in my stomach.

Our bed.

It's so silly. Those simple words shouldn't make me so happy.

But they do.

I lie back with him, giggling against his mouth. I let him undress me, even help him along.

I know I'll put the clothes back on when he falls asleep again, but for now, hidden in the darkness, the feel of him can chase the chill of winter and lies from my bones.

Chapter Sixteen
Ronan

"Some can see Sihetva move in the body, some feel it in the world. Some can see how it moves in metal or leather. You bear its mark and need only find your connection."
- The half-remembered teachings of Da

Lessiyara moves away, reaching for her clothes again. I hold still, though I'm far from asleep.

I need to see, to know if my eyes deceived me.

I peer into the darkness, searching her back, her sides, as she pulls clothes on. For a moment, I consider calling for Sihetva's assistance, reaching into the wind to tug at the tent flap.

But I can't bring myself to do it.

Guilt already swirls through me even just hoping to see. Forcibly gaining the knowledge seems like outright betrayal.

And then, I don't have to do anything.

The tent flap swings of its own accord, just a touch, just enough to see the dark line that moves down her spine. It splits into many lines, reaching to trace her ribs, to curl on her hips. The firelight gleams on the tip of a tiny horn, half-buried in that little bump of hair she keeps so carefully pinned in place.

My jaw drops.

She lied. She wasn't cold.

I almost laugh, but I think better of it, knowing she won't appreciate it, not on this matter. But the implications reverberate through my mind.

She's half Soorahk.

Not only that, Sihetva chose her.

I close my eyes as she pins her hair back into place, content to let her tell me in her own time. She clearly isn't ready to do so now.

She pulls back the blanket, nestling in against me and planting a soft kiss on my chest. I slip an arm over her waist, wrap my legs with hers. I look at her, a shadow among shadows, and smile.

"Did you get cold again?" I ask.

"You know, we have to sleep," she says with a sweet laugh. "You can't just keep warming our bed all night."

I chuckle and pull her closer. She relaxes against me, and I let out a deep breath.

I try to come up with something that might have compelled a Soorahk woman to lie with Berinasten but come up with nothing.

And then, it doesn't matter anymore.

The warmth of her lulls me, tugging at my eyelids. Lessiyara's hand slides to my back, traces my spine. I shiver at the touch, and a moan eases past my lips. Her hand comes to rest on my lower back.

Her breath crashes on my chest as she whispers, "Goodnight, Ronan."

"Goodnight," I whisper, wrapping my arms tighter around her shoulders, her waist.

***

With our camp disassembled and stowed in the pack, we set off into the snow. My eyes trace the trees, hunting for smoke rising from Berinasten's camp, but I find nothing. Either they went without a fire, or they set off far earlier than we did.

My brows furrow.

I hope they had no fire.

I hope they froze.

My hands curl into fists at my sides as my head fills with the sight of my Sword Siblings cut down, my father and friends slaughtered last year. My heart twists in my chest as I recall Lessiyara's panic when she heard him catching up to us.

And suddenly, freezing is too kind a death for him.

I need to tear the life from him myself.

My teeth grind together. Sihetva gathers around me of its own accord, and the air around me ripples with the heat of my fury. The snow at my feet melts away.

Lessiyara steps up beside me, puts a hand on my back. Sweat beads on her skin in the heat surrounding me, and I close my eyes, dispelling the power that Sihetva granted as it rallied with my emotions.

"We'll get there in time," she whispers. "We'll warn your people."

I look at her, half tempted to correct her, to say *our* people. But I hold my tongue. Pulling in a deep breath, I say instead, "Are you sure?"

The words are an echo of last night, but the sentiment couldn't possibly be more different.

She nods. "I know this mountain, far better than they do. I've spent as much of my life out here as I could. And I know this wind. I can feel them moving within it."

She raises an arm, points to a section of trees off to the north, just barely further down the mountain than us. "He'll push them hard. They'll set off early every morning. But I know the quickest way down."

A laugh bubbles up in her, and she looks at me, ice blue eyes far warmer than I ever supposed such a color could be. "Well, the second fastest way."

And just like that, I'm laughing again. "I only fell off two cliffs. How long are you going to tease me about that?"

"As long as I can," she says.

Her smile dims as she considers me, but it doesn't disappear. Before I can ask what she means, she's moving forward, stepping lightly through snow drifts. I trudge after her, startled by how much the idea of parting from her pains me.

My brows furrow.

This is exactly why I didn't need to get close to someone. What was I thinking?

But I can't bring myself to fully regret what we shared last night. I blow out a sigh and shake my head.

My eyes drift to the north, trying to pick out their path, trying to imagine what it must be like to feel people moving in the wind. I turn my gaze forward, intending to ask, only to find her far ahead. She casts a glance back at me, lingering on the edge of a copse of trees. A smile hangs on her lips, but her eyes hold no trace of it.

For half a breath, I fear she'll slip the mask back on, fear she'll hide away from me. But every step I take toward her shows me the sadness that lingers in the depths of her eyes just a little more clearly.

The wind whistles through the mountain peaks, carries her long white hair over her shoulder. She closes her eyes, listening to it, feeling it.

My heart races, watching her, watching Sihetva try to comfort her.

Her eyes open, and she says, "We should move. We have time to warn them, but not if we dawdle."

I almost ask what's wrong, almost ask why she dressed in the night, almost ask about the sadness lurking in her eyes. But I nod, knowing she's right.

We have to move while the sun shines, and the pace she keeps in the snow steals the breath from my lungs.

I can ask later.

***

"Where are they?" I ask as I tear into the jerky Lessiyara offered up for lunch. We trudge forward, walking slowly as we eat.

She pauses, takes a bite of her food, and closes her eyes. The wind sighs through the trees, and the branches whisper overhead.

"We've drawn up even with them," she says, pointing straight north. "They might get a bit of a lead in the morning, but the path there," she moves her hand, gesturing further down the mountain, "curves and winds around. It'll take some extra time for them to pass it."

In every direction, I see trees, fallen needles, and snow. But somehow, she sees past them, *feels* past them.

Lessiyara opens her eyes, moving down the mountain. I follow in her wake, moving straight down toward my village. No curving or winding. She warns me of rocks buried in the snow, shows me where to step.

Pine needles catch in my hair as we pass beneath branches. They crunch underfoot when we leave the snowdrifts behind. My fingers trail over the bark of a tree trunk, and I try to feel the mountain as she does.

I feel Sihetva moving nearby, feel it as it interacts with me. But I don't see everything it holds.

The sun slips behind the clouds, but her eyes light up as she looks upon the snow that falls around us as if those snowflakes can tell her anything she wanted to know. Maybe they can.

"This way," she says, leading me out of a thicket of trees.

A rocky precipice waits ahead, ready to plunge us to our deaths. Jagged stone reaches up, desperate to trip me. But she reaches for Sihetva. She takes the wind in her hands and blows the snow from their dark surfaces to show me where not to step.

And Sihetva moves as she wishes.

I turn to follow her, rubbing my hands together to fend off the chill of the open air. My face burns with it, and I blow into cupped hands.

The slope to our left rises, forming another jagged cliff to loom over us, and we walk along a narrow path. I reach out, using the rock wall to steady myself.

This can't be it.

I can't fall here.

I can't come all this way, meet her, lose so many others, and fall off a third cliff.

I peek over the edge, and my heart stops.

This fall would be fatal.

I gulp back a breath.

But Lessiyara walks on, steady as ever. Her hand trails over the rocks, just as mine does, but she doesn't cling to it. Her tail sways back and forth, slow and easy.

When she turns to face the wall, she casts a glance my way, then disappears within a cave I hadn't even noticed. I shake my head, thankful yet again for the strange connection she shares with Sihetva.

I follow her in, assuming we'll wait out the storm and keep moving. But she opens her pack, takes out the makings of our bed.

This can't be it for the day. We didn't get far enough.

I turn to face the opening of the cave and the cloudy sky beyond. Soft grey turns dark and brooding in the distance. Snowflakes fall, drifting through the air, and I want them to stop, want them to go away. Tension builds, tying my muscles into knots and furrowing my brows.

I need to get to my village.

"The clouds stretch too far. They won't let up until after dark," she says. "I'm sorry."

My brows furrow at the absurdity. "For what?" I ask.

She gestures to the snow beyond the cave entrance. "That we won't get further today."

"You didn't bring the storm," I say. Then, teasing, I add, "Or did you?"

She shakes her head. "Of course not. I just… I know you want to get to your people."

Our people.

Sighing, I reach out to her, hauling her against my chest. "Unless you're strong enough to stop an entire storm and just chose not to, you don't need to apologize."

"I can't…" she whispers, staring out at the sky. "I'm not enough for that."

My heart twists in my chest, and for the moment, I forget the agonies of the blood-stained snow, forget the rage that boiled in my veins at Berinasten's taunts. The world centers on this marvelous woman and the pain she carries.

I touch her chin, tip her head back. She watches my chest, refusing to meet my gaze.

"You're more than enough," I whisper.

Her eyes find mine, and her lips part as if to speak. But she doesn't say a word. She leans against me, resting her head on my chest.

Chapter Seventeen
Lessiyara

Unbeknownst to the Vaikahlen people, the mountain doesn't have to be so cold. Sihetva froze it by degrees, year after year, in a gradual, subtle rebellion against their control.
- The ways of Sihetva

Ronan tightens his grip, pressing me to his chest. I lean my head against him, staring out beyond the mouth of the cave. The wind whips past, whistling shrilly against the opening. The world dulls to shades of grey and white as a fresh coat of snow lays itself upon the earth.

A chill comes over me, and tension builds within. My feet itch to move, to get Ronan home, to warn his people. But my heart aches to hold us here, hopes for the storm to drag on, fears he'll leave me behind as soon as he gets home.

Guilt trickles through me at my wishes for a delay, but the storm holds Father and his Enlightened in place too. They can't reach the valley, can't travel at all right now.

I hope they freeze.

I shiver, and Ronan's arms tighten around me.

"You don't happen to have kindling stored away in another camp nearby?" he asks with a chuckle.

"Not quite," I whisper.

Reluctantly, I pull away from him and slide my bag off my back. We spread blankets and lay back against the wall, watching the storm rage beyond the cave opening. The valley below drifts into obscurity.

Ronan puts an arm around my shoulder, pulls me close, and I nestle into his warmth. Tugging the blankets up to my chin, I sink into him. A great breath lifts his chest, and he exhales slowly.

His lips find the top of my head, just behind the pins. My heart skips a beat, but he's well behind my horns. I swallow, toying with a snow-white braid.

My stomach flips.

He could've found out.

A small part of me wonders what he would do. Would he shove me away? Would he beat me as I know my father, my neighbors, would?

It doesn't fit with what I've seen of him.

My mind fills with memories of Father and of my true father. Cold eyes on the former. Warm, joyful eyes on the latter, dark and sweet.

I glance up at Ronan, at the tenderness in his eyes. It reminds me of the looks my parents shared before Father found us, and for a moment, my mind fills with the blood of that afternoon, the little valley home transformed from safe and sunny to a bitter thing that haunts me in a matter of moments.

Ronan leans in, brushing his lips softly against mine, clashing with the chaos in my head.

I close my eyes, trying to just be here, to focus on him and push my memories away. I drop my braid, resting my hand on his stomach. He takes a deep breath at the touch, drawing my attention fully into the cave, into the moment.

His hand touches my jaw, tipping my head back, and his thumb moves slowly over my cheek. "Lessiyara?"

I force my eyes open, staring into the dark warmth of his gaze, but I find his brows furrowed.

He touches the place between my brows with one finger, moves to smooth his thumb over the skin beneath my eye, caresses the corner of my lips.

All the places that give me away.

I still my features, pulling on the mask out of habit.

"What's wrong?" he asks. "You don't need to hide. Maybe you don't want to show these things around your father but… You don't have to hide with me."

My throat grows tight, and I try to swallow. My breath hitches.

He stares into my eyes, offering up his own emotions in the set of his features. A soft smile lifts one corner of his lips. Concern draws his brows together.

Concern for me.

The realization settles over me, and my jaw drops. I touch his jaw, his cheek, his lips. He wraps his hand around mine, pulling my palm to his lips for a gentle kiss.

"So…" he whispers against my hand. He kisses my palm again. "What's wrong?"

My life crashes back into focus for an instant, but I shake my head, sending it all away. I don't want to think about all of that now. I want to think of him.

"Later," I whisper, trying not to wonder if he'll stick around long enough for that conversation, if I'll ever be strong enough to speak those words.

I pull our joined hands from his lips, settling my palm on his chest. Leaning forward, I kiss him, glad to savor him for as long as I can.

Our mouths dance, and his hand tightens on mine. Sliding to my waist, his other hand pulls me closer.

My heart pounds, and blood roars behind my ears. I clutch his shirt, delighting in the way he grips my waist in response. Everything in me begs for more, but I can't finish what I've started. My stomach drops at the realization.

Even with the storm clouds, too much light fills the cave.

He'll see what I am.

I hesitate, pulling away. I release his shirt, hand limp on his chest. But I can't meet his gaze.

Ronan's chest rises beneath my palm. He releases my hand, tips my head back. "Lessiyara..." he says, exhaling my name. "It's okay to talk."

And it all comes back.

Father. My dead parents. The years of abuse that followed in their wake.

I keep my eyes down, focused on his chest, on my hand lying limp. My vision blurs with tears, clearing for a moment when one trickles over my cheek. My mouth opens as if to speak, but nothing comes out.

I shake my head.

"I can't…" My voice comes out weak, croaking. When Ronan's shoulders fall, I force myself to add, "Not yet."

I brace for repercussions, for demands.

But he nods, accepting my answer easily.

Finally, I look up.

He smiles at me. "It's okay not to talk too," he whispers. "If you can't, if you need to figure out how to say it…"

I take a deep breath. Slowly, I nod.

Something inside me seems to break open. Tears prick at the corners of my eyes, but I wipe them away. Swallowing, I nod again.

He kisses me, soft and quick, hand brushing my neck. Falling back against the cave wall, he seems to settle in.

But I follow him back, pressing my lips to his, aching to show him that what he said means something to me, even if I can't say it. His hand slides to the back of my neck, tangling in my hair.

I pull back, just shy of throwing my leg over his lap.

My stomach flips, but I force words past my lips. "Is it okay if…" My voice fades beneath the weight of my words. "Can you not look?"

His brows reach for each other, but the corners of his lips lift. Nodding, he says, "I won't look. I'd love to see you, but I can wait until you're ready."

His eyes lock on mine for a breath, then he closes them.

My heart flutters, and for a terrifying moment, I'm gripped by the fear that he may know, somehow. For another moment, a foolish moment, I hope he does, that he's somehow figured it out and hasn't turned away from me.

I untie the knot above my tail and slide my pants off below the blanket, heart beating madly. I keep my eyes glued to him, to the dark lashes fanned over his cheeks, making sure he doesn't look.

My stomach flips.

But he keeps his eyes closed.

Holding the blanket in place, I climb atop his lap. I lean my forehead against his, kiss his lips, relishing the feel of him kissing me back. His hands slide up my bare thighs, cup my buttocks. Reaching down, I untie the laces of his pants, freeing him.

But my hands go still as he whispers, "Can I look now?"

I hesitate, fingers stilling on laces undone. My breath comes quickly, hovering somewhere between nerves and desire.

"Can I look at your face, at least?"

I let out a breath, nodding.

Realizing that he can't see me, I swallow and say, "Okay."

Dark eyes open, shining up at me. Gold flecks sparkle within their depths. They drop to my lips as his hands rise to touch my neck. Soft and sweet, he kisses me, and I melt.

Taking him in, I move my hips, delighting in the rasp of his breath, the moan riding on his exhale. Heat builds within me, but I move slowly, shifting, torturing us both.

His hand tangles in my hair, and he pulls me in, deepening our kiss. The taste of him drives me mad, and I settle further upon his lap, taking him in deeper.

One hand grasps my hip, fingers sinking into the soft flesh of my backside. He writhes beneath me, eyes locked on mine.

I slide an arm around his shoulders, slip a hand into his dark hair. My breath comes fast, but we move like a falling feather, slow and achingly tender.

Our lips meet, and Ronan slides his hand up my back, beneath my shirt. His fingers splay across my skin, sliding as he wraps his arm around my waist. He pulls me down harder, grinding against me.

My body burns, and the world collapses around me. I arch against him, straining against the hand tangled in my hair. He bends, kissing my neck, nipping at the soft flesh.

My breath catches, and everything within me shatters. Stars explode behind my eyes.

His breath burns my skin, ragged and hot. He pulls me down hard one more time and gasps against my neck as he erupts, fingers digging into my backside.

His chest rises and falls quickly, colliding with mine.

I rest my forehead against his, staring into heavy-lidded eyes, dark with the beauty of what we've shared. He tastes my lips, the movement gentle and perfect. He touches my neck, fingers light as they slip down from my chin to my collarbone.

I cup his cheeks, slide my hands to his jaw, hold him in place. Something shines in his eyes, delicate and warm and gentle. I want to memorize it, want to capture that look in my mind to ease the loneliness I'm sure will come for me when he goes back to his village.

My breathing slowly evens out as I watch him, but his eyes never stray, never dip below my face. His hands move beneath the blanket, tracing the sensitive skin of my thighs, my buttocks, my lower back.

But he never looks, never sees the swirls on my hips.

Shock spreads through me as I marvel at him, and I swallow. My heart expands in my chest, growing far too large for the little cage it lies in. Tears prick at the corners of my eyes.

When they fall, he brushes them away with gentle touches. Concern lines his face, so clear, so crisp. "Are you okay?"

I nod, dislodging a few more tears. I drop my gaze, and a small, embarrassed laugh bursts from me, spluttering through lips now slick with salt.

"How are you feeling? Better?"

"Good," I whisper. "Is good an emotion?"

He chuckles, his deep voice rumbling through me.

"Happy," I whisper.

Ronan meets my gaze, face aglow with the smile that parts his lips. "Me too."

My heart jumps into my throat, and my chest grows tight. He kisses me, leaning back against the cave wall and taking me with him. Tugging the blankets up around us, he wraps his arms around me.

After a moment, I slip from his lap and pull my clothes back on as he ties his pants. He lays down, and I nestle against his chest, shoulders falling as I relax into him. Something soft and gentle takes up residence in my chest, and a fuzzy warmth flows through me.

Ronan's lips press against my forehead as my breaths even out, and I let myself drift off to sleep.

Chapter Eighteen
Ronan

"Down in the valley, Savage and free,
Down in the valley, Where laughter runs free
That's where you'll find my heart, my heart"
- The half-remembered songs of Ma

Lessiyara falls asleep curled up against me. I breathe in the scent of her, and the warmth of our time together almost lulls me to sleep.

A shrill wind blows, screaming past the cave opening, and my eyes jolt open at the sudden chill. Lessiyara nestles in closer but doesn't wake. I pull her tighter against me, tucking her into a tight embrace, and stare out at the snow whipping about on the breeze.

How accustomed is she to cold winds and snowstorms?

I'd chalk it up to living on the mountainside, but they have stone cottages in the villages. Surely, they have hearths to warm them. Her time out here alone must be why the chill barely seems to touch her.

I look down at snow-white skin and hair the color of frost. My eyes trace thick dark lashes splayed on her cheeks and the hint of a drowsy smile playing on her lips.

Such a far cry from the tortured whimpers and tears that have plagued her sleep in nights past.

Berinasten...

The name coils through me like a serpent's hiss.

The man who killed my father, my friends, my Sword Siblings.

The man who beat Lessiyara and sent her off into the snow.

My fingers curl, hands balling into fists on Lessiyara's shoulder and waist. The fabric of her shirt bunches in my hand, and I force myself to relax, to release her clothes from my grip lest I wake her.

She deserves a few moments' rest without the horror of her father hanging over her head.

My mind fills with the attack on the village, and again, I see death on every side, see the fury I unleashed upon the mountainside in a wall of fire and lightning, desperate to take them out even if it cost me everything. That determination fills me again, just as it did every day while I languished in bed letting my body heal, while I climbed the mountain with my Sword Siblings, only to lose them all halfway up.

My breath comes hot and fast, puffing out in little clouds, because now, with my arm resting lightly on Lessiyara's back to keep from hurting the bruises, I have even more reasons to squeeze the life from Berinasten.

I look at her face, peaceful but not blank.

Happy.

And resolve fills me.

No one hurts the people I care for and gets away with it.

***

After a meal of dried foods and bread, Lessiyara and I huddle beneath blankets again.

We warm each other, and in the darkness, she lets me explore her body once more. I fight the urge to trace the marks she wants so badly to hide. My hand splays on her hip, fingertips landing where I know Sihetva's mark spirals. My breath catches as she pulls me closer, lifting her hips to meet me.

Our bodies melt together, and I work her to a fever pitch with caresses and roving hands. She shudders beneath me, gasping my name. My body clenches, and I follow her into oblivion.

Spent, we lie together under blankets. She nestles against me, bare skin hot to the touch. Knowing she'll dress in the night, I touch every bit of her that I can, relishing the feel of her.

She doesn't pull away, doesn't reach for her clothes, but sleep tugs at my eyelids, warm and seductive.

And I know she'll wriggle from my embrace soon.

My breathing grows even, soft, and I mumble, "Don't get your pants."

She breathes out a soft laugh, but it holds no real humor. "Not yet," she says.

Her hand slides up my back, then her fingertips drift down, tracing the mark Sihetva bestowed upon me. If I didn't know she bore the same mark, I might wonder how she knows it so well.

Is she trying to tell me?

I dismiss the thought, mostly.

It follows me as I drift off to sleep, nipping at my heels.

***

I startle awake as Lessiyara moves, shaking her head against my chest. I loosen my arms, pulling back to look at her in the dull light of near dawn. Her brows knit together, and a tear hovers in her dark lashes.

She mumbles groggily, "I know, I know, I know..."

Sleep hangs heavy on her words, but they're clear enough. Sweat drenches her shirt, and I wonder when she put it on, why I didn't wake when she moved from my arms or when she came back.

"I know," she repeats, louder this time, face a scrunched mask of pain. "No one wants me. I know!"

I freeze, hating the conviction in her voice.

"I'm a savage..." she whispers.

My heart breaks, twisting in my chest. A lance of pain spears me, and I touch her face, kiss her forehead.

"Lessiyara," I breathe, cupping her cheek, desperate to wake her, to free her from whatever nightmare plagues her. "Lessiyara, please, wake up. Come back to me."

She jumps, pulling away, flinching as if from an impending beating. My hand stills midair, reaching for her, and my stomach drops.

Her eyes search the dim cave, coming to rest on me. Her chest rises and falls, far too quickly in the panic of small prey.

"Lessiyara..." I whisper. "Come here?"

She swallows, throat bobbing as she nods. "Sorry," she whispers. "I didn't mean to wake you."

I wrap my arms around her, tucking her against my chest. "No need for that," I say.

She burrows into me, arms slipping around my waist.

"You're not a savage," I say. The words cross my lips before I can talk myself out of them. Softly, I say, "If Berinasten is civilized… I'm happy to be a savage."

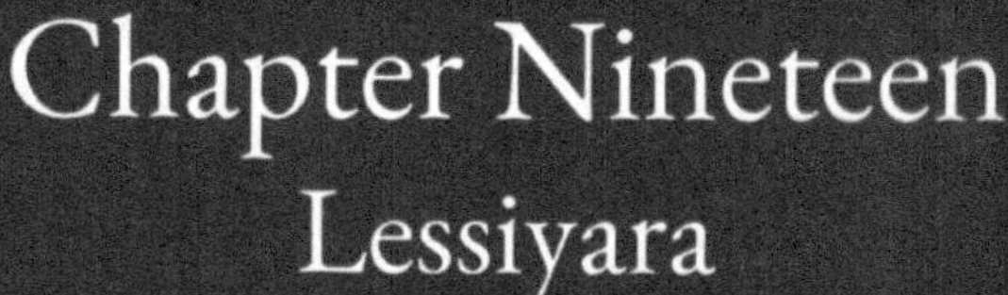

Chapter Nineteen
Lessiyara

"The magic has feelings, my darling."
- The half-remembered teachings of Da

The wind whips around me as we trek down the mountain. It's angry still, but not with us. As if working with me, the wind shows us mercy, releasing us from our cave while pinning Father and his Enlightened in place for the time being.

I reach out, feel the bite of the wind, feel the shape of it. The precipice we wound down looms high above us, and the wind screams through the opening of the cave we vacated this morning. I breathe the wind, feel the rage that moves within it, bending trees on the path Father travels.

But I never noticed the rage in the wind before.

The rage that feels so much like that which boils in my belly as Ronan's Sword Siblings flash through my mind, broken and bloody in the snow. Like the rage that burns my veins when I think of Mother and my true father.

The wind feels like...

It feels.

A memory floats up from the depths of my past, and I see him, see Da, my true father.

The sunset shone brilliantly behind him, sparkling on his black horns. His dark hair hung well past his shoulders, and his eyes twinkled in the late-summer sunlight. He reached out to it, whispering that he could feel it, feel the happiness of it.

"The magic has feelings, my darling," he said. "It chooses people who feel as strongly as it does. Through that kindred spirit, it works with us, moves with us, communes with us."

Light coalesced before him, gathering, swelling with joy, and I felt it. He turned his warm eyes on me, holding a star in his palm, offering it up.

"It chose you, my darling. Let it commune with you."

I stared at the ball of light hovering above his palm, golden and perfect. I reached for it, unafraid of its warmth, my heart bursting with the same happiness that pulsed within it.

My eyes prick with the promise of tears as the memory of my true father fades away. He was so gentle, so warm. He handed me a star and told me I could hold it, feel it.

But I forgot.

My heart spasms in my chest.

I spent so much time pushing my heart away...

I pushed him away too.

My insides clench, and I blink back tears lest they freeze on my cheeks.

I'll remember him more.

I'll try.

I push forward, leading Ronan through snow drifts, between pines, and beneath heavily laden boughs. My heart twists as I try to remember more of my real father.

I see flashes of him running with me, laughing as I climb a tree like a squirrel, smiling with my mother as they work together in the kitchen.

In my memory, he kneels beside me, brows knitted together in concern as he appraises my skinned knee. In another memory, he weeps at the news of a friend succumbing to the winter's chill.

I flinch as the last memory I have of him and Ma comes back, and I push that one away.

I don't want to see him like that.

Sifting through memories, I think of the times we spent together in our happy little home instead.

I cast a glance over my shoulder at Ronan. He smiles at me, eyes light, cheeks tinted pink with exertion.

My heart leaps into my throat, and my face warms.

I turn back, eyeing the trees we pass and letting the wind guide me. My mind fills with his words, spoken in the night.

"If Berinasten is civilized… I'm happy to be a savage."

Those words, so simple, so straightforward, stole my breath. Now, they ripple through me, resonating with all the cherished memories of my time with Ma and Da.

I don't want to be like Father-

I catch myself, correcting my thought.

I don't want to be like Berinasten.

I want to be like my mother, my real father.

I cast another glance back at Ronan, and this time, he's looking out at the forest, at the icicles hanging from a nearby branch. Wonder shines in his eyes, plain for all to see.

I want to be like Ronan.

***

The clouds part above us as we make camp and eat our meal. Darkness falls, and the full moon shines down upon the mountainside. Beside me, Ronan gazes up at it, eyes alight. "It looks so much bigger from the mountain," he says, voice hushed.

My heart flutters, and nerves dance in my belly.

I remind myself of my resolution earlier.

I don't want to be like Father. Berinasten.

I take a deep breath, letting my features relax as I exhale. A smile tugs at the corners of my lips.

I reach for Ronan's hand with my heart in my throat and lace our fingers together. He pulls his gaze from the moon to smile down at me, dark gaze warm and tender.

My heart flips.

Somehow, that simple smile, the touch of our hands, feels more intimate than a nighttime visit from a Vaikahlen man.

I lean against him, staring into the flames before us. My eyes trace the impressions where the rocks sat at the edge of the fire before I buried them under our tent.

Ronan shifts, and I look up, only to find him watching me. My stomach flutters as he searches my face. He touches my cheek, and heat spreads through me. The corners of his lips lift. Kindness shines in his eyes.

My gaze roams over him. I take in the lines that grow deeper with every smile, every laugh. The soft warmth in his gaze washes over me, and I ask, "What was it like? Growing up in the valley, I mean."

Was it like my years with Ma and Da?

How different might my life have been?

How different might I *have been?*

"Well, for starters, it's a lot warmer," he says, eyes twinkling with mirth. "I don't know how you survive up here with all this snow."

I smile, and with his laughter caressing my ears, it isn't hard to let my lips curl upward. "It just takes some getting used to."

I shivered almost constantly for months after Father- Berinasten took me away.

"Being born to it might help," Ronan says.

"Maybe."

Not that I'd know, having been born at the mountain's base.

Ronan draws his knees up and pats the ground between his legs. "Sit here. I'll tell you a few things."

I leap at the chance, settling between his legs and reclining against his broad chest. His arms wrap around my waist, and he rests his chin on my shoulder. I run my hands down the lengths of his arms, twining my fingers with his.

"My father was a Child of the Sword. He wasn't chosen by Sihetva," Ronan says.

I turn to look at him, brows knitting together. "Sihetva…" I whisper the word I haven't heard in years.

Ma said it. Da said it.

Another thing I lost.

"The magic," Ronan explains, but it's coming back to me.

They call it by name. They see that it feels and moves of its own will, and they work with it rather than control it.

"It knew my father felt strongly," he continues, "but not as strongly as it feels. Sihetva found no kindred spirit within him, but he grew to be a great warrior. My mother had no taste for fighting, but Sihetva did find a kindred spirit in her. It helped her tend our gardens, helped her mend minor wounds."

I close my eyes, sighing as I relax into his embrace.

"I remember lying in the grass paths in our garden while she picked velsta flowers. It was one of the only times my sister and I were allowed to stay up late. The velsta plants only bloom beneath the full moon, so it was a special night. The blooms are these huge, purple things, as big as my head, and the sivets love them."

I imagine it all as he speaks, see him lying on the ground with his sister as his parents move through lush greenery to pick flowers by moonlight. A sigh eases past my lips.

"My sister, Coren, and I had a competition, every velsta night. We'd sit as still as we could, with one hand touching one of the blooms, and we'd wait. We'd listen to the sivets chirp, watching their silvery feathers glint in the moonlight."

His arms tighten around me, and his voice drops to a whisper, hushed by that long-ago night.

"We had to be quiet and as still as the earth. It wasn't easy, of course, but if it worked, a sivet would perch on our fingers for just a moment before stepping into the flowers." He chuckles and adds, "Their little feet would be slick with velsta nectar when they stepped back out onto our fingers, and beautiful as those things are, the nectar smells awful."

"Then why would you want the birds to track it onto you?" I ask with a laugh.

"They were just so beautiful. The moonlight didn't just shine on their feathers, it was a part of them. Our ancestors said that the sivets are actually descended from the night sky, pieces of stars that fell and broke apart. Holding one, even for a second, felt like reaching beyond the sky."

My breath slows, evens out. Warmth spreads through me, moving beyond the reach of the fire.

He goes on to speak of his sister, of the baby she'll have soon if she hasn't had it already. My head drops back against his shoulder as he whispers of his hopes for the child, for the life it might lead.

"I want it to have a peaceful life. Sihetva chose me, communes with me on the battlefield. I want to give Coren's baby a better life."

I smile, and drowsiness pushes words to my lips. "And your babies. They should have a good life." The words come out as a mumble.

But he hears them.

A trickle of embarrassment moves through me, and the warmth of half-sleep disappears. His shoulders lift in a sigh.

"I won't have any until I know they can live in a good world," he finally says. "There was…" He swallows. "There was a woman, before. She wanted to make a life with me, wanted a family. But I couldn't. Not with our people being attacked, not with Berinasten trying to cleanse us all from the valley."

My blood runs cold, and I lift my head from his shoulder.

"She didn't want to wait, found someone else. She had her fourth child a few moons ago."

"Four? Already?"

"Already?" He laughs, leaning forward to peer into my face. He shakes his head. "I haven't been with her for years. I only mentioned it because you mentioned my future children."

My heart stutters, still struggling to beat normally.

He kisses my cheek, my neck. "Relax," he whispers. "There's been no one serious for a long time."

I breathe a sigh of relief, despite myself.

"And you?" Ronan asks. "Anyone serious?"

A derisive laugh bursts from me. "No. Some… not so serious. But nothing more than a night. No Vaikahlen man would be interested in someone like me."

I freeze, clamping my lips shut. The truth lies perilously close, ready to spring from my mouth. Some small part of me wants to tell him, just to see what he would do.

He's different. Maybe he wouldn't mind.

But fear slips through my veins, stills my tongue.

"Someone like you?" Ronan prompts, leaning to look at my face again.

I close my eyes, breaths coming faster. My throat dries up, growing tight. Even if I wanted to say it… I can't.

My hands ball into fists.

"Do you mean… someone strong?" Ronan says. He kisses my neck. "Or maybe you mean someone kind?"

His lips find my neck again, and warmth blossoms through me. Slowly, the tension eases from my muscles.

Sighing, he says, "I know you probably weren't going to say either of those things…" He nuzzles his face against my hair. "Whatever you were going to say, you *can* say it now, but you don't *have to*."

I nod, swallowing back the lump in my throat.

We sit quietly, staring up at the stars. But I stew over what I almost said, over the change I've worked in the mood around us.

"Want to go to bed?" Ronan asks.

I nod, and we climb into our blankets, warmed by the hot rocks buried beneath. He wraps his arms around me, pressing me to his chest.

"I'm sorry," I whisper. "Some things are just… hard to say."

"There's no need for apologies," he says, pressing a kiss against my lips.

I nestle into him with tears trickling over my cheeks. He holds me tight as I shudder, crumpling beneath the weight of everything he doesn't know, of what he might think if I told him.

I can't even say it, can't even tell him what kind of thing I am.

I'm a coward.

My tears fall faster, and my heart twists in my chest.

But I can almost hear his gentle assurances to the contrary, the words I *think* he'd say.

And slowly, softly, I drift off to sleep in his arms.

But my mind doesn't find darkness. It finds a memory.

I sit in a field surrounded by tall grass, holding Da's hand.

He looks at me, dark eyes sparkling with mischief, and presses a finger to his lips. "Quiet," he mouths.

Giddiness swells within me, and I suppress a laugh. He squeezes my tiny hand, completely enveloped by his.

In the field, Ma hangs clothes from a line, and not for the first time, I wonder why Da brought me here. But then, I get my answer.

Ma's voice carries toward me, but I've never heard it like this before. It rises and falls, lilting and trilling.

My heart skips a beat.

Ma sings...

We sit quietly as Ma's quiet voice joins with the wind, swirling around the field, swaying with the grasses. She sings of Sihetva, of helping it break free from Vaikahlen control.

My jaw falls, and tears prick at the corners of my eyes.

I look to Da. The smile on his face, the sunlight shimmering on tear tracks, makes my throat grow tight.

Turning back to watch my mother, my beautiful Ma, I settle into the grass, folding my legs beneath me. Her voice sweeps through me, peaceful and beautiful, and I wish I could see her face, wish I could rush up to her and throw my little arms around her waist.

I've never heard her sing before, and it's so pretty!

But Da holds my hand, holds me here, and I wonder if she only likes to sing in private.

Her snow-white hair swirls about her face, and the sun sparkles on the pale skin of her arms. Her dress floats around her ankles, swaying with the wind and her words.

But she cuts off quickly, turning in place to stare in our direction, face a mask of horror.

For a moment, I think she's heard us, that maybe she's embarrassed. I open my mouth and say, "Ma, it's okay! I love your song."

But Da turns, looking behind us, and I realize Ma isn't looking at us. She's looking behind us.

"Vasret, take her," Ma says. "Take her and run."

Chills skitter over my skin.

Da's grip on my hand tightens, and waves of fear surge through my veins. I turn but see only the pines I've known all my life. But I feel the wind, feel the way it moves around something, *someone*, in the trees.

"Da, what's wrong?" I ask, but my voice comes out as a squeak.

"Sureenassa, come on," Da says, staring at Ma. He rises, pulling me into his arms. "We have to go."

I almost argue, almost tell him I'm big enough to walk, but the shock in his eyes stills my tongue.

Ma rushes over to us, blue eyes frantic. Her hands tremble as she touches my face, my hair. "Go with Da, baby."

Tears slide over her cheeks, and my breath catches.

"Ma, what's wrong?" My mind reels, and I grip her hands. "Where are we going?"

"You're going with Da," she says, pressing soft lips to my forehead.

"Sureenassa, no. You're coming with. We've talked about this," Da says, voice firm.

Panic fills me, and my tears fall freely. Questions form, but my voice won't work. My throat's too tight.

I shake in my father's arms.

"You know I can't," Ma says, meeting Da's eyes. She touches his cheek. "Now that he knows, he'll keep looking for me. If I go with, he'll follow. I can't bring him to the village, you know that. I can't."

Her voice breaks as she says, "Go!"

She steps away from us, hand trailing over Da's face, over mine. Her fingers leave me, and I wail.

"Ma, no! Where are you going?" My heart shatters in my chest, and agony rips through me.

She turns, wiping tears from her face.

And then, she runs.

"Ma!" I scream, but she doesn't come back.

Da tries to shush me. He puts a hand to my neck and cradles me, pressing my face against his chest.

And he runs away from Ma.

I stare over his shoulder, gripping his shirt and crying out. "Ma, don't leave! Please!"

But pines and shadows swallow her.

I bounce against Da's chest as he runs past our cabin, past the shed full of food for the animals. "It's too far, it's too far, it's too far…" Da breathes, voice shaking with each step.

A scream rips through the air, and a sob breaks from his lips.

"Ma!" I whimper.

"Shhhh, darling," Da says, but his voice wavers and cracks.

The earth bursts open behind him, a line of roots and dirt exploding into the air, moving straight for us. A scream flies from my lips, and Da looks back, just in time for the ground beneath him to erupt.

We careen into the air, tumbling forward. I slip from Da's grip as we hit the ground, sliding forward, finger bending backward. Agony ripples through me, and I scream again.

Da's face goes pale, and he scrambles toward me on hands and knees. His eyes dart toward the village we visit every couple of weeks, a dark spot on the horizon.

"Cover your horns," he whispers, frantically pulling my hat from my pocket. The tiny stubs hide easily within my hair, but he puts the hat over my head regardless.

"But Da..." I whimper. "It's too hot out." Tears cascade over my cheeks, and I cradle my broken finger to my chest. "Da, it hurts!"

His hands shake as he smooths my hair. "I know, darling. I know. Sihetva can fix it," he says, voice breaking. Tears stream from his eyes, and he whispers, "Always hide your horns and Sihetva's mark. Your Ma and I love you. Remember that! Please, darling, always remember that."

"Da, I don't like this. What's happening? Is Ma okay?"

His chest bucks with a sob, and he shakes his head. "She's not, and I won't be. But you can be, okay? As long as you're careful."

A man looms over Da, blurry through the tears swimming in my vision. A scream catches in my throat.

Eyes as cold as ice stare down at us, and his white skin reflects the sun, nearly blinding me.

He moves his hand, and a spear of ice bursts through Da's chest.

A scream rips through me, echoing through the air. Hands shake me, and I sit upright, shivering in the tent.

My breath comes in gasps, and my cheeks are wet. My throat aches with the scream that's still coming, that won't stop.

"Lessiyara," Ronan whispers, pulling me against his chest. His hands move over me, smoothing my hair, sliding in circles on my back. "Lessiyara, it's okay. It was just a dream."

But it wasn't.

I bury my face in Ronan's chest. Another scream threatens to come, but I clench my jaw, grit my teeth, refusing it passage into the world. I grip Ronan's shirt to stop my hands from shaking.

But I can't stop the tears.

Or the fury that roils in my stomach.

Chapter Twenty
Ronan

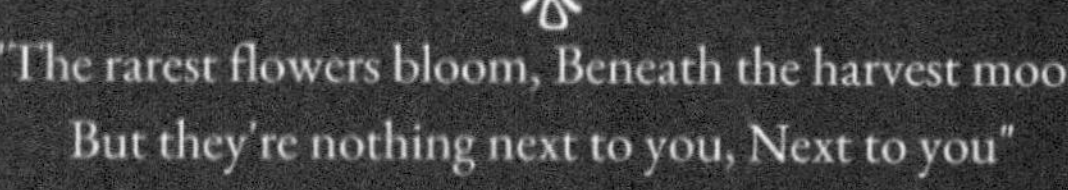

"The rarest flowers bloom, Beneath the harvest moon
But they're nothing next to you, Next to you"
- The half-remembered songs of Ma

I jolt awake, head aching with the scream that fills the air. Lessiyara tosses in my arms, letting loose an ear-shattering screech. Her cheeks shine with tears.

Panic fills me, and I shake her shoulders. “Lessiyara!” Concern coats her name as it falls from my lips.

My brows knit together, and I shake her harder.

She sits up, throwing my arms off as she moves. Her body shakes, and still, she screams.

I sit up, whispering, “Lessiyara,” as I touch her back. Her scream cuts off, and I pull her against me. I smooth her hair and rub her back, but still, her shoulders shake.

“Lessiyara, it’s okay,” I whisper into her hair. “It was just a dream.”

She buries her face in my chest, gripping my shirt. Her tears soak into the fabric, and I wrap my arms tighter around her.

She shakes her head, face moving against my chest. I pull back, touch her face. Tension clenches her jaw shut.

I tip her chin up so she'll look at me. The little bit of firelight that seeps into the tent sparkles on tear tracks, and I smooth my thumb over them, brushing them away.

No new ones take their place.

"Why did you shake your head?" I ask, voice gentle.

"It wasn't just a dream," she whispers, voice raspy, and the tears start up again. They flow over her cheeks, and her lips tremble.

I kiss her forehead, feel the lines melt away beneath my lips, and pull her against my chest again. She slides her arms around my waist, and I let one hand rest on the back of her head, cradling her against me.

"Sometimes, it helps to talk about things," I whisper.

She shakes her head again, and a sob breaks from her, flowing out on a hiccup. "You wouldn't…" She turns her face into me, and the next words come out muffled in the fabric of my shirt, "You wouldn't want me if you knew."

I blow out a soft laugh. "Something tells me you're wrong about that."

I search my brain for anything that she might say that could make me want her less, and shock spreads through me at how much I care for her already.

She stares up at me. The tent flaps sway with a breeze, and a patch of firelight casts golden light over her face. It glitters on her tears. Shadows play in the lines marring her pale skin, and she chews at the inside of her cheek. Her eyes drop to my chest.

"You can tell me," I whisper, dipping my head to meet her gaze.

Her blue eyes blaze with fear and anxiety. But she nods.

"Just know that… I'll still take you to your people," she assures me. "Even if…"

The wind slips away, and shadow falls over us once more. But it doesn't hide the way her throat bobs as she swallows.

She pulls away, setting my arms in my lap. Her hands trail over my skin, reluctant to relinquish the contact. But she lets me go.

"I don't want to feel it when you…" Her voice breaks. "When you know what I am."

My heart shatters. I reach for her, throat tight, but she moves further away.

I let my hands fall to my lap and sigh, ready to wait for her words.

The phrase, "when you know what I am," races through my mind, over and again, and I know the secret she plans to tell me, know I have no intention of pushing her away or doing any other awful thing she might have in her head right now.

"Father—" She cuts herself off and starts again. "Berinasten isn't my real father. He just… thinks he is."

I nod. This makes more sense than the idea of such a *purist* laying with a Soorahk woman.

"The dream… wasn't a dream. It was a memory. Of the day he…" Lessiyara trails off, shaking with a sob and covering her mouth with her hand. After a moment, she pulls her hand away, forcing herself to go on. "The day he killed Ma and Da. She'd left him for Da, found herself with child not long after. We were so happy for a few years…"

Horror fills me, and again, I reach for her, hating how alone she's been, how alone she clearly still feels.

She shakes her head, staving me off. Tears flow over her cheeks, slipping down her neck. Firelight reaches in again, caressing her face, shimmering on the tear tracks that line her skin.

"Da was…" She pulls in a deep breath, fortifying herself. "He was Soorahk."

The corners of my lips turn upward, offering comfort and acceptance. But she doesn't look up, won't meet my gaze.

"He was so kind, so warm. Ma… she was too, most of the time. Sometimes, she seemed far away. I didn't know then, but she was just falling back into the habit of hiding herself, *controlling* herself."

Something you *do.*

I nod but let her speak.

"Da would touch her face and say, 'Come back to me.' And slowly, she would. She'd smile again, or even sing."

Finally, she looks up at me, just a glance, before her eyes fall back to her hands balled in her lap. Silence falls on her, and she stills.

I reach out and cup her cheek. Tipping her head, I meet her gaze, see the lines carved into her face, the anguish trickling from her eyes.

I lean forward, brush my lips over hers. When I pull away, she stares at me, statue still.

Not wanting to spook her with any sudden movements, I whisper, "Come here?"

In stops and starts, with slow moves and a watchful gaze, she moves across our bed, closing the distance between us. But she doesn't touch me.

Hoping to ease the tension so evident in her drawn-up shoulders and her tight expression, I smile. Gently, I reach up and pull pins from her hair, letting loose locks and braids fall about her face. Two small black horns glint in a line of firelight, and my smile widens.

"I already knew," I whisper, making my own confession. My hand rests on her cheek. "I saw Sihetva's mark, saw the tiny hint of horns buried in your hair. The first night that we shared our bodies. Not when we were together, but after. You were dressing, and the tent flaps moved. The firelight showed…"

I let the words trail off, staring into her eyes. She waits, brows digging trenches in her forehead. Her breath comes in shuddering gulps.

"You knew?" she chokes out. "But we… after that, you still…"

I nod. Leaning forward, I kiss her forehead, then press a soft kiss to the tip of each horn, so much rougher than they should be. When I pull back to look at her again, I find her eyes scrunched shut, tears pouring out.

"You're beautiful, Lessiyara."

She opens her eyes, looking up at me through a veil of tears.

I pull her against me, holding her as sobs rack her frame. She wraps her arms around my waist, burrowing her face into my chest. Her tears soak my shirt, and her shoulders shake.

I kiss the top of her head, hold her tighter.

The wind tugs at the tent flaps, reaching in toward us. Firelight caresses her soft skin, glints off the blunted points of her horns, highlighting the rough edges left by a file.

My heart lurches at the thought of her efforts to conceal herself.

Slowly, the tension eases out of her. She looks up, face still shining with the trails left by her sorrow. With furrowed brows, she asks, "You really don't mind?"

I chuckle, smoothing her hair back and wiping the tears from her face. "I really don't mind." My hand finds her neck, and my thumb moves over her jaw. "I care about you. Whether you're Soorahk or Vaikahlen or both. Or some other kind of person we haven't met. It doesn't matter."

She searches my gaze, breath coming fast. And with every beat of my heart, every moment where I don't look away, don't pull away, the panic and fear slip from her features.

I smile, glad to finally have this out in the open, glad she finally knows that I couldn't care less as long as she's this person, this kind, strong, smart person.

She leans forward, eyes dropping to my lips before meeting my gaze again. Testing the waters.

I brush my lips against hers, and a fire burns within me. I try to hold it at bay, but she tangles her hands in my hair, pulling me into a kiss that chases the thoughts from my mind.

She climbs atop my lap, rips my shirt up over my head. Her lips find my neck, my shoulder. Her hands trace Sihetva's mark, sending shivers through me as her fingers trail my spine, my ribs. Frustrated by the pants I still wear, she stops short of tracing the part of the mark that swirls on my hips.

I chuckle, breath rushing out over her neck. Easing her shirt upward, I revel in the feel of her skin, and she shudders. Hungrily, I fall upon her bare breasts. I drink in the soft sounds she makes.

My hands come to her ribs, fingers parted to trace the marks on her sides, trailing up her spine, then down again. When my hands meet the waistband of her pants, I slide them under the fabric to splay over the spirals on her hips.

She sighs, breath caressing my ear.

Freeing my hands, I untie the knot above her tail, letting the back of her pants fall loose. Slipping beneath the fabric once more, I grip her backside, pulling her against me.

Our lips meet again, and she tangles a hand in my hair, clutching me as if for dear life.

Gently, I lay her back on the blankets. I shudder as her hands move over me, untying my trousers. She slides them downward, using her feet to push them off. The soft fur of her tail wraps over my leg, tickles my thigh.

My body begs me to rip her pants away, but I force myself to move slowly. I slide them down, hands trailing over her soft skin, her strong thighs. I tug her pants off, then slip my hands all the way back up. She shivers at the touch, and I smile. Kneeling between her legs, I kiss her neck, feel her warmth as I brush against her.

Her hands move down my back, and she grips my hips, pulling me in. I shudder, and she arches against me. I kiss her neck, moving slowly, gently, within her. She clutches my back, nails digging in. Her legs wrap around me, pulling me deeper, and I gasp against her shoulder.

I slide an arm beneath her, cup the back of her head, fingers tangling in snow-white locks. Our lips meet, hungry and desperate. My body burns for her, begging me to move faster. A sweet, hot ache builds within me, roaring through my veins.

She moves with me, hips working in time. My hand slips between us, thrumming carefully, and she moans against my lips.

The world disappears. Every fiber of my being tenses, begging for release.

My fingers move faster, push her higher.

She cries out, nails scraping skin as she clutches my back. I drive myself deeper, once, twice, and then, I splinter.

Stars explode behind my eyelids, and I gasp, shuddering as my heart pounds. Lessiyara's breaths come hard and fast, shaking her, pressing her breasts against my chest.

She cups my face, tilting my head up. She kisses my forehead, my cheek, my nose, my lips.

A soft chuckle bursts from me, ragged and broken by labored breaths. She giggles beneath me, smiling against my skin as her breath hitches.

Still shaking, I fall to lie beside her, pulling her to face me. She nestles in close, tugging a blanket up over us. Not that I need it now, but we will later.

Slowly, my heart slows its frantic rhythm, and my eyelids droop. A tear slips from her eyes onto my arm.

When I pull back to look at her, she rushes to say, "I'm okay. Happy tears."

I pull her closer, reaching up to hold the hand pressed against my chest.

And this time, I don't worry that she'll pull away to dress after I fall asleep.

***

Sunlight reaches through the flaps of the tent, and smoke drifts in from what remains of our campfire. I pull in a deep breath, and locks of long white hair stick to my face.

I blow them away with a laugh and kiss the top of Lessiyara's head. She's rolled to face away in the night but grips my arms, still tightly wrapped around her.

Her soft warmth presses against me, bare and perfect.

But she's tense.

I prop myself up on my elbow, and my hand trails over her ribs, around to her spine. Up, then back down, only to trace the spiral on her hip. I kiss her neck and whisper, "Good morning."

She lets out a breath, shaky and ragged. A soft laugh bursts from her, tinged with disbelief, lifted by wonder. Her shoulders shake, and tears seep out through scrunched eyes.

"Lessiyara?" I whisper, touching her chin. I turn her head to face me. Stroking her cheek, I wipe a tear away. "What is it?"

"I thought…" Her voice trails off, choked by a sob. She covers her face with her hands before saying, "I thought you'd regret it."

Gently, I pull her hands away. She meets my gaze, but only for a second.

My heart twists. A lance of pain shoots through me, and I shake my head. "I don't regret it."

She rolls to face me, arms slipping around my waist. She burrows into my chest, tiny horns pressing against my skin.

I wrap my arms around her, tangling my fingers in long white hair, and her tears streak over my skin.

Chapter Twenty One
Lessiyara

Throughout their youth, those who bear Sihetva's mark are taught to commune with Sihetva, not as a means for power, but for kinship.
- The ways of Sihetva

We set off down the mountain once more, and for a while, my heart soars. The wind sighs around us, and I feel the joy within it. Each step toward the valley takes a bit of the chill I've known most of my life from its bite, and the gentle breeze grows almost... warm.

I reach out to it, let it slip around my gloved fingers, and it seems to greet me. I feel the happiness within it, and my smile widens.

He doesn't mind.

Better yet, he already knew and still wanted me.

I can still hear the words he whispered last night. "You're beautiful, Lessiyara."

They echo through my mind, expanding to fill my heart. They're so much easier to bear than the words that have plagued me through most of my life.

Savage.

Abomination.

Weakling.

Some from Berinasten. Some supplied by my own mind, guided by his cruelty.

I step through a snow drift, cold soaking into me, every bit as cold as the gazes I've lived beneath for years.

Beautiful.

I take a deep breath, trying to fit the word over myself, to wear it like armor.

Memories of Ma, of Da, reach out to me, and this word fits so well with the life I had with them.

I want to be that person, the person I could've been if Berinasten hadn't killed them.

That day threatens to spring up in my mind, to pull me down again. For half a breath, a single step and then another, I close my eyes.

I can't cry now, not out here in the cold. In Ronan's arms in our tent, sure.

But not now.

The wind reaches for me again, whispering against my cheek, and I wonder if my tears would even freeze now. Already, it's so much warmer than it is up high, and I wonder how I forgot how nice it can be closer to the ground.

Life with Ma and Pa in our little corner of the valley felt warm and special in my memories all these years. But I never thought about how much warmer it actually was.

Again, Ma's scream, Da's anguished whispers fill my mind.

But this time, no tears spring forth.

I see the cruel emptiness of Berinasten's face as he dragged me from Da's bloody body, feel the vicious power of his hand curled around my tiny wrist.

I remember the walk through the forest, up the mountain. The threats that quickly turned to reality as he beat me for crying, restrained me from hitting him back, incapacitated me for wielding the power of the elements against him.

That fury comes back, boiling within my veins. My hands curl into fists, and I grit my teeth.

The sight of Ronan's bloodied Sword Siblings, the thought of his father killed in an ambush, the words Berinasten spit at me just days ago, all come back, trying to sink their teeth into me.

But now, they only strengthen my resolve.

I'll take him down.

***

As we snake down another cliff, I listen to the birds chirping in the trees around us. The slope evens out just enough for us to walk straight down rather than winding back and forth, and the valley seems to rise to meet us, moving closer and closer, bringing with it air that doesn't try to lock my joints into place.

Ronan walks beside me in the thin layer of snow that speckles the rocky ground. He ducks under branches that I pass beneath easily.

He laces our fingers together, bare skin warm against mine. I stuff my gloves deeper into my pocket with my free hand, glad to be rid of them.

Our feet trod over rocks and soft snow, and Ronan tells me of Sihetva, of the rift that grew up between it and the Vaikahlen people.

"Legends say that Kohlvensterba felt very little. Only greed and jealousy. He seldom laughed, and often coveted," Ronan says, thumb moving slowly over the back of my hand. "And even those precious few emotions that he did feel never got the better of him. He hid them, controlled them. Used them."

The tale is so different from the one Vaikahlen children hear that it shocks me. On the mountain, he's lauded as a hero, the man who made his heart heel and forced magic to do the same. The man who brought magic to anyone strong enough to control it, who taught them to tame it and make it theirs.

"He stuffed his feelings down, reached past them," Ronan continues. "He felt Sihetva in the elements around him and forced it to do his bidding. It took him years, but once he figured it out, he showed all the Vaikahlen people who weren't chosen by Sihetva. And then, he fed them lies, told them Sihetva's chosen were afraid of them, that that was why the chosen kept them from Sihetva, even though it's only because Sihetva can't reach them. Then, he pushed them to slaughter."

I shiver.

Slaughter.

Not cleansing. Not revolution. Not any of the pretty words used on the mountain for what Kohlvensterba led the Vaikahlen to do to their family members, their friends.

"They hunted the chosen rather than work with them. They killed them, carved Sihetva's mark from their flesh, and flew it like banners as they staked out territory on the mountain," Ronan says.

My stomach turns, and I shudder, having never heard that part of Berinasten's family legacy.

Ronan squeezes my hand and says, "So, the Soorahk people grew their prowess as warriors, anticipating trouble. Our chosen communed with Sihetva more often, becoming more and more 'savage' in the eyes of the enemy."

"Does Sihetva know?" I ask, voice quiet as we move further down the mountain.

My legs ache at the steep incline despite years of this rugged terrain, and I wonder how he must feel, having spent most of his life in the flatlands of the valley.

"Know?" he asks. "That we're persecuted for our connection to it?"

I nod.

"Yes," he says. The weight of grief hangs on that solitary word. "Sihetva knows our pain. It wants to help."

Swallowing back a lump in my throat, I marvel at the thought of such a powerful thing wanting to help us.

To help *me*.

"So, how do I commune with Sihetva?" I ask, desperate to do my part and bring Berinasten down.

And apparently, free Sihetva from the clutches of people forcing it to bend to their will.

A shiver rolls through me at the thought of pushing another living, thinking, feeling thing to move in ways it doesn't want to move. Guilt swirls in my gut as I realize I've been doing that, or at least trying to do that, for years.

I'm no better than Berinasten.

"It seems like you already commune with it, a little anyway," Ronan says.

I breathe a sigh of relief, and tears prick at the corners of my eyes. "How can I do it more? I don't want to force Sihetva. I don't want to be like… him."

A soft laugh slips through Ronan's lips. "You're not like him," he says and squeezes my hand. "Did your Da ever tell you anything about Sihetva?"

My throat tightens, but I force myself to speak. "He said…" I clear my throat, trying to push the lump down. "He said it feels, that it chooses people who feel as strongly as it does. He said I should let it commune with me."

My heart drops, and I glance at him before admitting, "But… I don't know how to do that."

"So, you were learning the basics when Berinasten killed your parents…" Ronan squeezes my hand again. "How old were you?"

I watch the rocky ground, count the tiny blades of grass that punctuate the moss. "I don't know exactly. I think I was six years old, maybe seven. I've been on the mountain for sixteen years."

Sighing, I wait for him to speak, mouth too dry and throat too thick with emotion to utter another word. Pebbles skitter down the mountain ahead of us, dislodged by our feet, and I listen to the whispering rustle of their movement, feel the gravity that pulls on them, the sinking feeling of plunging over the edge.

"Well," Ronan says, pulling my thoughts from the pebbles and Sihetva's feelings within them. "Sihetva has feelings. It thinks. It wants to guide the world according to its heart and the hearts of those strong enough to show their feelings to it. And that's what you do. Let Sihetva see your feelings, and it'll give you the elements you need."

I scrunch my brows, shake my head. "That doesn't make sense…"

"Sihetva doesn't deal in sense," Ronan says with a chuckle.

"But… How does Sihetva know what element we need?" I stop, tugging on his hand to turn him toward me. "Can you show me?"

Ronan's smile widens, and he nods. Bending, he lifts a twig from the ground. He rises, holding it up. "When I want a fire, I can show Sihetva memories of either anger or of warmth and happiness," he says.

"The fires you make sometimes burn recklessly, far too chaotic for natural fire or for a fire that a Vaikahlen would make," he says with a smile.

"That's why I think you already let Sihetva commune with you sometimes. I think you give it your anger, maybe unintentionally. And the thing you do with the wind, feeling the forest through it, feeling where things and people are, I think maybe you show Sihetva your fear or your curiosity. Also, without realizing exactly what you're doing."

His dark eyes soften as he gazes at me. His chest rises with a deep breath, and he pulls himself back to the task at hand.

"Now, when I want a campfire or to light a candle or a stove, something small, I draw on warm memories. Nights spent with my family and friends, laughing and smiling. The feeling of pulling in a good harvest or coming home safe after a patrol in the forest," he says.

"I offer them up for Sihetva, and it gives me the warmth necessary for the fire. And since it's of joy, of happiness and serenity, the flames don't try to consume everything. The fire simmers, perfect and sustainable."

I stare up at him, brows furrowed, and nod. "Okay. So, it's all about choosing the right part of ourselves to show Sihetva?"

"Essentially," Ronan says. He holds the twig out to his side and steps closer to me. "Right now, just to show you how it works, I want this twig to burn. But Sihetva doesn't like to be forced to do things. It likes to feel… less alone. Like it can relate to someone. It's a lot like us in that way. So, if I show it my feelings, if I respect it enough to let it in, it lends me some of its strength."

He slips an arm around my waist, eyes burning as he gazes into mine. He glances at my lips, then meets my gaze once more.

The pine needles on the twig spark and sizzle. The flames move downward, and sap bubbles out. The fire grows hotter, reaching upward, burning more and more fiercely.

Ronan steps closer, and the air between us swelters. I gulp back a breath as he pulls me closer, pressing me to his chest.

And the flames lick higher, reaching into the air.

"For a fire that changes and grows but doesn't destroy everything immediately," Ronan says, "I show Sihetva desire."

I reach for him, my hand sliding up his chest.

"Want to give it a try?" Ronan's voice comes out husky.

I drop my gaze to his lips, thinking of all the things I want to try.

But that isn't what he means.

Swallowing, I nod.

Ronan shakes the twig, extinguishing the flame. He hands me the remnants and says, "Give Sihetva a warm memory."

I freeze, wracking my brain for something, anything. I nod, finally deciding on one. I close my eyes, concentrating on a day in the garden with Ma and Da. I feel Sihetva in the twig, feel it reaching out, longing for someone to commune with.

I fill my head with their smiles, sharing the joy of picking blooms as Ma sang, the warmth of Da's laughter.

But their deaths weigh heavily on my shoulders.

Ice moves over the twig.

I pull in a deep breath, frowning up at Ronan. "Sorry…"

"No need to apologize," he says. "You let Sihetva commune with you, just in a different way than you meant to. Try again."

Nodding, I try to think of a happy time that isn't tinged with regret and loss. The little cabin with Ma and Da won't work, twisted as it is with loss. The mountain held only pain.

But sitting with Ronan by the fire, the feel of his arm around me, listening to him speak of his family…

That memory holds only warmth.

Soft, comfortable warmth.

A gentle fire moves over the twig, melting the ice away.

I smile, stunned by the flaming stick in my grasp, and Ronan kisses my temple.

Chapter Twenty Two
Ronan

Sihetva depends on those who bear its mark, not for influence over the world, but for friendship.
- The ways of Sihetva

We watch the flames for a moment, letting them burn lower and lower. When the fire nears her hand, Lessiyara settles the twig on the ground and stamps it out beneath her heel.

Yet, I can't help but wonder what happened with her first attempt. Gaining power over the element of ice when seeking fire is... unusual. I ask, and her face falls.

She says, "I thought of my parents and the garden we used to have. It's such a nice memory, I thought..."

I nod, and say, "But it isn't just a happy memory."

Shaking her head, Lessiyara leans her head on my shoulder. I slip an arm around her waist, and we walk like that, ambling down what remains of the mountain. The grass grows more plentiful with every step, almost lush, and the trees thin.

"I imagine your Da was likely working with you a little on this, but most don't master it for years," I begin.

Years you didn't get...

“Letting Sihetva commune with you isn't just about sharing the right thing at the right time," I say. "You have to understand yourself and how you feel. You have to learn how something you feel might affect the world around you so you can learn what to show Sihetva and *if* you should use the power granted."

"But then, isn't…" Lessiyara shakes her head. "Never mind."

I stop walking and turn to her. "What is it? Unasked questions help no one."

She fidgets, staring at the ground. "Vaikahlen magic forces Sihetva. But isn't this just manipulation?"

I chuckle. "If you commune with Sihetva only when you need its power, perhaps. If Sihetva had no choice but to grant us power when we reach for it, perhaps."

She finally raises her crisp blue eyes to mine.

"But we commune with Sihetva frequently, showing it what we feel throughout the day out of *kinship*. And it doesn't have to grant us power. It chooses. Sometimes, that choice is not to share power with us,” I say.

"But then," Lessiyara says with a shake of her head, "how do you know it'll help you?"

We resume walking as I answer, footsteps silenced by the soft growth covering the earth.

"I don't,” I tell her. “But I trust Sihetva to know when I need it, to choose correctly whether or not it should share its power with me."

My shoulders rise as I fill my lungs, breathing in the air, feeling Sihetva's shimmering presence within it. The breeze whispers over my skin, and I feel the joy in it, the celebration that one of Sihetva’s chosen is coming back to it.

"Once you reach out enough, once you share enough of yourself with Sihetva, friendship blossoms. It connects with you."

To my surprise, Lessiyara tenses against my side. I tip my head forward, peering beneath the white locks that fall over her face now that her hair isn't pinned to cover her little horns. She chews at her bottom lip, face scrunched up.

"So, all these years… I could've had a friend," she mutters, so quiet I barely hear it.

The wind whispers over her cheek, drying the tear that falls, brushing the hair from her eyes.

"You *had* a friend, the whole time," I whisper, eyes pricking with the promise of tears. "See how it reaches for you?"

I trace the quickly drying track the tear traveled, the parts of her face that were concealed by hair. A single braid falls forward again, and I push it back behind her ear just as Sihetva did a moment ago. My eyes trace her face, and when she finally looks at me, realization hovers within her gaze.

She touches her cheek, now fully dry.

***

My mind wanders as we move further down the mountain. My eyes follow the pillars of smoke rising into the sky from chimneys, and my heart spasms in my chest, torn between relief at being home, excitement for Lessiyara to see my village, and dread.

I'll have to tell them.

My Sword Siblings flash through my mind, smiling on the trail as we climbed together.

Then, dead and bloody in the snow.

I swallow, but the lump in my throat goes nowhere.

Reti's parents and siblings, Skarsi's partner... I'll have to break their hearts when I get there. I can already see their tears, feel their anguish, their rage.

Every step takes me closer to tearing their lives apart, and for half a breath, I wish we'd been kept in that cave, held up by the storm for another day.

But another day won't make it any easier.

The bodies will be colder, but their families will feel the loss just as keenly.

Sighing, I try to put together the words to tell them, but nothing comes. What words could ever be sufficient? A simple sentence or two could never be a substitute for the people lost to Berinasten and his Enlightened.

A wave of apprehension sweeps through me.

They'll be angry, which of course, makes sense. I'm angry too.

But...

I cast a glance at Lessiyara, at the tiny horns that peek out above her hair. My stomach flutters.

They won't be angry with her... Will they?

Will they blame her?

My blood runs cold as my mind fills with the sight of my people, my friends and family, drawing weapons against her. A flash of Lessiyara sprawled out with an axe in her neck fills my mind, and my stomach drops.

I shake my head, try to slow the breaths that come too quickly.

I barely keep my hands from curling into fists. My mind spins, and I almost stop walking, almost tell her to go back up to her little plot of land on the mountain.

No.

They wouldn't hurt her.

Tivasta isn't so cruel as that.

I pick through memories of our chieftain, searching for any scrap of her behavior that might suggest such brutality possible against an unarmed, innocent woman simply because she isn't fully Soorahk.

But I find only the caring nature that led Tivasta to nurture and raise three orphans as her own. I find the practicality that helped guide her away from the wastefulness of chieftains past, forsaking the gluttony that stretched their garments to bursting long after their hunger was sated. I find the woman who left behind their useless pursuit of lavish tributes from other villages in addition to the cost of trade.

Tivasta is kind. She's smart.

She'd want to learn from Lessiyara, seek Berinasten's weaknesses.

She wouldn't kill her on the spot. She'd give me a chance to explain why I brought Lessiyara along.

And then, she'd take her in.

I blow out a long breath, trying to slow my frantic heart. I squeeze Lessiyara's hand, and she rubs her thumb over mine, a smile dancing on her lips.

When she faces the path, I look at her, stark white hair and skin vibrant against the lush green pines, the red needles littering the earth, and the grass poking out between them. Her braids and locks of long hair swirl about her face as Sihetva sends a breeze to brush them from her eyes.

She turns, gazing up at me. Her eyes soften, and her smile widens.

Warmth builds deep within me, and I find myself smiling back at her.

Even if they tried to hurt her, I wouldn't let them.

Realization sweeps through me, and suddenly, I know I'd step between my people and her, between their blades and her.

And not just because she saved my life.

***

The pine trees thin as we approach a stream. The water babbles as it moves over pebbles, cascading down the mountain, winding between banks crowded by lush greenery. I glance up, staring at the stream, tracing its path, and my jaw drops.

I know this stream, know its falls and switchbacks. I've stared up at it at some point in the day every day of my life.

It's the reason our village was built where it is. It nourishes the valley, feeds our crops.

Every spring, the snows melt on the mountain, everywhere except the highest peaks, and the stream overflows its banks.

But the grounds around it produce the best plants.

I trace the path we've taken and see that we got close to it, over and again.

We've been close to my people the whole time, just upstream.

At the top of a cliff, a section of dark rock looms, and the grounds at its base are littered with rocks.

"Is that where I fell?" I ask, pointing it out to Lessiyara.

She squints, then extends a hand into the breeze to feel its edges. "It is."

I trace the rocky outcroppings and the trees atop them. "So that," I say, moving my hand over, "is your camp?"

Lessiyara nods.

How many times have I looked at this mountain, looked up at her, without even realizing it?

***

The sun hovers over the peaks, ready to dip behind them and plunge us into darkness. The stream burbles nearby, whispering the promise of home.

We'll be there soon.

Tomorrow, even.

A trickle of fear slips through me, but I push it away, shaking my head. My palms sweat, but I tell myself not to worry, even as I glance nervously at Lessiyara.

Tivasta will let me explain.

She'll have questions for Lessiyara, especially with all my Sword Siblings dead.

But my mouth goes dry.

I close my eyes and breathe deeply.

Trust in your chieftain…

She's never led us astray before. She won't now.

Pushing the doubts away, I let my eyes trace the plumes of smoke rising from the homes below. A breeze drifts by, almost warm as it tickles the bare skin of my arms. The chill of the mountain barely reaches us here.

I stare out at the valley, wondering if my mother and sister got the early seeds into the ground, as Lessiyara settles onto the ground beside stacked twigs. I squint at the field we started tilling before I set off up the mountain with my Sword Siblings, though there's no way I could see any seedling from here.

An ember sparks to life beside me, and the twigs sizzle. Fire spreads, forming a perfect campfire. Soothing heat seeps out.

I smile at Lessiyara. "You found a good memory to share with Sihetva," I say.

The breeze slips past us, but Sihetva moves in the flames, keeps them steady and gentle. I cross the space between us and sit beside her. I hold my hands out, soaking in the heat of the fire and reveling in Sihetva's presence.

Lessiyara's hands fidget in her lap, and I knock her shoulder with mine.

"What did you share?"

Her cheeks flush pink.

Chapter Twenty Three
Lessiyara

"Your marks make you lucky, darling,
For never need you be lonely."
- The half-remembered songs of Ma

Ronan waits, eyes on me. But I can't speak, can't force my lips to part. Heat spreads over my skin, and I drop my gaze.

"Now, I really want to know," he says with a chuckle.

I swallow.

I can't tell him that I shared the soft heat that moves through me when his arms slip around me in the night, chasing the thoughts from my head. I can't tell him that I thought of the sound of his voice when he woke, when he called me beautiful.

When he made me feel... Accepted. Wanted.

Even if it only lasted a moment before my thoughts turned to doubt, even if my heart could barely handle it.

But I focused on the good part of the memory, and some small part of me wants him to know that I separated the pieces, that I managed that scrap of control and awareness.

It certainly wasn't easy.

Pulling in a deep breath, I whisper, "I thought of you. I shared… the way it feels when your arms wrap around me in our bedroll."

Ronan stills beside me, and my heart beats faster.

But I force myself to go on, to show him that I'm trying, that I've succeeded in something.

"I shared the way it felt when you woke up and called me beautiful… the morning after I told you…"

Swallowing, hands fidgeting with the hem of my shirt, I continue. "It took me a while. I wanted to make sure I didn't mess it up. I had to sift through the memory and separate the feelings, had to share just a little piece of it, the piece that I like… Not the other ways I think of myself."

It flashes through my mind again. The way it felt to pick it all apart, to see the doubt for what it was, to pull that terrible feeling away from the joy of his words, his acceptance.

"I wasn't going to say it, but… I wanted you to know that I'm trying. I want to learn this. I don't want to force Sihetva. I want…" My voice trails off.

I want the friendship I could have with it.

Ronan touches my chin, lifts my face. His dark eyes meet mine, gaze soft and tender.

My stomach flips.

My hands go still.

He leans in, brushing his nose against mine, and my heart flutters.

"You're learning quickly," he whispers against my lips.

Heat pools within me, and I swallow.

His free hand touches my neck, slides into my hair, leaving a trail of fire in its wake.

My breaths grow shallow, and I search his gaze. Some small part of me seeks a sign of treachery, of disgust, in his eyes. But I find only heat, only tenderness, in those dark eyes.

His thumb traces my lips, and I part them.

"I'm glad you told me what you shared with Sihetva," Ronan says, voice low. "I'm glad you think of me so warmly."

I blush, but I can't look away, can't pull my eyes from his.

And I don't want to.

Those eyes have seen me, really seen me, and they found something good.

I lean forward, brushing my lips against his. I stare into his eyes, trace the lengths of his thick eyelashes with my gaze.

A sweet, delicate ache builds within me.

I touch his cheek, feel the sharp line of his jaw. My hand slides to his neck, and I revel in the feel of his pulse, beating hard and fast, in his neck. I move my hand lower, relishing the way his chest rises and falls with quick, hot breaths.

A smile plays on his lips, crinkles the skin around his eyes.

A smile for me.

Leaning in, I press my lips to his, heart hammering in my chest. His hand tangles in my braids, pulling me closer. Our mouths move together, lips parted and tongues dancing.

My breath comes in gasps, rasping through me as he tips my head back to ravish my throat. Fire spreads over my skin at the touch of his lips on the sensitive skin of my neck, my collarbone.

His free arm tightens around my waist, pulling me to my knees. He slides my shirt up, hands trailing over my stomach, my ribs, my arms. The cool evening air nips at my exposed flesh, but he warms me. Casting my shirt aside, he kisses me, fingers slipping down my spine and sending shivers through me.

I reach for him, heart skipping a beat as my hands splay over his muscled chest. Our eyes lock, and something beautiful shines in his dark gaze. Something aching and sweet.

My heart swells in my chest, and a blush spreads over my bare skin.

I lean my forehead against his, and he whispers, "How did I get so lucky as to find you?"

Something flutters within me, and a soft laugh slips through my lips. "You only say that because I pulled you up the cliff," I whisper. I move forward, kissing him once again.

But he shakes his head.

"No," he says. "That isn't why."

I swallow, brows furrowing as I stare into his eyes. And there it is again. That sweet, delicate emotion shines in his eyes.

He kisses me, slow and soft, burning the world down around us. His hands splay across my back. One slides up to my shoulders, and the other grips my hip. I tug at his shirt, pull it up over his head, hating the distance between us as the fabric comes between our lips.

But it's thrown aside quickly, and our mouths dance again.

Reaching behind me, I untie the bow above my tail, and his hands slip down beneath the fabric to grasp my backside. I gasp softly, relishing the feel of his hands on my hips, on my thighs, as he pushes the dreadful clothing down. I settle into the soft grass to kick my pants off, then rise to my knees.

He takes my hand, pulls me atop his lap.

My hands move over his chest, his stomach. I kiss his neck, letting my hands tangle in his long, dark hair. He grasps my thighs as I move against him, as I press my breasts to his chest.

But it isn't enough.

His hands move between us, unfastening his pants. Lying back, he lifts his hips against me, pushing the fabric down. I bow, trailing kisses over his abdomen, delighting in the rough breaths that shake him.

I sit up, eyes roaming over him. The firelight dances on his tanned skin, and shadows play in the outlines of his muscles.

He pushes himself up, holding my gaze. Words seem to hover on his lips, ready to leap out.

I settle myself onto his lap, taking him in, and his dark eyes never leave mine, even as he gasps, even as he clutches my hips. My tail curls around us, and we move together, slow and gentle. My arms wrap around him, threading one hand into thick locks of hair.

We gasp the same air, leaning our foreheads together as my hips sway and swirl. He clutches my back, wraps an arm around my waist.

And my heart expands, swelling to fill my chest to bursting. An ache builds within me, and my breaths come hot and fast and desperate.

But still, I move slowly, luxuriating in the feel of him, the warmth of his eyes on mine.

Heat builds, pushes me, begs me for release. My body tenses, and my hand curls into a fist in his hair. The other digs nails into his shoulder.

"Ronan…" I whisper, voice husky.

His arm around my waist pulls me down, plunges him deeper.

And the world shatters inside me. My legs shake, and my nails dig deep into his shoulder. I gasp, falling apart around him.

He kisses my lips, my neck. His grasp tightens, and he raises me up, pulls me down hard again.

His fingers dig into my soft flesh as he splinters beneath me. He cries out, "Lessiyara," voice low and deep. A desperate moan shakes through him, and he tightens his embrace.

The convulsions stop, and he lifts his head from my shoulder. Our lips meet, and the warmth of the fire caresses my skin.

***

We lie in the grass, skin bare under the nearly full moon. Ronan's hands move over my back, gentle and reverent. He kisses me, but his eyes are dark when he pulls back.

"My chieftain, Tivasta…" he begins but trails off. He opens his mouth to continue, but no words come out. A deep breath fills his chest, pressing his bare skin to mine.

I tense, going still in his arms. I close my eyes, waiting for the goodbye I knew would come.

When he says nothing, I force myself to speak. "She won't let me into the village, will she?" I open my eyes. "I shouldn't…"

I almost say that I shouldn't exist, but I clamp my mouth shut.

Ronan won't like me speaking of myself that way.

I almost voice the terrible thought just to hear him refute it, to see the compassion he somehow finds for me.

Instead, I say, "I had a feeling that going to the village would mean goodbye."

Ronan's face shifts, brows furrowing as he considers me. He shakes his head. "What? No. That's not what I meant."

"It isn't?"

"No," he says, pressing a kiss to my forehead with a chuckle. "I just… I know people will be angry that my Sword Siblings were killed. They're hurting, and they wanted this dealt with. They wanted Berinasten dealt with. Losing more people, more family members, more friends…"

He sighs, eyes closing, and I touch his cheek.

Swallowing, he meets my gaze and says, "They'll be angry. I don't think they'll be angry at you, but rage doesn't always follow a sensible path. Once we explain, once they know what you've suffered, once they see that you're half Soorahk and that Sihetva chose you, I know they'll welcome you. But…"

His words hang in the air, and my heart hammers as I wait for him to go on.

"Just say it. Please," I say.

"In case I have to convince them to hear you out, to hear *us* out," he says, smoothing my hair back, "stay behind me when we get there tomorrow. It should be fine, but… I don't want to take any chances. I don't want to lose you."

I gape at him, heart fluttering as my mind struggles to comprehend his words. A warm blush spreads over my skin. "R-really?"

"Really," he says with a nod. "Did you really think all of this," he gestures to our naked bodies, "was just something to do until we got back to the village?"

My blush deepens, and suddenly, I can't hold his gaze. I stare at his chest, swallowing nervously.

His shoulders go slack, and he whispers, "Lessiyara… I wish you thought better of yourself."

He cups my cheek, thumb moving slowly back and forth. I offer a half-smile, but it doesn't reach my eyes.

Ronan pulls me close, tucks me against his chest, and I burrow into him. A soft breeze whispers over us, nipping at my skin.

I mumble, "Should we get into the tent?"

He pulls back, staring into my eyes, searching. His lips find mine, warm and tender. My heart clamors in my chest, filling with a sweet ache.

Our lips part, and I stare into his warm eyes. Heavy-lidded and compassionate, his gaze is everything I could want.

But guilt sweeps through me.

"I'm sorry…" I whisper.

"Why?"

"For doubting you. For thinking you'd just leave."

With a deep breath, Ronan says, "You weren't doubting me. You were doubting yourself, doubting your worth."

I go still in his arms.

Ronan rises, tugging me up after him. We gather our clothes and settle into the tent in silence. My mind fractures, struggling to process his words.

Because he's right.

I stare into the darkness, still reeling.

He slides his arms around my waist and pulls my back against his chest, fitting me against him. His hands on my bare skin send tingles through me, but I barely move. He tucks my hair behind my ear.

"Believe me," he whispers, breath hot against my neck, "you're worth sticking around for."

***

My stomach ties itself in knots as we pack up camp, a task that takes far less time than I'd like it to. My eyes drift to the village below, time and again, and my palms sweat.

The grey light of pre-dawn seeps over the mountains, showing me sleepy homes and smoke trails. One or two people walk the paths, heading for fields and market stalls. I take a deep breath, watching them.

The wind slips over me, brushing strands of hair from my face.

It's not just the wind. It's Sibetva.

I close my eyes, reveling in the comfort this being, this energy, offers me. My eyes prick with tears as I wonder how often I've failed to notice it, how often I've overlooked the attempts of my oldest friend to help me in times of need.

Thank you...

I beg Sihetva to see this, to feel the acceptance and regret and joy that war within me. Energy buzzes through me, an offering, a commiseration.

Forgiveness?

A tear slides down my cheek.

I stare out at the village once more, brows knitted together. My lungs fill with the cool morning air, so much warmer down here than it is high on the mountain.

Ronan approaches, smiling wide, and I tell myself not to worry.

He's here.

He doesn't want to leave.

I review our conversation last night, and my heart soars. But I can't stomach the thought of him stepping into harm's way on my behalf if his chieftain deems me unworthy.

He wipes my tear away with a tender hand. Dark eyes soften as they roam over my face.

"It'll be alright," he says, voice calm. "Tivasta is reasonable and kind. She won't harm you if she knows you're not a threat."

But will I get the chance to tell her I mean no harm?

I don't voice the thought, instead forcing myself to trust him, to trust Sihetva. My nerves wind tight, and my heart races.

But I nod.

And though every fiber of my being begs me to run, to hide, to protect myself from someone else who will no doubt call me an abomination, I take him at his word.

He takes my hand, and we move down the last stretch of the mountain.

Chapter Twenty Four
Ronan

When a child is born in the valley, a new flower blooms.
- The ways of Sihetva

The trees seem to part for us, granting us easy passage. The slope of the mountain smooths out, gentle as a rolling hill, sweeping us forward. I gaze across the stream and the fields, at the place I've known all my life, the people I've grown with.

And for the first time, the sight fills me with worry.

I squeeze Lessiyara's hand, eyes roaming, searching for whoever might be on patrol. An archer peers out of the tower at the village center, but I can't see who it is.

A flash of light glints as they raise a glass to their eye, staring straight at us. Turning, they ring the bell once, and I cringe at the sound.

They only rang it once.

Caution, not imminent threat.

Even so, I tug at Lessiyara's hand, sweeping her behind me as we approach. People stop their tasks, abandon their market stalls, and come to the edge of the village. They stare at me, straining their necks to see the person tucked behind my back.

My heart leaps into my throat, and Lessiyara's grip tightens on mine. My toes touch the edge of the field, the dirt freshly turned and awaiting seed.

Tivasta rides forth, saber cat eyeing me carefully as it carries her out between stone cottages. Her linen clothes and fur cloak billow in a soft breeze, and her dark braids whip the air.

Lessiyara steps out beside me, and I turn.

"What are you doing?" I ask.

"I won't let you get hurt for my sake," she says, eyes fierce. "If they wish to eliminate an enemy, I won't have you go down with me."

"You're not the enemy," I say. Frustration seethes within me.

"They don't know that," she whispers. Her neck bobs as she swallows.

"Then let me tell them before you offer yourself up." I turn to face them, stepping in front of Lessiyara once more.

Tivasta perches on her mount, mere fathoms away. The massive cat sniffs the air, and my heart skips a few beats.

"Take the Vaikahlen woman into custody," Tivasta commands, voice as sharp and cold as ice.

The guards behind her rush forward, eager to do her bidding. Their fur cloaks flap as they move toward us, and their leather armor gleams in the sunlight,

"Tivasta, wait!" I shout. "You don't need to do this. She means us no harm. She saved my life."

"Has she forced her control onto you as she does to Sihetva?" Tivasta spits sardonically.

But Sihetva doesn't frost the air around her words, doesn't grant her the power her cold fury might otherwise earn her.

I breathe a sigh of relief.

Sihetva knows Lessiyara too well to treat her as a threat.

"And what of your Sword Siblings?" a guard calls, voice jarred by every step he takes. "You would betray them by bringing her into our village?"

Lessiyara's hands move, brushing my back, and the air around us shimmers for a single heartbeat. She leans her head against my back, breathing heavily.

The shimmering stops, and I realize she's put up another ward. She steps out beside me, and this time, I don't stop her.

I turn, taking her face in my hands. The bright sunlight shines on her tiny horns, and tears stream over her face.

The guards running toward us skid to a stop. They gasp at the show of emotion, as does Tivasta.

"Please," Lessiyara whispers. "They don't want me here. I can't stay, but you should. They need you."

She starts to pull away, but I hold fast, shaking my head.

"No. I won't let you go live alone and miserable." My heart thuds in my chest, and words fall free. "I'd live up there with you before I'd let that happen."

She stills, and so do I.

My eyes flutter, shocked by the revelation, but I forge ahead. "I can come back to visit them. I can still fight by their side when needed. But I won't abandon you."

She stares up at me, open-mouthed. Her breath comes quick, and she falls against me, burying her face in my chest.

I wrap my arms around her and kiss the top of her head. Lifting my gaze, I stare at my chieftain.

Tivasta's long dark hair swirls on a gentle breeze, sliding past her awestricken face. She shakes her head. "Are you..." Tivasta trails off, clears her throat. "Your mother and father, were they Vasret and Sureenassa?"

Lessiyara lifts her head, brows knitted together. She nods. "You knew them?" Her voice breaks beneath the words.

"I did," Tivasta says, voice gentle. A sigh drops her shoulders. "I always wondered what happened to you."

My heart pounds, and my stomach flutters as I eye the nearby guards. Their weapons hang idle at their sides, and they stare at us with curiosity rather than malice.

But I don't let go of Lessiyara yet.

"You mean…" Lessiyara squeaks. "You knew me?" Her eyes fill with tears once more.

"I did," Tivasta says, tears glimmering in her eyes. "Come. It's time we share a meal."

My shoulders sag beneath the weight of my relief, and I blow out a breath. Taking Lessiyara's hand in mine, I ask, “Ready?”

She nods, and we step beyond the limits of her ward.

We walk the path between fields, following in the wake of Tivasta and her saber cat. Its tawny tail swishes through the air, brushes the dirt.

People I've known all my life stand in doorways and gardens, staring openly. Their dark braids and their linens sway in the wind, but they stand, unmoving. They don't speak, merely watch as Tivasta leads us between stone cottages.

I grip Lessiyara's hand, and she trudges along beside me, eyes darting around the village.

Does she remember anything about this place?

Did she ever come here before her parents were killed?

I gaze at her, trusting my feet to guide me. Her soft blue gaze washes over the homes, the people, the flowers all around.

With white braids and loose locks flowing about her, she stands out. Her snowy skin shines brilliantly in the sun, and her tail sways behind her.

But those horns peek out, dark and undeniable, and everyone we pass stares at them.

If only they knew about the mark beneath her clothes…

My skin flushes at the thought, but a familiar voice calls my attention away.

"Ronan?"

My head jerks up, and I search for her. A smile spreads over my features as I take in Coren, and my heart soars. A few dark braids hold her hair from her tan face, framing midnight eyes. A fur cloak rests about her shoulders, split wide by her belly.

My sister steps past a group of guards, young men and women who have yet to be promoted to my rank. She rushes to me, waddling as quickly as possible.

"Ronan! You're okay!"

I drag Lessiyara along with me as I rush forward. "Coren!"

She smiles up at me, eyes streaming as she throws her arms around me. I lean forward to wrap an arm around her without hurting the baby still tucked away in her belly. My hand plunges into the soft fur of her cloak, gripping tightly to hold her to me.

"How's Ma?" I ask. "How's the baby?"

She chuckles. "Ma's fine. And the baby is stubborn. It won't come out."

I laugh into her hair.

"I'm so glad you're back," she whispers. "Sihetva was so restless... Where's everyone else?"

Coren pulls back, black eyes searching the fields, the mountainside.

Sighing, I shake my head. My teeth grind together, and I hiss, "Berinasten and his Enlightened killed them all."

Coren's jaw clenches. She reaches up, touches my cheeks. "We'll get him," she says. Her eyes soften as she adds, "I'm so glad you made it back."

"Only because I fell off a cliff."

Coren stares at me, openmouthed.

"Two, actually," Lessiyara whispers.

Despite everything, I chuckle.

"You fell off two cliffs?" Coren asks, brows drawn together. "What were you doing?"

I shake my head. "I have no idea."

"Clearly," Coren says with a teasing smile. She turns her gaze to Lessiyara. "Now, when are you going to introduce me to—"

Tivasta clears her throat, drawing our attention. "Perhaps you'd like to join us, Coren? You're more than welcome, but I'd like to do this inside so everyone will get back to their day," she eyes the people of the village, still standing, watching.

Coren takes my free hand and falls into step with us, sneaking glances at Lessiyara from time to time. "Two cliffs? Really?" she mock-whispers, conspiring with Lessiyara already.

A smile blooms over Lessiyara's face, stealing my breath.

"I'm never going to live that down, am I?"

"Never," Coren says. Leaning forward, she adds, "Thanks for telling me so quickly."

Lessiyara giggles.

I squeeze Coren's hand and smile at her, a silent thanks for already trying to welcome Lessiyara into the fold.

Chapter Twenty Five
Lessiyara

After his refusal to send Swords up the mountain to search for Lessiyara, Sihetva never granted power to the former chieftain again.
- The ways of Sihetva

Ronan's sister leans past him, smiling conspiratorially at me, as if we share some private joke. Her black eyes sparkle in the afternoon sun, and a long braid slips over her shoulder to dangle freely.

My cheeks flush, and I drop my gaze. She's so warm, so nice.

So much like Ronan.

Though I can't hold her gaze, I force myself to keep the mask tucked away, to let my smile remain on my face.

The woman on the saber cat, Tivasta, leads us to her home with dark locks and braids swishing over her furs. The feathers twined into her hair flutter in a gentle breeze.

I lift my hand, feeling the way the wind plays and whispers over my fingers. Sihetva slips through, warm and gentle, comforting. I pull in a deep breath, silently thanking it, thanking Ronan for showing me its presence.

I watch the ground as I walk, tracing the dirt path, the soft impressions of the saber cat's paw prints. My heart speeds up with every step we take, and I cling to Ronan's hand.

It's okay.

I sneak a glance at the Soorahk chieftain, trying to convince myself that she no longer means me harm, that she'll hear me out. After all, I have information for her.

I can tell her of Father— Berinasten's progress down the mountain. I can tell her how many are with him, how many he lost to the warriors she sent up the mountain.

I have answers for her.

I steal another glance at her and catch her looking to the side, smiling at a child playing in a garden. Wrinkles spread around her eyes, crinkling softly.

I take a deep breath.

Maybe she has answers for me.

After all, she knew Ma and Da. She knew me.

I swallow, heart racing.

Tivasta leads us to a stone cottage surrounded by gardens. Children laugh among the rows of plants, tossing freshly plucked weeds into small buckets.

Slipping from the saber cat's back, the Soorahk chieftain beckons us into her home. I barely raise my eyes as we meander over the threshold, scarcely sparing a glance for the herbs hanging on the walls. The bottoms of tapestries dangle in my view, just brushing the flagstones.

"Come," Tivasta says, voice soft and warm. "Have some cider."

Finally, I dare to lift my gaze to find her filling tankards at a large wooden table. She smiles at me, eyes soft and sad as she chews at the inside of her cheek. Then, her gaze falls away from me.

Ronan's hand deserts mine, only to find the small of my back, guiding me toward the table. He pulls out a chair for me, scraping wooden legs across the stone floor.

My heart rattles in my chest as I search his gaze, but I find only compassion. He smiles, reaching out to push a lock of hair behind my ear. His fingers trail over the furred tip in a soft caress.

I close my eyes, savoring the touch, breathing in the woodsy scent of him. With another deep breath, I stare up at him. I cup his cheek, thumb moving slowly over his cheekbone, and he leans into it, turning to kiss my palm.

As I settle into the seat he offers, Tivasta hands me a mug of cider. Steam wafts up from the tankard, and I wrap my chilled hands around it, swallowing uneasily.

She settles across from me, casting a delicate smile at the shuttered window. The voices of her children filter through, cheery and oblivious to the pain the world can bring.

But that's how it should be.

How my life should've *been.*

I stare at the shutters, at the rays of light peeking in through the slats and the dust motes floating within them. My lungs struggle, searching for air they can't quite find.

I could've had a life like this.

I could've laughed and smiled without being beaten. I could've cried when I was hurt, when I was sad, and no one would've taken a whip or a cane to my back.

Tivasta's soft voice drifts through the room. "You know… You're the reason I took them in."

I come back to the world, the present, and my gaze darts to her. With furrowed brows, I shake my head. "What?"

The fire in the hearth crackles as she closes her eyes, listening to the kids outside. Ronan squeezes my knee beneath the table, and I pull one hand from the mug to lace my fingers through his.

"I always wondered what happened to you," Tivasta says, warm brown eyes strained, and lips drawn tight in a frown. "I felt terrible. I tried to get your parents to move to the village. I tried…"

She shakes her head.

"They didn't want to endanger us. Your mother, especially." A breath rushes from her, and she closes her eyes.

But I sit stunned, waiting silently. I grip Ronan's hand with my mouth hanging open.

"We heard her scream when he came for you," Tivasta says. "I wasn't chieftain yet, but I gathered my Sword Siblings, and we ran for your cottage. But Vasret was dead when we got there. You were gone…"

That terrible day flashes through my mind. I do everything I can to push it away, but I feel Da running, carrying me, desperately repeating, "It's too far." I see his face, see the agony in his eyes when the ice spear pierced him.

Ma's scream fills my head, echoes through my bones.

"We searched for your mother, combed the woods until we found her. They're buried here in the village, together."

My chest heaves.

They're here?

All my life, I've tried not to think of their bodies, left to rot.

But they found them.

They buried them.

Tears sting my eyes, slip down my cheeks. My stomach clenches.

"I wanted to go up the mountain, to bring you back. I swear I did. Sihetva wanted us to," Tivasta says, voice desperate. "But our chieftain…"

A deep breath fills her chest, and Ronan's grip tightens on my hand.

"He was a coward," she finishes, chewing her lip. She turns to the window once more. "After the ambush last year, there were children without homes, and I… I couldn't let them suffer. Not after failing you."

Her face softens, and some of the tension falls away as she listens to them playing happily outside.

I stare at the tankard in my tight grip and force myself to release it. Breathing heavily, I drop my gaze to the wood grain of the table.

"I hope you can forgive me… in time," Tivasta says, returning her gaze to me with a sigh. "You're more than welcome here, and I'll take you to their graves if you'd like. Would you mind…"

She clears her throat. "If you don't mind, I'd like to hear about your life, about what Berinasten has done, what he plans." She reaches across the table and wraps her hand around mine. "Whether you tell me of him or not, I want to know about *you*, darling niece."

My heart races, and my breath comes in gasps. I glance at Ronan, find his mouth agape, and turn back to his chieftain.

Niece?

My eyes fill with tears, and I stare at her anew. I shake my head, dislodging the tears.

"I… I'm your niece?"

Tivasta nods, her tan face streaked with tears. She smiles and squeezes my hand.

I have… family?

Chapter Twenty Six
Ronan

"A coward has no place at the reins."
- The wise words of Tivasta

My jaw hangs open, and I look back and forth between Lessiyara and Tivasta, searching for some resemblance. But Vaikahlen looks run strong in families.

And from the sounds of it, that may be the only reason Lessiyara didn't die alongside her parents.

Turning to me with creased brows and tears in her eyes, Lessiyara whispers, "Did you know?"

I shake my head.

Maybe my mother or father would've known. Maybe I should've tried to learn more about my chieftain's past.

But I was young when her brother, apparently Lessiyara's father, died.

And she wasn't yet our chieftain.

Vague recollections of a pale girl with horns slip through my mind, just a toddler holding a tall man's hand in the market, but the memory holds no detail. I don't remember his face, just a warm laugh.

"No," I say. "I might've seen you in the market once when we were both really young, but I forgot. And I didn't know he was Tivasta's brother."

A deep breath fills her chest, and she nods.

"Did he teach you anything of Sihetva?" Tivasta asks. "You were young, and Vasret's mark was only faint. But he could feel Sihetva sometimes. Did he tell you?"

"A little," Lessiyara says.

She closes her eyes, and I can almost see her fighting the mask that threatens to slip over her features. She breathes heavily, but her frown smooths out. Tears hover in her eyes, but the lines between them disappear.

Turning in my seat, I touch her neck. She stares up at me.

"You don't have to hide here," I whisper. "No one will hurt you for feeling things. You can let it out."

She grits her teeth, breath coming fast as she struggles to keep the tears from falling. "Not yet." She wipes her tears away. "I have to tell your chieftain…" Her eyes flutter, dislodging a tear. "…My aunt… I have to tell her about Berinasten, first."

Reluctantly, I nod.

Lessiyara clears her throat and begins. She speaks of Berinasten's attack on my Sword Siblings. Tivasta's face falls, but she nods, likely guessing as much since no one returned but me.

They're in Sihetva's care now.

Lessiyara reaches out to Sihetva, lifting a hand to the wind. I watch her face as she feels the contours of the mountain, feels the way the wind bends around trees and stone and bodies in a way I never thought possible.

Tivasta's jaw drops as she watches, taking in Lessiyara's actions and their meaning.

Lessiyara tells us of the fourteen bodies that lie tangled with our people, of the sixteen more they left along the trail after they succumbed to injuries sustained in the attack. "There are still ninety of them, plus Berinasten. And we only have about three days before they reach us unless another storm delays them," Lessiyara says.

My stomach drops.

Beside me, Coren gasps.

Ninety wouldn't be so bad if they hadn't just slaughtered our best Swords up on the mountain. The village holds mostly children and farmers, merchants and the elderly.

Only about seventy Children of the Sword stayed behind.

My mind works feverishly, searching for ways to even the odds.

Wards are too small to cover the whole village.

Maybe traps on the path?

Keeping watch might not be enough to alert us, not if they come by night.

Sihetva...

Please help us.

"If you can… *take care* of those coming down the mountain, most of the villagers can't control Sihetva," Lessiyara says. "Those who can are usually pushed into the rank of Enlightened."

"And the other Vaikahlen villages? What do you know of them?" Coren asks.

Lessiyara shakes her head. "Very little. They're mostly cut off. Traveling to them is difficult, even in summer. Impossible in winter."

I take a deep breath, nodding.

No wonder Berinasten took so long to muster his forces after last spring. If he sent for aid or trained new Enlightened… that takes time.

"I'll speak with Vestrol," Tivasta says. "We'll have eyes on those paths all day and night. We'll figure this out." Her voice falls to a whisper, and she adds, "I'll send word to nearby villages, asking for aid."

"Will they help?" I ask.

I don't mention our tendency to stay neutral in intertribal conflicts, but I know she's aware of the resentments that might bring, regardless of the logical reasons for our neutrality.

"It would be in their best interest. They can't afford to lose our mine to Vaikahlen control," she says.

But she chews at her lip, and her tension seeps into me, quickening my pulse.

"Ronan?" she says, dark eyes falling on me. "Why don't you take her to the burial grounds. Her parents are three rows in. On the side near the river."

I nod.

"After that, come back here," Tivasta says, rising to her feet. Her black braids swing forward to brush the table before she straightens.

She comes around the table as Lessiyara, Coren, and I rise. Her kind eyes sparkle, and Tivasta wraps strong arms around Lessiyara's shoulders, pulling her in close. Tivasta's hand presses against white hair, and she cries softly.

My heart warms as Lessiyara slowly raises her arms, tugging her hand from mine, to embrace Tivasta. She stares at me over the older woman's shoulder with wide eyes.

Chapter Twenty Seven
Lessiyara

"Garden graves bring our loved ones back
to us, time and time again."
- The wise words of Tivasta

The Soorahk chieftain presses a gentle hand to the back of my head, arms wrapped around me. Slowly, I embrace her, never tearing my eyes from Ronan.

My aunt.

I have family, real family.

Not Berinasten.

Tears prick at the corners of my eyes, blurring Ronan's dark countenance, blurring Coren beside him.

"I'm so sorry we didn't get you back," Tivasta whispers into my hair, voice breaking. "We thought..."

Pulling back, she cups my cheeks. "You're here now, though. You're welcome to stay here with me or..." She casts a glance at Ronan, and my cheeks burn. "Wherever you want to stay, you're welcome in the village. I want to know you. I want to know what you endured and who you became. Could we talk tonight?"

My throat tightens, and words desert me. A tear rolls down my cheek.

She wants to talk to me. She wants me to stay.

I search her gaze, looking for any hint of hatred, any semblance of the fury I always feared would show itself if I came here. I wait for her to call me an abomination.

But she only smiles, eyes bright despite her tears.

Those warm brown depths promise safety and acceptance, and my heart begs me to take it.

So, I nod.

It's a small movement, so easy to miss, burdened by lingering fear, but she sees.

Beaming at me, she says, "Ronan will take you to see your parents' graves. I have to speak with Vestrol immediately, otherwise, I'd come with. I promise I would."

Her voice cracks once more, and she smooths my hair down, wipes a tear from my cheek with her thumb.

And I believe her.

She would come with me. She'd comfort me and let me cry as long as I wanted, as long as I needed.

She wouldn't judge me or hit me.

The look in her eyes tells me she'd do exactly as she's doing now. She'd hold me and tell me she understands, somehow convincing me that she really does.

I let out a slow, shaky breath and offer up a smile.

"I'll see you soon," Tivasta whispers.

And then she's off, bustling out the door without drying her face, comfortable showing her tears to the world.

***

Soft grass springs up to greet my feet, and birds chirp overhead, such a far cry from the mountain. Winter holds that land in a death grip, but here, spring is already waving hello.

The soft breeze cools my skin, so much warmer than I've felt in recent years.

But my heart freezes in my chest, and dread builds within me.

What will it be like?

I've never seen a Soorahk grave, never seen the way they mourn. Vaikahlen funerals are emotionless things, a carefully controlled fire, a pile of ash, a single blank expression on every face as the body burns, and no one waits to say goodbye.

Life goes on, and families pretend they feel nothing. The ashes filter through cracks in the rocks, and no one pays them any mind, no one looks at them.

But I'm sure it'll be different here.

A low stone wall surrounds a plot of land, separating it from the rest of the village. Smaller stones outline rectangles in the earth, and within each small border, plants burst from the earth, carefully cultivated.

There's one little rectangle that stands out, looking just a little different from the rest, and I know.

My throat grows tight.

I walk ahead, leading Ronan through the rows. Even if Tivasta hadn't told us where to look, I would've known it.

Within the border of stone that outlines my parent's final resting place, beautiful green vines intermingle with the tall silver stalks of the slanta plant. White buds decorate the shining branches, and a few have opened, spreading petals like feathers to the early spring sun.

I gasp, eyes filling with tears.

"Ma loved these…" I whisper.

In my mind, I see her tending them in our garden one winter, one of her rare smiles sparkling in her eyes, pulling me back in time until I can hear her voice once more.

"They bloom so much faster here," she says, kneeling next to me to point out the tiny white buds.

"They should be everywhere!" I shout, reaching for them with childish enthusiasm, yet unbroken by the life I ended up living.

"They can't grow here all year like they do on the mountain," Ma says, taking my hand. "The summer gets too warm."

"How do we have them?" I whisper, staring at them with reverence.

"I save the seeds and replant them every year."

Now, staring at the flowers growing from their grave, my jaw falls at the effort they've put into remembering her, and I wonder who kept the seeds as Ma used to, who planted them again and again.

Tivasta…

My aunt did this, in memory of the woman who became her sister.

I reach out, running a finger over the gossamer strands of the petals.

My knees wobble, and I settle on the ground. Ronan touches my shoulder, and my eyes slip to the luscious green vines of the bastevi plants, winding up the stalks. Dark green leaves surround tightly closed red buds, and I can almost see the glorious flowers that I know open at the summer solstice.

Pa's favorite flowers.

Tears trickle over my cheeks, and I trace the vines.

Slowly, Ronan eases down beside me, slipping an arm around my shoulders. I lean into him, tears cascading over my cheeks.

They've done so much to remember them, to honor them, and I barely remember them, at all.

Guilt sweeps through me, weighing me down. I shrink into myself, curling forward, dropping my head into my hands. Sobs shake my body, rattle my ribs.

Ronan rubs my back, but I don't deserve the comfort he offers. I deserve the beatings Berinasten gave me, even if he doled them out for a different reason.

"You don't have to..." I choke out.

Ronan leans forward, hand gentle on my back, and for a moment, I wish the bruises were more prevalent, wish it hurt the way I deserve it to.

"Don't have to what?" he asks.

"I don't deserve this," I whisper.

"No one deserves to lose their family the way you did," he answers, voice so soft it hurts me to hear it, to hear the compassion laced into every word.

I shake my head. "I don't deserve your comfort." I move away from him.

He stares at me, stricken, and I hate the lance of pain that pierces my heart.

"Of course, you do." His brows furrow, and he reaches for me.

My chest aches, desperate to fall into his embrace. But I sit still, shaking my head, smoothing my features. The mask slips on so easily, an old enemy locking me away yet again.

"I didn't remember them how I should've," I say, voice flat now that I've regained control. My heart splinters, but I hold it in my grip, iron tight. "I didn't honor them. I left it for someone else to do. I've no right to mourn now."

Ronan's face softens. A tear glitters in one dark eye.

And my facade begins to crack. I feel it, feel the fracture in the mask, the line between my brows. One breath hitches, an echo of the tears I shed a moment ago.

"Lessiyara…" he gentles. "That isn't how grief works. You have every right to mourn now that you can. You didn't have a choice before." He touches my cheek.

I swallow, grit my teeth, trying so hard not to fall apart. I want to argue, to tell him that I should've at least remembered them more, should've thought about them more.

But my mouth is too dry, too gummy, and my throat tightens painfully at the thought of speaking.

"Loss is still loss, even years later," he says, sliding his thumb over my cheekbone. "I still mourn my father and the friends I lost last spring. I still mourn the aunt I lost as a child, even if I go a full moon without thinking of her at all. And *I* had the chance to mourn properly at first. It wasn't stolen from me like this was stolen from you."

My breath hitches again, and my mask slips. My lips pull down at the corners.

"If you'd set up a little garden to remember them, what would've happened?"

My mind fills with Berinasten plucking the flowers, one by one, tossing them into the fire and watching them burn. I can smell the smoke, see the cane he would've reached for.

I crumple, eyes filling with tears, spilling over.

Ronan pulls me into his arms.

And this time, I don't pull away.

Chapter Twenty Eight
Ronan

"An open home and a warm hearth can
ease many burdens."
- The wise words of Tivasta

We walk to Tivasta's house when the sun sits atop the mountain peak. Lessiyara grasps my hand tightly, and though her grip is strong enough to make my hand ache, I don't ask her to loosen it.

That blank expression slipped over her features so easily at her parents' grave, frighteningly swift. Her voice fell flat without a second of warning.

I'll gladly take the slight ache in my fingers just to know she isn't hiding.

She kicks a small rock with her step, sending it skittering ahead of us on the path. When we reach it, I do the same. We pass it back and forth like that all through the village, and she keeps her head down, eyes trained on it.

I smile.

Though she dips her head, though she doesn't meet anyone's gaze, she doesn't wipe the frown from her face either. She's here. All the way here.

"Ronan!" a voice cries.

I jerk my head up, searching. Ma stands near Tivasta's cottage with a hand pressed to her chest.

I beam at her as she rushes forward, throwing her arms around me. She squeezes hard, shoving the breath from my lungs, and I laugh. Her black hair puffs out with my breath, sending the feather tied into a slim braid spinning.

She pulls back, hands on my cheeks as her eyes search my face. With a step back, she grips my shoulders, looking me over for injuries.

"I'm okay, Ma," I assure her with a smile. I touch her shoulder. "Really, I'm okay."

She nods, and finally, her attention turns to Lessiyara, saying, "And I hear I have you to thank for that."

She doesn't falter, just pulls Lessiyara into the same bone-crushing hug she gave me a moment ago. My smile widens, and a tear pricks at the corner of my eye.

Startled, Lessiyara slowly raises her free hand to touch my mother's back. I squeeze the hand I still hold, then release her.

She embraces my mother. Softly. A little awkwardly, with stiff arms and careful breaths turned away.

But she does it.

Ma pulls back, searching Lessiyara just as she did me. With her hands on Lessiyara's cheeks, she looks for bruises or scrapes. She puts firm hands on shoulders, searching for bigger wounds elsewhere.

"And you? Are you hurt?"

Lessiyara shakes her head, eyes wide with shock and lower lip trembling.

I barely refrain from mentioning the bruises I know aren't fully healed yet. She doesn't seem to mind them, so maybe they're further along than I thought.

I'll have to check later.

"Alright," Ma says. "Come along then."

She moves to Lessiyara's other side, slipping an arm through hers. I fall in behind them, smiling as we approach Tivasta's cottage.

No one plays in the garden this time, but cheery voices ring out through open windows. Dishes clank and thud against wood inside as we pass through her yard, stepping up to the door.

"All set, Ma," one of Tivasta's kids says. Maybe the oldest boy.

A young girl's voice carries out the window. "Can we go to Valeek's house now?"

The older boy shushes her. "What are you doing? I want to meet Lessiyara, first."

The little girl squeals with excitement inside the cottage. "How did I forget? Never mind, Ma. I want to meet her too."

I chuckle, pressing a kiss to Lessiyara's head before I lean past her to knock.

She looks up at me, eyes wide, and whispers, "They want to meet me?"

"Of course," Ma answers, drawing those beautiful blue eyes away from me. "They've helped Tivasta care for your parents' grave. They may not be your cousins by blood, but Tivasta raised them, and that's close enough."

Lessiyara stares, eyes swimming in tears and lips lifting in a smile, but I chuckle. I hadn't even thought of their relation to her, hadn't put it to words, anyway.

But she's getting a very full family today.

The door opens, and Tivasta beams at us. She steps aside, waving an arm to beckon us forward. In the soft light of the hearth, her four children wait, smiling in linen clothes dusted with dirt from the garden.

The oldest, Tratven, reaches out a hand. His voice cracks as he introduces himself to Lessiyara, clasping her hand joyfully.

Beside him, Kresta waits her turn, eyes shining. Intricate braids hold her black hair back around her horns, framing her dazzling smile. As soon as Tratven releases Lessiyara's hand, she rushes forward, throwing tan arms around her. "I always wanted an older sister. A cousin is just as good."

Tivasta chuckles. "Your new best friend is named Kresta."

Blushing, Kresta pulls back.

Lessiyara smiles at her, tears shining in her eyes and cheeks even redder than the young Soorahk girl's.

Bleven waves shyly, muttering his name with furtive glances at his new cousin.

And then, little Selista jumps up and down, braids smacking against her shoulders. "It's my turn! I'm Selista! Are you really my cousin?"

Her plump cheeks widen as she grins up at Lessiyara. Given a nod and a smile, the five-year-old grasps Lessiyara's hand and jumps even faster. "Yes! I hope I'm as strong and pretty as you one day. Ma said you pulled Ronan up a cliff! But he's so big! How'd you do it? You must be really, really strong."

Laughter fills the room as her words continue to flow, unceasing.

"Breathe, darling," Tivasta reminds Selista with a smile.

The girl makes a show of it, gulping in large breaths and then blowing them out quickly, all the while jumping and flapping Lessiyara's arm.

With a soft chuckle, Tivasta says, "Why don't you all race to Valeek's house? You can tell me who wins when you come home."

Selista shrieks with joy, tugging laughter from us all. Lessiyara stares on with her mouth agape as the children pull boots on, joking about who will win the race.

Despite her boundless energy and confidence that it'll be her, I suspect Selista will be second. Bleven doesn't boast, but he's quite fast.

In an instant, the two youngest are out the door. Kresta and Tratven stroll out, casting shy smiles at Lessiyara, but as soon as they're through the door, their feet thud against the ground, clearly trying to catch up.

We settle in at the table, and Tivasta assures us that preparations are underway.

"Don't fret over what will happen in a few days. Right now, I just want to learn about you, darling," she says, reaching across the table to squeeze Lessiyara's hand.

I turn, gazing down at snow-white hair and small black horns. Lessiyara looks up at me, eyes smiling though she chews at her lip. She shakes her head slowly, opens her mouth silently.

Dropping her gaze to the table, she whispers, "Where do I even start?"

"How about the beginning?" Tivasta offers, gaze softening. "How did he get you up the mountain? You've always had such a strong connection with Sihetva. It's a wonder you didn't bring a tree down on him, even then."

"I tried..." Lessiyara whispers. "But he stopped it, shoved it away. I don't remember what happened after that. Everything went dark, and when I woke up, I was in his house. I think he might've hit me, but I'm not sure. My head hurt a lot."

Her gaze falls to her hands. "It's not exactly hard to imagine he would've."

My heart twists in my chest, and I wish I could've helped her, could've pushed him away and brought her to the village.

But I was only a kid then.

Even if our old chieftain had been willing to send people up the mountain to search for her, it wouldn't have been me. My father would've gone. Tivasta, too. My aunt if that was before she died.

But not me.

"After that," Lessiyara continues, "he raised me. He thought I was his daughter, thought Ma ran away with me. He didn't realize... I hid Sihetva's mark, filed my horns. I tried to act like them, to control myself. But I was scared and angry."

"Of course, you were," Tivasta says, eyes gentle.

"Anytime I was weak, anytime I was emotional, he'd punish me. At first, he used a whip, but after last spring," Lessiyara looks up at me before continuing, "he had his cane."

My stomach drops, and sickness writhes within me. "No..." I whisper, shaking my head.

Guilt washes over me.

I gave him the weapon...

Her eyes soften, and she says, "It's okay. The cane hurt less than the whip. It was more likely to break and absorb some of the force. And I was never afraid it might tear my clothes and show him my marks."

A knife twists in my chest, and I stare at her, at this girl who was thankful to have been beaten with one weapon over another. While I laid in bed healing and laughing with family, she was happy not to worry that her beatings would reveal her marks and bring death down upon her.

Tivasta sobs quietly across the table, and Ma grinds her teeth together.

But I don't tear my eyes from Lessiyara.

Tears shine on her dark lashes, and deep lines like caverns gather shadows at her brows. "Really," she says. "Don't feel bad for injuring him as you did. The cane was much better."

"But it shouldn't have happened," Tivasta whispers. "It shouldn't have."

Fury roils within me, and I feel it in Sihetva too, feel the fiery heat of rage in the air. The flames in the hearth grow, reaching high into the chimney.

Through gritted teeth, I say, "I will kill him."

Lessiyara shakes her head, and I almost argue. But she whispers, voice firm and steady, "No. He's mine."

Her eyes turn dark and hard, and violence flickers in the shadows of her features.

I nod, vowing to let her do it, denying myself the revenge I crave, because even if Berinasten killed my father, she's clearly suffered more at his hands over the years than I have.

If I can't kill him, I'll take as many of his Enlightened down as I can.

Chapter Twenty Nine
Lessiyara

Sihetva's emotions run deeper than any ocean, climb higher than any mountain peak, for it is in the very center of the earth and the farthest reaches of the sky.
- The ways of Sihetva

We talk until the children return, and Tivasta rises to her feet. Wrapping her arms around me, she cups the back of my head and says, "I'm so sorry I wasn't there."

Again, I reassure her. She didn't know I was alive, after all.

But when she pulls back, hands resting on my cheeks, sadness hovers in her dark eyes. "You can stay here if you'd like. I don't think Kresta would mind sharing her room," she offers.

I glance at Ronan, unsure what to say. I hadn't given my sleeping arrangements much thought, simply assuming I'd be sent away.

"You can stay here if you want. Or you can stay with me," he says with a smile. A flicker of hope shines in his eyes as he offers to share his bed, sending waves of heat through me. But still, he adds, "It's your choice."

Tivasta smiles when I look at her, eyes twinkling knowingly.

I blush, dropping my gaze, hiding out of habit despite everything.

But I take Ronan's hand.

Tivasta nods, and Ronan's mother approaches. She embraces me, somehow not angry or disappointed in the slightest that her son has taken an interest in me of all people.

"The two of you should come over for breakfast in the morning. I'll have it ready just after dawn," she says.

I nod, heart aching and soaring at the same time.

She hugs Ronan, bids Tivasta a good night, and slips out the door.

We wish the chieftain, *my aunt*, goodnight, bid my cousins farewell, and follow Ronan's mother out. Already, the darkness has swallowed her up, wrapping around her black hair, her tan skin.

Ronan squeezes my hand, and I smile up at him as he leads me to his home. I turn my gaze to the village, to the people who seem willing to accept me into their world.

My heart skips a beat, not quite able to accept this turn of events as reality.

But for once, I let myself hope.

I gaze at the homes we pass, at the smoke trailing up from chimneys, at the gardens. Laughter and soft voices filter through shutters. The whole place feels warm, despite the lingering chill in the air.

I lift my eyes to the harsh mountain and its frigid peaks. My gaze traces the route from the village, the scar of a path leading down. I reach out to Sihetva, feel the wind move over the bodies of Ronan's

Sword Siblings, frozen and bloody in a clearing. Reaching again, I feel the camp Berinasten and his Enlightened lie in for the night.

My head fills with the memories of beatings, and my back aches with the ghosts of old bruises. Memories of Ma and Da, of their laughter and their screams, flood my mind.

My free hand curls into a fist.

I will kill Berinasten. I'll protect my new family from the sham of a family he forced me into.

No matter the cost.

Ronan turns to look at me, squeezing my hand gently.

I gaze up at him, and my resolution strengthens.

He leads me through the village, passing between stone cottages and livestock pens. The beasts shuffle softly in their barns as we pass.

Sihetva moves softly around us, shining in the moonlight, twinkling in the stars, whispering on the breeze. It reaches for me, gentle and reassuring.

But I feel the way the wind screams through the trees on the mountain, feel it seething beneath their control as they build a fire and boil their water. They force it, bend it to their will.

Yet it shows kindness here, compassion, for Ronan and me, for the people of this village.

I close my eyes, filling my lungs with its gentle sweetness. Breathing out, I gaze upon the village again.

Ronan leads me through a wooden gate tucked into a low stone wall. A cozy cottage sits amid the beginnings of wildflowers, their tall stalks defiantly green. Two tall trees guard the place, nestled up close.

Their branches brush the stone walls and the windows, filling the air with the fresh scent of pine.

A plot of dirt lies waiting for seed, just like the fields outside of town, and I wonder if he dug it before going up the mountain or if someone did it for him.

Vaikahlen people help with planting and harvest, but only out of pragmatism. It makes sense to work together. It's more efficient to have a team of people plant while another team builds and another team hunts. Everyone learns their trade, learns their place.

They develop their skills.

Somehow, here, in this place where people embrace and laugh, I think they might help each other for an entirely different reason.

Maybe just to help someone.

Maybe just because they care.

"Ready?" Ronan asks. "It'll be warmer inside."

I turn to face him, cheeks burning at my distraction. I swallow hard.

He watches me with amusement dancing in his eyes and a smile on his lips. The door stands behind him, already open and waiting while I gawked at his flowers, his tilled garden plot.

"Sorry," I mutter.

Ducking my head, I walk the little path to the door. His hand comes to rest on the small of my back as I pass him, and he follows me in, closing the door behind him.

I meander further into his home, boots loud on the stone floor. The hearth lies cold and empty, and Ronan steps past me to stack wood within it. My gaze wanders over the mantle and the little wooden figures atop it. Behind each one, a candle stands, unlit but partially melted.

He lights the fire, and soft warmth radiates through the small space, gently sinking into my bones.

What memory did he share with Sibetva?

Turning in place, I consider the cabinets beneath a window on one side and the little hatch that likely leads down to a root cellar. A door hangs open in a wooden wall, and a large bed hides in the shadows.

My cheeks color at the sight of a large stone wash basin in a corner by the hearth, partially hidden by a dark green drape of fabric hung from the ceiling. It perches atop a platform of dark stone, and I try not to imagine Ronan's muscular frame within it, tan skin bare to the warm air.

A strange wooden cylinder juts from the wall, protruding above the basin. It piques my curiosity, drawing me closer, and I find a hole within the basin that leads to another wooden cylinder, this one stoppered and angled down to a hole in the wall.

A drain.

Ronan comes up behind me, hands sliding around my waist. "Do you want a bath?" he asks, words whispering against my ear.

I shiver.

Pointing to the cylinder above the basin, I force myself to ask, "Why is that there?"

"There's a barrel outside," he says. "It catches the rain. It's easier to fill the basin that way. Just uncork the little pipe from the roof, and it runs in."

I nod slowly, marveling at the ingenuity. On the mountain, any barrel of water not kept near a fire would freeze. But here…

"I can fill the basin for you if you'd like," he offers.

I turn to face him, relishing the feel of his arms around me. My hands slide up his chest, over his shoulders, into his hair. Our lips meet, and my body burns. A sweet ache builds within me.

Just say something.

I brush my nose against his, gathering the courage to speak. "That's… an awfully big basin… for just me."

He pulls back, throat bobbing as he swallows. He stares into my eyes, gaze dark and heady. His chest rises and falls quickly, pressing against mine.

But he says, "Not tonight."

Reaching up, he taps my nose with one finger.

And my cheeks burn as realization sweeps over me.

"I must say," he whispers, leaning in to kiss my neck. "It's rather handy, knowing when seed would take root." He kisses my neck again, then growls, "But also very inconvenient."

He pulls back, meeting my gaze with a soft, rumbling chuckle.

"How long does yours last?"

"A day and a half," I whisper as the ache inside turns to disappointment.

"Well, your nose turned pink this morning." Ronan rests his forehead against mine and says, "So maybe tomorrow night?"

I nod. My eyes close, and I thank whatever quirk of nature spared me the risk of an unsought child. Briefly, I wonder if it was nature, or if the Vaikahlen people forced the body, the little pieces of Sihetva that move within us all, to show that sign.

Ronan touches my face, and I open my eyes to find his brow furrowed.

"It isn't you," he whispers, voice strained. "I don't mean to offend, I just… I can't bring a child into this world until Berinasten and his Enlightened are dealt with." His eyes shine in the light of the fire, so earnest and kind.

I smile. Shaking my head, I say, "I know. I wouldn't want that either."

"Okay. Good," he says, then kisses my forehead.

I sink into the sensation, letting words flow through my lips. "I never really wanted kids. I always assumed it would only come to that if Berinasten wed me to one of his Enlightened, and I just… couldn't stand the thought of that. It would've happened eventually. That's why I wanted to build my own cabin and live by myself. I never thought there might be other options."

Ronan's arms tighten around me, pulling me closer. "You don't have to have that life, alone on the mountain," he whispers, burying his face in my hair. "You have more choices than you realize."

My heart leaps into my throat. He rests his chin atop my head, but I pull back, staring up at him.

"What choices might those be?" I ask, voice teasing though every part of my body aches with a hope I dare not speak aloud.

He opens his mouth to speak, then closes it again. A wry smile twists his lips upward and he says, "I can give you a full list after we deal with Berinasten. But for now, do you want a bath? Or tea?"

"Yes, please," I answer with a laugh.

But disappointment swirls through me.

He nods and says, "I'll be right back."

His arms leave me, and he disappears through the door into the night. I meander to the hearth, letting the fire soak into me as I trace the carved wooden figures on the mantle with one finger.

A steady drumming draws my gaze to the basin and the water that trickles out of the little pipe. My jaw drops as I gaze at it.

Chapter Thirty
Ronan

"Sihetva is in everything, Darling Daughter.
More present in some things than others."
- The half-remembered teachings of Da

I stand near the barrel, gazing up at the moon and listening as the water drains. My heart thuds in my chest, and my mind whirls.

What am I doing?

What have I done?

Panic spreads through me at all I've shared with Lessiyara, all I want to share with her. I want a life with her, a future, a family.

My gaze strays to the mountain, to the thin trail of smoke drifting into the sky from Berinasten's camp, and cold terror washes through me.

I needed to go into this battle with clear thoughts, with nothing to lose.

But now...

If Sihetva needs a vessel, a funnel... Can I do it?

The life I always wanted, the life I always thought I could never have, is so close.

My heart spasms, twisting in my chest. My throat grows tight. I close my eyes, running a hand over my face. I leave it there, covering my mouth as I shake my head.

I cast a glance at the barrel. The water shimmers in the moonlight, sparkling with the reflections of stars. It drains slowly, reaching the mark that denotes a full basin's worth of water, and I grab the metal rod with the cork on the end. After stopping up the pipe, I turn my gaze skyward, reaching out for Sihetva.

"What do I do?" I whisper.

I make my feelings plain, letting Sihetva in to see my guilt at betraying it, my desire for a future, my hatred for Berinasten. I need Sihetva to know, to see that I still aim to do everything I can.

But my heart isn't my own now.

I can't give it so wholly to this cause now that it's hers. I can no longer throw myself upon a blade without hesitation.

Sihetva reaches for me, warming the air. The stars shine brighter for just a moment, and in it all, I feel Sihetva. Pain and betrayal mingle on the cool breeze, but they're soft and distant. The warmth of the light, of the air swirling around me, fills me with a sense of knowing and acceptance.

A sense of joy.

Sihetva shows me its companionship with Lessiyara, its desire to see her happy.

I wonder for a moment if Sihetva found a kindred spirit in her when Berinasten trapped her on that mountain, forcing her hands as he forces Sihetva.

The breeze warms, brushing my hair, and I know I've understood.

"I want to make her happy," I whisper to Sihetva, and again that soft, warm breeze caresses my skin.

I want to be happy.

And I want to free you.

"We just have to survive the battle," I say. "We just have to win. We'll pry their cold fingers from you."

The task before me settles on my shoulders, far heavier now that the stakes are higher. Victory is one thing.

A victory that I can walk away from is another beast entirely.

And then I remember my promise to Lessiyara.

She wants to kill Berinasten.

Dread pools in my stomach, and my heart sinks into it. My mouth goes dry at the thought of losing another person I care for to this vile man.

And suddenly, I feel just as helpless as I did for months after the ambush last spring.

Sihetva reaches for me, brightening the moon and wrapping me in warm air like an embrace. I close my eyes, trying to soak in the comfort it offers.

But the chill of fear still pricks at my heart.

"Thank you," I whisper. "I'll find a way to free you. I just hope we can all survive this."

With a final glance at the moon, I grab the small bucket of water I filled from the barrel and climb down the stairs off the roof. Nighttime insects sing a gentle lullaby as I walk the path around the cottage, and an owl hoots as I step inside. The warmth of the fire wraps around me, gentle and full of Sihetva's care and kindness.

I'll figure out a way to free you.

I pull the door shut, hang my coat on a hook on the wall. Lifting my gaze, I find Lessiyara leaning over the basin, her hand in the water and clothes on the floor. Heat sweeps through me at the curve of her backside, her strong thighs. Her tail curls, draping around the side of her leg.

She glances over her shoulder at me, alabaster skin glowing in the firelight. Cheeks as pink as her nose, she smiles.

I swallow as she steps into the basin. She doesn't flinch, though the rainwater can't have been warm.

But curls of steam rise around her.

She must've asked Sihetva to warm it.

My mind fills with images of us together in that basin, and my body tenses with need. I force my feet to move, pushing myself to the cabinets.

Nothing can happen tonight.

I grab the tea leaves and a pot. Closing my eyes, I pull in a deep, steadying breath, then turn toward the hearth. I fill the pot and hang it over the fire, then settle into my chair near the flames.

The curtain sways, drawing my gaze up to the basin. Lessiyara's leg rises above the water as she scrubs up, and I close my eyes, hoping tomorrow night comes quickly.

The heat of the fire settles into me, and I let my head fall to rest on the back of the chair. A hint of smoke mingles with the smell of pine and herbaceous soaps, and I fill my lungs with it all.

The water splashes softly, and Lessiyara whispers, "Ronan?"

I lift my head and open my eyes to find her leaning forward, gazing at me with one arm over the side of the basin.

She smiles. "I wasn't sure if you were awake."

I chuckle. "Very much so."

She drops her gaze, but her smile doesn't fades.

My heart flutters.

Lessiyara settles back into the water, staring out the window. The light of the fire glows on her skin, and the moonlight dances in her eyes. Her expression softens, turning thoughtful.

"What is it?" I ask.

She rolls her head to face me, tiny horns sparkling in the light. "Last year… They came back with burns. Father— Berinasten's leg was badly burned, so I know it was Sihetva. But…" She lets out a slow breath. "How? How did you do it? How did you keep him from suppressing Sihetva?"

I close my eyes, trying to keep it all from playing out in my mind again.

But it doesn't help.

In my head, I watch my friends charge into battle, swords and axes held aloft. I sprint, headlong, grabbing an axe on the way. Boulders roll, and my father charges for Berinasten.

My heart leaps into my throat.

I try to swallow, try to look away. But the ice spear pierces his chest, and his blood flows.

Again, I feel the surge of power as Sihetva funnels through me, pouring out in a solid wall of flames, too wild, too powerful, for Berinasten to tame.

And then, the darkness.

Sighing, I open my eyes and tell Lessiyara, "I let Sihetva use my body as a funnel. That concentrates the power, lets it surge forward in extreme amounts. It overwhelmed Berinasten. And me."

"What do you mean?"

The water ripples as she moves, sending reflected starlight shimmering over the ceiling. She braces her arms on the side and resting her chin on her hands. She watches me, snowy skin glowing in the firelight.

"It nearly killed me," I say simply. "We aren't meant to hold that much power. Sihetva is meant to be separate from us, for the most part. We all have part of Sihetva in us, part of its energy, but that much…"

I shake my head slowly, letting out a breath.

"So, it's like giving a fire too much air or a garden too much water?" she asks.

I nod. "It exhausts the body. I didn't wake for many days after that. Even then, I was too weak to rise from my bed for a few moons. I felt so helpless… I hated it."

Sihetva stokes the fire, sending comforting waves of warmth my way, and I feel the apology in it.

My eyes fall to the floor, faltering before her steady gaze. "I pushed everyone away… I couldn't stand who I was, didn't want them to see me like that. I was humiliated. I've worked every day since, trying to rebuild myself, to get back to where I was before."

"Ronan?"

I look up and find her soft gaze trained on me.

"You don't need to be embarrassed. You didn't need to then, either," she whispers. "Warriors come home battered. I'm sure people here know that."

I nod slowly. "That they do."

Silence falls over us, broken only by the crackling of the fire. Lessiyara stares into the flames, brows furrowed in concentration.

After a moment, she rises, muscular thighs glistening with droplets of water. Sihetva's mark stands out sharply against her skin, and her tail curves in imitation of the swooping lines, the spiral on her hip.

She climbs out, taking a towel from the stool next to the basin. I rise as she wraps herself up and step past her. I dip my hand in the water, and heat seeps into me.

She must've warmed it again.

Smiling, I step behind the green curtain. I raise a hand to the buttons of my shirt, undoing them and letting the garment fall. My pants drop quickly after, and I turn.

Lessiyara stands before me, towel wrapped around her chest. She leans into me, arms slipping about my waist.

My heart quickens, and I hold her tight, my body tensing at the feel of her. She gazes up at me, eyes soft, but a hint of sadness lingers in the furrow of her brow, the slight downward tilt of her lips.

Leaning down, I kiss her, gentle and slow, bringing a hand to her cheek. "What's wrong?" I whisper, lips brushing over hers.

She shakes her head. "I'm just worried," she says, eyes falling to my chest.

I hold her tighter, resting my chin atop her head.

Me too…

Chapter Thirty One
Lessiyara

"Foolhardiness makes for the dumbest deaths or the bravest heroes."
- The wise words of Tivasta

I stare into the flames as Ronan bathes. The air fills with the sound of the crackling fire, the gentle splashes of water as he cleans himself. Breathing deeply of spiced soaps and wood smoke, I try to let the tension seep out of me.

But my conversation with Ronan runs through my head, repeating over and again.

He pushed Berinasten back, kept Sihetva free, by letting it use him as a funnel. Concentrated and wild, Sihetva batted away Vaikahlen attempts at control.

It's such a perfect solution, such a simple sacrifice.

But can I do it?

My heart stutters in my chest. My hands tremble, and I ball them into fists to steady them. Swallowing, I try to focus on Ronan, to let myself enjoy the time I have with him just in case this is all the time I get.

I have a couple more days to decide, after all.

Give myself to Sihetva to protect him, to protect the family I never knew I had... Or risk losing them all.

My breath catches, and I close my eyes, trying to shove it all down, just for the evening.

Water sloshes in the basin, and soft footsteps draw me from my thoughts. I turn to find Ronan standing beside the basin, patting a towel over his glistening body. His long, dark hair frames his tan face, water dripping from the strands. Sihetva's mark reaches over his ribs, curls on his hips, and shadows play between his muscles.

My heart flutters when his eyes find mine and a smile spreads over his face.

He approaches, hangs the towel to dry near the fire, and turns to me. Strong arms wrap around my waist, and he touches the tip of my nose with one finger.

Leaning down to whisper in my ear, he says, "If only…"

My lungs falter.

Our lips meet, brushing softly together, and every bit of me clamors for his touch. When we pull apart, I stare into smoldering eyes as he caresses my cheek.

Of course, my fertile day would rob me of a night joined with him when I might only have a couple left.

My lips turn downward, and my brows furrow. I try to wipe the frown from my face before he sees it, smoothing out the crease in my brows, relaxing the muscles around my eyes.

But Ronan doesn't miss much.

His hand slides down my neck, thumb tipping my chin up. Staring down into my eyes, he searches my gaze. "Come back to me," he whispers, pressing a kiss to my forehead.

I relax into his arms, and my face falls again.

"There you are," he says, lips turning up into a gentle smile. "Now, what is it?"

"I just…" My eyes close, and I lean my head against his chest. "I want more than just a couple of days with you."

His arms tighten around me, and his chest puffs out as he breathes in. My hair ruffles beneath his exhalation, and he says, "I know. Me too."

I clutch his back, and he pulls me tighter against his bare chest. My heart stammers, stuck between a flutter and a full stop.

"We'll get through it," he whispers. "We'll have more than just a couple of days." His soft tone tries so hard to thaw the ice within me.

But my heart cracks, frozen and falling to bits.

***

The morning sun burns brightly overhead as Ronan and I work in the wheat field. All around, townspeople bend to their tasks, working the land and sowing seeds. They laugh and smile, even as they toil and sweat. Children giggle and play, making games of their tasks.

My heart swells with the beauty of this place, of the community and family that I've finally found.

If only I could keep it.

Again, I run the numbers, trying to imagine a situation where the few Children of the Sword left could overpower Berinasten and his Enlightened. Again, I find nothing that could turn the tide in our favor.

At least, nothing but letting Sihetva use me as a funnel.

Taking a deep breath, I lead Ronan down another row of turned soil. Seeds spill through my fingers, as fleeting as the time I have left, and my heart cracks just a little more. Each thud of dirt behind me as Ronan shifts the soil over the tiny seeds feels like dirt on my grave.

I look up to the mountain, to the path that Berinasten and his Enlightened travel, and my heart twists.

There's no other way.

I sigh and accept my fate. I'll do what I must to protect them, to make sure Berinasten doesn't hurt them anymore.

Sihetva moves around us all, shining joyfully in the sunlight, whispering through the breeze, oblivious to my decision. It reaches for us, brushing leaves from the field, joining in the celebratory air that I just can't sink into the way the others here do.

With a deep breath, I send a silent plea to Sihetva.

Please… Let me survive this.

Chapter Thirty Two
Ronan

The sun shone bright and warm with Sihetva's joy
the day the Soorahk tribes made peace.
- The ways of Sihetva

I pull a clean shirt over my head, thankful to be home, to be somewhere that traveler's musk no longer dogs my heels. Wafts of soap and sun-soaked air reach out from the fabric of my clothes, and I breathe it in.

Lessiyara stands near the window, wrapped in a blanket as her clothes dry near the fire. She stares up at the mountain with a blank expression.

But her shoulders are hard, her arms crossed.

Walking up behind her, I slide my arms around her waist. My lips press against the back of her head. After a moment, she leans into me, clutching my arms tightly.

"We'll be alright," I say. "Tivasta will be here soon. She said she had news. Maybe she figured something out that could help."

Her shoulders lift further with a deep breath, but she doesn't speak. She nods slowly, but it doesn't feel like she believes me.

Maybe it'd help if I believed it, myself.

Turning in my embrace, Lessiyara touches my face. Clear blue eyes stare up into mine, framed by furrowed white brows. A faint hint of pink still touches the tip of her nose.

"Berinasten will die. I won't let him walk away from here again," she says, voice fervent.

But her words unsettle me.

Rising onto tiptoes, she kisses me, soft and sweet. Another deep breath presses her chest to mine, and she nods slowly.

"I'll go get dressed. Tivasta should be here soon." She smiles as she pulls herself from my arms, but a chill settles in my heart.

She moves away, sidestepping the bed without a look back. I stare through the doorway, stomach turning uneasily.

Taking a deep breath, I move to the hearth, turning the rabbit on the spit as Lessiyara ducks into the bedroom with her clothes to dress. I almost follow, almost try to get her to talk, to tell me what's going on because it seems like so much more than what she's said.

But a knock at the door draws me away from her.

I welcome Tivasta in, and she wraps me in a hug. She settles a jug of her meade on the table and helps me set out plates and tankards.

Lessiyara joins us as I pull the rabbit from the spit, settling it on a platter with root vegetables and a loaf of my mother's bread. Tivasta regales us with tales of Lessiyara's parents and the day they came down the mountain, of the day of Lessiyara's birth and the first time she came to the village.

A gentle smile warms her, reflected on Lessiyara's face.

But every so often, those blue eyes turn from me and Tivasta, and Lessiyara glances out the window, mournful as she watches the mountain.

Hoping for something to buoy Lessiyara's spirits, I ask, "So, Tivasta, you said you had news?"

Face brightening, Tivasta says, "I've heard from Vahken. He readies his Children of the Sword even now. They should be here tomorrow afternoon."

Relief washes over me, rushing from me in a great exhalation. My head falls forward, and my eyes close. I mumble a silent thanks as weight falls from my shoulders.

"How many does he send?" I ask, lifting my head.

"One hundred," Tivasta says, eyes sparkling in the firelight.

My heart skips a beat. I smile at Lessiyara, taking her hand in mine and squeezing it gently.

She tears her eyes from the mountain, finally showing something other than dull resignation. A spark of light shines in her gaze.

"Will that be enough? Without Sihetva, will that be enough?" she asks, voice urgent. She grips my hand tighter, staring intently at Tivasta.

"It should be," our chieftain says.

My spirits soar at the thought of having more Swords, but Lessiyara's hand loosens on mine.

"*Should* be?" she asks.

"No battle is ever certain," Tivasta says. "But this does even the field."

Lessiyara nods, eyes darting to the window for a single heartbeat. She rejoins us quickly this time, and a genuine smile slips onto her face.

But Sihetva coils around her, hanging heavy in the air in a comforting embrace.

My mind whirls, trying to puzzle out what she's not telling me. But when she meets my gaze and her smile widens, another weight slips from my shoulders.

Maybe she really was just worried about the battle being so uneven. I *certainly was.*

I consider her, bring her hand to my lips for a gentle kiss on her palm. Her features soften, and a light blush spreads over her cheeks.

Sighing, I tear my gaze from her as Tivasta speaks of the evening's planting festival and the meade and wine stores she's amassed. Hope blooms within me, just as it always does on the day of the planting festival.

But this time, it's more than that.

It's the sweetness of an ally lending help in a time of need.

The warmth of meade and the feeling of a day of good work.

The gentle promise of a night with a love, a lover now that Lessiyara's nose has returned to its pale white.

We finish our meals, and Tivasta rises. "I'd stay and talk longer, but I have to gather the kids for the festival. I'll see you there?"

Lessiyara nods, eyes never leaving the ground. She squeezes my hand.

"Of course," I say.

We see Tivasta to the door, and she wraps Lessiyara in a hug. She whispers something against soft white hair, and a smile tugs at the corners of Lessiyara's lips.

When the door closes, Lessiyara turns to me. "A festival? I only have these clothes, they're hardly appropriate for a celebration."

"It isn't formal," I tell her. "Everyone's usually so worn out from the day's work that they go exactly as we are now."

She nods, sliding her arms around my waist and leaning against me. "Will everyone be there? Will they… Will they want me there?" she whispers, voice muffled by my shirt.

I chuckle, kiss the top of her head. "Of course, they will." I pull back, cupping her cheek and staring into her eyes. "You belong here."

In this village, with these people.

In this cottage.

With me.

She kisses me, hand wrapping in my hair in a delicate tease of what this night will hold.

I offer her a wry smile before leading her out into the setting sun and through the village.

The first strings of instruments call out, plucked gently, tentatively, testing the tune. By the time we reach the torch-lit village center, music fills the air and the earliest revelers dance. Meade and wine flow from barrels into tankards, and laughter swirls around us.

I squeeze Lessiyara's hand, and she smiles up at me, eyes alight.

Chapter Thirty Three
Lessiyara

"I'm sorry I fade to the mountain, my heart,
I'm sorry it calls me back.
Please bring me back from the mountain, my heart,
For I never want to go back."
- The half-remembered teachings of Da

Meade warms my belly, and music fills the air. People dance and laugh and sing. Their feelings bubble out into the air, free and wild.

But nothing about it feels savage, as Berinasten might say.

The burden of the coming battle lifts, buoyed by their joy, by the news of other Children of the Sword coming to help.

Maybe I'll survive the battle.

I gaze at the torch-lit revelers, at the smiles they offer me and the brilliant sparkle of their eyes as they celebrate a successful day in the fields. Spring will come soon, and the days of rationing preserved food to last the winter will come to an end with the harvest of early crops.

But will I be here for it?

Even with the newcomers, I owe Berinasten my vengeance.

I owe him for Ma, for Da.

For every beating I suffered at his hands.

My chest puffs out with a deep breath.

Ronan squeezes my hand. His eyes search mine, worried by what they find, but he doesn't ask me to come back to him. He doesn't have to.

I'm already here.

My face shows my concern, plain for all to see, and I know I won't go back to hiding. But for his sake, for my own sake, I'll put the battle from my mind for the evening.

I deserve one celebration, one good night spent with people who might actually care if I'm okay… Don't I?

The question echoes through me, and though I don't know the answer, I know what Ronan deserves. He deserves to enjoy himself. He deserves freedom from the burdens of my doubts.

I glance at the people dancing between market stalls, skirts and tunics fluttering around them. My eyes roam over the children chasing each other, giggling all the while.

He deserves this.

I smile and turn my gaze back to him.

Dark eyes soften as concern melts from him, and he squeezes my hand again. "May I have this dance?"

Excitement flits through me, but my nerves tighten. I look at the dancers, twirling and skipping in time with the music.

"I don't know if I can," I say. "We don't… I never danced on the mountain. No one does."

"I'll show you how," Ronan says, pulling me against him.

He puts a hand on my waist, and the other takes my hand, raising it as high as my shoulder. He shows me a few steps, slow and even.

Simple.

But the song is much faster than this. The other dancers skip about, twirling and giggling with abandon, trusting their feet to lead them true.

Releasing my waist, Ronan touches my cheek, guides my face back until I look at him instead of them.

"We'll get there," he says with a smile. "But we have to start here."

My cheeks burn beneath the intensity of his gaze, and I wonder just how many things he's saying with those simple words, how many promises he's making.

He puts his hand back on my waist, leads me through the steps again. The music leaves us far behind, but his smile never wavers.

Coren dances past us, arms stretched to embrace her partner around her belly. She smiles, brushes a hand against my shoulder as she draws near again.

"I'm glad you came!" she shouts over the music and the laughter. "If only we could have a drink."

I smile at her, cheeks aflame.

She's glad I'm here.

It isn't just Ronan.

My eyes trace the shape of her stomach, wondering what kind of life her baby will have, and I reaffirm my vow to take Berinasten down.

But that's not a problem for tonight.

I turn back to Ronan, and he whispers, "Ready?"

"For what?"

He nods at the other dancing couples, and I pale. I watch them, trying to trace the patterns their feet beat into the ground.

“I don't know…”

“We can wait if you want,” he says. “But I should warn you. This is the slowest song they’ll play.”

My head jerks back toward him, and my jaw falls.

He chuckles, placing a gentle kiss on my forehead. “It’ll be okay. Just follow my lead. If you miss a step, no one will notice. They’ve all had a fair bit of meade, I'm sure.”

“Except Coren,” I say.

He laughs, throwing his head back with abandon. “As if she could judge. She’s a terrible dancer. Her poor husband is likely thankful for her belly. She can’t step on his feet with the space it puts between them.”

A laugh bursts from me, and some of the tension falls away. I nod, and Ronan leads me into the crowd.

He spins me around, skipping gracefully between market stalls and revelers. Ronan watches me, his dark eyes bright and his smile wide.

My heart pounds, and my blood roars through me. For a moment, I try to hold back the giggles that bubble through me, but soon, I let them fly, let them mingle with the sweet night air.

The moon shines brilliantly overhead, and the stars sparkle. A gentle breeze sweeps the hair from my face as Sihetva reaches for me. Laughter and cheering and singing fill the air, swelling and ebbing, filling me with soft warmth.

And in all of it, I feel Sihetva, welcoming me, urging me to stay.

***

The hearth in Ronan's cottage crackles, mingling with the warmth of the meade, and I sink into his arms. He holds me close, swaying gently as he hums.

I close my eyes, rest my head against his strong chest. His deep voice rumbles softly beneath my ear as he sings a quiet tune of rolling fields and plentiful harvests to come.

His fingers trail up my spine, and heat courses through me. He touches my neck, tipping my head back. Our eyes meet, and we share a soft smile.

I lift my lips to his, brushing them together, and his hand tangles in my hair. My breath quickens, and I pull him tighter to me, hands gripping his shirt.

We break apart, and his thumb traces my lips. His eyes open, dark and smoldering, and my heart falters.

He kisses me again, pulling me close, and I relish the feel of his hand sliding down to my waist. His lips brush my skin, hot breath whispering over my neck.

We tear our clothes away, and our hands land on bare skin. My body burns, aching for more. I kiss his neck, his chest. My fingers trail over his stomach, his ribs. I trace his spine, and he shudders against me, gripping my hips, groaning against my neck. His teeth nip at my shoulder, and a shiver rolls through me.

I commit the feeling to memory, just in case.

My breath hitches, and I force the coming battle from my mind. But every touch, every sigh, every step as we move to his bed… feels almost like a goodbye.

He lays me back, gentle and sweet. I ache for him to move faster, to join with me, to move above me.

But I want to draw this out, want every heartbeat I still have with him to stretch into eternity.

I arch my back as he kisses my neck, my chest. A sigh slips through my lips as he clutches my thigh, and I brush my tail up the inside of his legs, tickling sensitive skin. He shivers, smiling down at me with hooded eyes.

Our lips meet, and I tangle my hands in his hair, holding him there, desperate to keep him, to never let him go. My heart pounds, begging me to hold on, to stay.

But I can't let anyone else get hurt.

My chest heaves, but I kiss the pain away.

Sitting up, I push Ronan back onto his haunches. I rise to my knees, taking his mouth with my own.

His hands drift up my thighs, clutch my buttocks. He pulls me forward, and I climb atop his lap, relishing the feel of him beneath me. I take him in, breath catching, heart screaming out for more, and he moans against my lips.

Gripping my hips, he pulls me down, and I cry out.

Eyes locked, we move slowly, lips brushing, bodies aflame. Slipping an arm around his shoulders, I pull him closer, hips grinding. Heat surges through me, and a delicate ache builds within.

His hand slips between us, fingers thrumming, working me to a fever pitch. I drop my head back, arching into him. He ravages my neck, kissing and nipping lightly.

I move faster, hips grinding in time with his until the world shatters. I cry out, voice shaking with the effort.

He moves faster, pushing me higher. My legs quake, and he tips me back onto the bed. His body presses me down, comforting and tantalizing in its weight.

Clutching my hip, he drives home, and stars explode within me again. My nails dig into his back, and I writhe beneath him.

His teeth find my shoulder as he shudders, joining me in the collapse. He pants against my neck, whispering my name.

We tremble together. His head rests on my shoulder, breath warming my skin. My breath comes in gasps, and my heart hammers in my chest.

Slowly, he lifts his head, gazing into my eyes as he presses a kiss to my lips. Smoothing my hair back from my face, he smiles, eyes alight in the flickering firelight that filters through the doorway.

He cups my cheek, leaning his forehead against mine.

And my heart falters.

I don't want this to be the last time.

My breath comes quick, hitching and heaving. I press my lips to his to hide the fear that slithers through me, and I remind myself that we have one more day. A day that will be consumed by battle preparations and greeting the Children of the Sword from the nearby village.

But one more day, nonetheless.

We part, and Ronan lies down beside me, arms slipping around my waist. He pulls me to him, and I tuck myself against his chest, letting the warmth of his body seep into me.

Words perch on the edge of my lips, waiting to be spoken, but they seem impossible.

We haven't known each other long.

He'd probably think me crazy.

Arguments against speaking fill my head, but really…

What have I to lose?

I likely won't survive the battle.

So, I whisper, "I love you."

Ronan pulls back, and a smile dances on his face. His eyes search my features, but I face away from the fire, hidden in shadow.

"Really?" he asks, voice hopeful.

I nod, heart lodged in my throat.

"I love you too," he says.

Shock spreads through me. His lips find mine, and my breath catches. He clutches me against his chest, and a warm silence falls over us.

I lie there, stunned.

He loves me?

Really?

Slowly, his breathing evens out as sleep claims him. I stare at him, at the smile that still lights his face, and my heart tries so hard to rejoice.

But my eyes drift out the window to the smoke trailing up from the mountainside, and my mouth goes dry. Dread seeps in, chilling me at the sight of Berinasten's camp a mere day's journey away.

A tear slips from my eyes, and I hold Ronan tighter.

Chapter Thirty Four
Ronan

Though Sihetva hates to see its friends suffer in the cold, it knows the world needs to reset every winter so that it may begin anew in spring.
- The ways of Sihetva

Sunlight slips through the shutters, pulling me from sleep. Lessiyara lies in my arms, motionless and peaceful. Dark lashes fan out over her alabaster skin. I touch her cheek, and her words from last night slip through my mind.

"I love you," she whispered in the dark, voice soft and tentative.

My heart soars, and I kiss her forehead. I pull her closer, tucking her head under my chin. I breathe in the soft spice of her, and a drowsy warmth washes over me.

She loves me...

And the other Children of the Sword will be here today.

I take a deep breath, thankful that Tivasta found a way to even the odds for the coming battle.

With that many to help us fight, surely, we'll be alright.

My tired mind assures me that we'll survive. Buoyed by Lessiyara's words, warmed by strips of sunlight through shutters, I drift back off to sleep.

***

The morning passes in a blur of whetstones and armor oils. Lessiyara works beside me, freshly sharpened sword gleaming as she holds it up to the light, inspecting the edge.

Sihetva moves restlessly all around us. It whips the wind this direction and that, tossing the loose dirt of my garden plot about. It warms the sun's rays and then cools them. In the distance, a sudden shower of rain falls over the fields we planted yesterday, then ceases just as quickly.

I lift a hand into the wind, sharing my hopes with Sihetva.

We'll be okay.

My heart glows with the future I might finally have after tomorrow, the life Lessiyara and I can build, right here in the cottage we lean against, once Berinasten has finally been dealt with. I can almost hear the approach of Vahken and his Swords, can almost feel the thumping of their boots and the feet of their mounts reverberating through the ground beneath me.

And for a moment, I wonder if I do feel it, hear it, as Lessiyara feels things in the wind.

Sihetva fidgets around us, unaffected by my attempts at comfort. It flounders, and I know it wants to help. I close my eyes, breathing deeply, willing Sihetva to slow its frantic worries.

"I know you want to help," I whisper. "But they'll only use you to hurt us. We have the people now to do this. We'll free you."

I open my eyes, hoping to find that I've had some effect.

But Sihetva only grows more restless, whipping my hair about in the wind, sending a cloud to block the sun and cool us, only to shove it out of the way.

And its frantic energy swirls around Lessiyara.

She sits, calm and unperturbed, in the middle of a maelstrom of Sihetva's power, brows creased at the display. A frown mars my face, and I stare at her, searching for anything that might concern Sihetva.

She knows how to use a sword.

I think of the armory in the village, of the pieces that will soon be gifted to her.

She'll have armor soon.

Surely, Sihetva knows all this.

But my gut twists at the apprehension in the shifting winds, the comforting warmth that hovers around Lessiyara, the chill that wavers nearby like a hidden fear.

Sihetva knows she can protect herself, has seen her do so with wolves in the woods. She told me of the encounters herself, recalling the way the wind warmed her and kept the hair from her face as she bent to the bodies afterward.

But what else does Sihetva know?

Though I've never wondered before, I wonder now.

Does Sihetva know when death comes for us?

Will Berinasten single her out when he sees her, truly sees her, here among his enemy?

I stare at Lessiyara, mouth dry. Fresh waves of dread flow through my veins, and Sihetva swirls around me. I put an arm around Lessiyara, silently vowing to Sihetva that I'll stay close to her.

I'll protect her.

I pull in a deep breath and lean down to plant a kiss atop her head. Her small horns shine in the sunlight, marked and grooved from the metal file she used for years to keep them small, to keep them hidden. I suppress a shudder at the pain that must have come from that effort.

"Is there something…" I begin, but words desert me.

She looks at me, waiting.

"Are you okay?" I ask.

She stares at the mountain, silent and still. My heart thuds in my chest, half expecting her to deny it, half expecting her to sob.

But she does neither.

She merely shakes her head. Slow and gentle, the movement would be easy to miss.

I set my sword and whetstone on the cloth laid out on the ground next to me and wrap my arms around her. She leans into me, but she doesn't cry or relax. Her sword clatters to the ground, and she wraps her arms around my waist.

But after only a heartbeat, her ears flicker, soft furred tips tickling my neck. She turns, staring in the direction in which the streams and rivers disappear, the direction of the nearest village.

"They're almost here," she says, voice too calm, too flat. After the ceaseless worry of the past days, it unsettles me. She looks at me, eyes dull despite the light that sparkles around her. "Shall we go meet them?"

I swallow back a lump, mouth dry, and nod.

We push ourselves to our feet, gathering our weapons and sheathing them at our sides. I take her hand in mine as we leave my little garden behind, moving through the village to Tivasta's house.

"I'll make sure he won't hurt anyone else," Lessiyara whispers, unprompted. Despite her low volume, her voice is fierce.

A chill slips down my spine.

I squeeze her hand. "*We'll* make sure he doesn't hurt anyone else," I correct, hoping to draw her gaze.

But she doesn't look up. Her eyes shimmer as a single tear slips over her cheek.

A sharp bark catches my attention, stills my feet for a single heartbeat. My eyes jerk upward to the village center, to the armored maurubeasts and their riders. The massive dogs paw at the ground, black coats shining. They stand with heads raised and tails down, well-mannered and obedient.

But my mind still goes back to the one that attacked when I was a child, the one that nearly killed my cousin. Even now, I see the beast's snapping jaws and slavering jowls.

But that one was wild.

Worse, it was sick, alone, and far from its home in the plains.

I blink the memory away, focusing on the Children of the Sword perched atop the maurubeasts, weapons and leather armor gleaming in the midday sun. Swallowing, I force myself to move closer, to approach Tivasta.

The leader calls the others to dismount, and my jaw drops.

I hadn't expected him to come, assuming he'd just send his Swords, but sure enough, Vahken taps his maurubeast's neck, and the massive dog kneels. Sliding down, the chieftain of the neighboring village approaches Tivasta. Determination shines in his black eyes, and he greets her warmly. Sihetva swirls around him, shimmering in the air, sending bits of wind through long black braids, every bit as free with this man as it is with Lessiyara.

"I'm sorry you lost so many," Vahken whispers, voice barely carrying to my ears. "We'll finish this tomorrow."

The sight of the two chieftains conversing would have filled me with hope mere moments ago, but the look in Lessiyara's eyes, the slant of her shoulders, puts a chill in my heart.

Chapter Thirty Five
Lessiyara

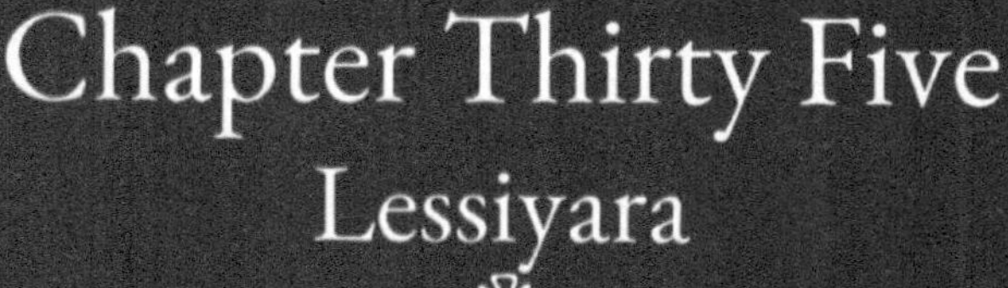

"A trinket saved from the ravages of time
is oft worth more than a fortune."
- The wise words of Tivasta

Tivasta turns to me, extending an arm. I glance up at Ronan with my heart in my throat.

He said I belong here.

Tivasta calls me family.

But these new people?

My palms sweat as I stare into Ronan's dark eyes, but he offers only compassion and a gentle nod. His hand deserts mine, only to find the small of my back. He eyes the dogs that loom over us, but only for a moment. Then, he leads me forward.

"Vahken," Tivasta says, addressing the neighboring chieftain. "This is my niece, Lessiyara."

He eyes me, dark gaze raking over me, assessing. A scar on his temple shines in the sunlight, disappearing into black braids. Light plays on his armor, dancing and glimmering.

I shrink before him, stepping back to Ronan's side.

Something dawns behind those dark eyes, a light flickering to life, and Vahken's mouth falls open. His head tips to the side as he says, "You're Vasret and Sureenassa's daughter, yes?"

The venom I expect is absent, and the words catch me off guard.

No taunts of abomination. No condemnations.

Only a question cushioned in a soft tone.

I nod, waiting for him to make up his mind about me.

"Where have you been since? Hiding in the forest?" he asks, brows reaching for each other.

I shake my head. "I…" Deep breath. I clear my throat. "Berinasten thought I was his daughter. He took me up the mountain."

Vahken blows out a breath, nodding slowly. "That can't have been pleasant." His eyes slip over my stubby horns.

"No. It wasn't." I close my eyes, trying to block out countless memories of beatings and blank stares.

Sihetva reaches for me on a gentle breeze, caressing my cheek. It warms the sunbeams that touch my shoulders, and light shimmers around me.

Despite everything, I smile at Sihetva's offer of comfort.

Ronan presses a kiss to my temple.

Looking up, I find the chieftain staring at me, eyes soft. "I've never seen anyone else with such a strong connection to Sihetva. Abused by Berinasten, locked away from your true potential… Perhaps it found a kindred spirit in you as it did with me."

I swallow. "Were you…"

He can't have been kidnapped by Berinasten too, can he?

I try again, asking, "Did Berinasten come for you too?"

He shakes his head, chuckling softly. "No, it wasn't Berinasten. The Soorahk villages haven't always been allies. I was taken as a child by one of the chieftains to the west." A devilish glint enters his eyes. "He didn't survive long. But I was old enough to have been given the tools to fight. You must have been very young."

"I was," I say, marveling at this man who knows all too well what it's like to lose everything.

"Well, I know Tivasta has likely told you, and it seems Ronan here has made it clear," Vahken says, sending a blush over my skin, "but I'm glad you're back in the valley."

My cheeks burn, and my heart twists.

"You don't have to fight though. You haven't been properly trained as a Child of the Sword. We can do this—"

"I will fight."

Rage boils within me, and Sihetva shimmers in heat waves around me.

Vahken's eyes trace the way it moves around me, and he nods approvingly. "You will fight."

***

With a plan in place and all civilians moving to the far side of the village, I stare at the path, watching the trail I know they travel. Sihetva bends around them, raked along in their wake as they force it to warm their bones, to clear their path. It seethes in their control, and my nerves wind tight.

I grit my teeth, hands curling into fists.

Behind me, Ronan and Tivasta busy themselves with a surprise for me. I keep my eyes trained on the mountain, looking away from them.

Heavy footfalls approach, armor clanking, and Vahken says, "They'll likely camp for the night. They're too far to get here this evening, but it won't be long after dawn."

I look up at him, considering this stranger. The elements seem to bend around him, with him.

Just as they apparently do with me.

"You feel how Sihetva bends around them too?" I ask.

He nods, dark eyes fixed on the pines at the mountain's base. "Your connection is more like mine than I realized."

My eyes drift over his black braids and the scruff of his jawline. His umber skin shines in the sunlight, soft despite the scars. His horns spear the air. Dark feathers, woven through his braids, sparkle in the light, and black rings adorn his ears.

He's my opposite in so many ways. Where he's soft and warm, I appear cold and unyielding.

But apparently, our connection with Sihetva is similar.

"No one else feels Sihetva the way we do. Tivasta wants us to keep watch just in case they press on to attack in the dark," Vahken says. "Would you like to go first or second?"

A sigh lifts my shoulders. I almost turn to look back at Ronan but stop myself to keep their surprise a mystery.

"I want time awake tonight, not in the morning," I say. "If that's amenable to you."

There's too much I'll rethink if I wake hours before the battle.

Vahken nods. "I wake well before dawn each day, anyway."

More footsteps approach, two pairs. The cheery voices of Tivasta and Ronan wander this way, but a strange, disjointed sound accompanies them. My brows furrow as I try to place it.

Clanking and swishing.

I shake my head, unable to make sense of it.

"Ready?" Tivasta asks, voice urgent and excited.

My heart leaps into my throat. Panicking at the unknown, some small part of me wonders if I'll turn and find her holding a cane, face and voice suddenly blank as she waits to punish me for my outbursts.

But I quiet that voice, shove it away.

This isn't the mountain, and these people aren't like Berinasten or his Enlightened.

Swallowing, I turn on my heel. Ronan's eyes twinkle, and a smile glitters on Tivasta's face. Slowly, my gaze drifts to the items in their hands.

Armor.

Dark leather shines. On the chest, delicate feathery flowers twine with vines and heartier flowers, all etched in bronze to match the buckles which wait to fasten it in place.

My jaw drops.

Tears prick at my eyes, and my feet pull me forward. I reach out, fingers tracing the intricate design. My breaths come quick.

"This... This can't be for me…"

But it looks like it'll fit perfectly.

"No, I thought Vahken might want a spare set," Ronan says. One corner of his lips quirks up. "Of course, they're for you."

"Ronan wanted armor for you. He was going to look through the armory, but these…" Tivasta strokes the intertwined flowers on the front with one finger. "These were your mother's."

The breath leaves me, rushing out all at once. My eyes flutter. "Really?" I choke out.

Tivasta nods. "She didn't want her white armor from the mountain anymore. She melted the metal armor down and burned the leather as soon as these were made. She wasn't wearing them that day, wasn't expecting an attack…"

Tivasta's voice cracks, and a single tear slides over her cheek. She takes a deep breath, then continues, "This armor couldn't help her that day. But it can help you."

My fingers curl around the edges of the chest piece, gentle and reverent. I lift the leathers from their hands. My throat tightens, and tears slip over my cheeks.

Ma's armor...

"You kept them?"

Tivasta nods. "I kept your father's too, but I don't think they'll fit you quite as well." A smile brightens her face, sparkling in her eyes.

I choke out a laugh.

"Can I put them on?" I whisper, voice thick with emotion.

Tivasta nods and touches my cheek. "Of course, you can, darling."

Chapter Thirty Six
Ronan

"A truth unspoken does not cease to exist."
- The half-remembered teachings of Da

Lessiyara and I lie in the grass near my home, staring up at the sky. My eyes trace the streaks of orange and red overhead as the sun sets behind the mountain, gone from view but still reaching for us with fingers of color.

But the peaceful feeling this sight would normally instill in me is absent.

My stomach churns nervously, and I squeeze Lessiyara's hand. She squeezes back, but otherwise, she may as well be a statue. She doesn't move, doesn't speak, barely breathes.

I turn my head to face her, eyes tracing her profile. The glow of the sky reflects in her eyes, lending them colors they don't normally possess.

But the emotions that have danced in them of late are nowhere to be seen.

Sihetva swirls around her, brushing grass against her face with gentle breezes, warming the air, trying so hard to comfort her.

I swallow.

"Lessiyara?"

She turns to me, and the sky's reflection falls from her gaze, revealing the shadows that lurk within. Her eyes are strained, brows just barely reaching for each other as if in need of comfort themselves but afraid to ask for it.

I touch her cheek, let my thumb smooth the tiny line at the corner of her downturned lips. "I know something's bothering you," I whisper.

She flinches, features slackening.

I sigh, wishing she could just show me what she feels, wishing she wouldn't hold back. I remind myself of all she's suffered for her emotions.

Be patient with her.

She searches my gaze, blue eyes flitting back and forth between mine, then lets her features shift into a frown. Her eyes drop, fall out of focus, staring at my shoulder without seeing it.

"Please, just talk to me," I whisper. "Maybe I can help."

She looks skyward, lifts a hand to hover just above the ground. Her fingers play in the breeze, and I wonder if she's checking, yet again, for Berinasten's position on the trail.

"I want more time here," she says, voice so quiet I almost have to ask her to repeat herself.

She takes a deep breath, then speaks again, this time a little louder. "I know we have more Swords at our back now. I know our odds are better. But I still need to be the one to do it. I need to kill him. For me. For Ma and Da. For everyone here. I won't let him keep hurting people, killing people. I might still have to—"

She cuts off, goes still. Her eyes close, and she blows out a breath.

My heart stops, waiting for her to speak.

She turns to me, finally meeting my eyes. "I was…" She trails off, tries again. "If I need to, I'll offer myself up as a funnel for Sihetva."

My blood runs cold, and the world seems to fall out from under me. I stammer, gripping her hand tight, shaking my head.

She'll die.

She's willing to die.

The thoughts repeat, over and again, and I close my eyes, pressing my fingers against them. A tear slips through anyway.

The grass rustles as she turns to face me. She touches my cheek, my chest. She grips my hand.

"Ronan, I'm sorry. I know you said people don't always survive that, but sometimes they do. You did."

"Barely," I say, voice hoarse.

"But you did." And then, her voice becomes firm as she says, "I can't let him keep hurting people."

"Please," I beg. "Please, don't do it."

I pull my hand away from my face, staring into her eyes through tear-blurred vision. "We have more people to fight at our side," I say. "We can do this without you killing yourself."

She flinches.

"You belong here. You have a home. You have your choice of homes if you don't want to live with me. You can live with Tivasta, or we can build you a home of your own if you want. But you have a place here."

I touch her cheek. My thumb wipes away a tear that slipped free to hover on her snow-white skin. She reaches up, wrapping her fingers around mine. Her chest hitches with a rasping breath.

"Tivasta would be devastated," I say. "And I…" A bleak future spreads out before me, barren without her now that I've finally let myself hope. "I can't… Don't do this," I whisper.

She stares at me, eyes welling with tears. They fall slowly, slipping over alabaster.

"If I don't have to…" she whispers, voice trailing off. Shaking her head, she closes her eyes, stealing that vibrant blue from me. "If I don't have to, I won't."

My heart falters.

That isn't quite the answer I hoped for.

"Lessiyara, please…"

She opens her eyes. Voice firm but quiet, she says, "Ronan, I won't let him walk away from here. I *will* kill him tomorrow. One way or another."

A lump forms in my throat, choking off my words. I grit my teeth and touch her neck.

Lessiyara props herself up on one arm, leans over me. Her lips find mine, soft and gentle, trembling as she kisses me. Her hand strokes my cheek. "I love you," she whispers. "And I love this place. I won't let him keep killing people. I have to stop him."

My mouth goes dry as her certainty falls over me like a pall.

I can't stop her, can't convince her not to do this.

My heart falters as I stare up at her. I trace the furrow between her brows with one finger, caress the lines where her lips turn down.

My earlier promise to let her be the one to kill Berinasten floats through my mind, sour with regret, and I pull her to me. She lies down, arm and leg thrown over me, and we watch the stars together.

I squeeze her hand on my chest.

"I love you too…" I whisper, voice hoarse.

***

I wake just before dawn and perch on the edge of the bed. Lessiyara sleeps at my back, white braids fanned out around her. Elbows on knees, I drop my head into my hands.

Maybe they'll come before she wakes.

Maybe we can do this without her.

But my head fills with all she suffered at Berinasten's hands, and guilt writhes within me at the thought.

She needs this. I can't steal it from her.

The sky turns orange behind the mountain, and light peeks over, peers in through the window. I turn to Lessiyara, gaze roaming over her peaceful features. A knock on the door sends her sitting bolt upright, eyes wide.

I sigh, nodding slowly when she meets my gaze, then go to the door. A Child of the Sword stands before me, dressed in dark leathers. Her weapons hang at her sides and on her back. Her dark eyes shine. "They're coming," she says, voice tight. "Dress and get into position."

Behind me, Lessiyara bustles about, readying herself for a war I wish she had no part in.

But she does.

The Child of the Sword turns and walks away, doubtless to inform others of the looming battle. I close the door softly, pressing a hand to the wood and breathing deeply before I move to the bedroom. Lessiyara has her arms bent at odd angles, trying to buckle her chest piece into place.

"Here," I say, voice gentle. "Let me help you."

I fasten the bronze buckle she fidgeted with, then move to the next. My hands come away, only to find her waist. I lean down, planting a kiss on the top of her head, right between her filed horns. A deep sigh leaves me, blowing strands of white around her face.

"Please, don't try to talk me out of this. I h*ave to* do this," she whispers.

My heart cracks. "I know." I pull her against me, arms tightening until I fear I may break her. "I know."

I blow out another breath and release her, hoping it isn't the last time I hold her.

A gentle silence moves around us as we don the rest of our armor, then slip larger farm clothes over top of everything. She grips my hand, and we meander through the village past homes emptied of occupants in the night. They wait in the safety of farther homes, and the air around us seems still with their held breath.

At the fields nearest the mountain trail, we join the Children of the Sword from our village and Vahken's. We all stash our swords and axes in feed troughs and wheelbarrows, on windowsills and propped against fences, then take up leatherworking tools, farming tools, anything to give the impression of a normal morning.

Lessiyara toils away with a shovel, breaking up dirt in a little garden patch with her hood up and back turned to the mountain. I chop firewood, eyes darting to the trail between swings.

But I needn't bother.

Sihetva moves around us, buzzing through the air. It grows frantic when they come into view, alerting me even had I not been looking.

My stomach drops, and my heart races.

But we give them a moment longer, let them close some distance.

As if we had no idea they were coming.

Free of the pine trees, they march closer. My palms sweat on the handle of the axe until I fear I may throw it on my next swing.

Bright white clothes and leathers gleam in the early morning sunlight, fitted carefully over metal armor. Their silver buckles glint, catching my eye.

Lessiyara stabs her shovel into the dirt and leaves it there. I drive my axe into a stump and rise.

People in the other fields and gardens and homes do the same, abandoning their tasks in a wave, following our lead or Vahken's, though I know some of them can feel the way Sihetva surges around us.

I reach for my sword, nestled against the woodpile, and Lessiyara grabs hers from the ground at the edge of her assigned garden plot. Our eyes meet, and I take a deep breath. She nods once, slowly, and turns to face the coming monsters.

The Enlightened freeze, just far enough for their stolen power to be useless against us. They stare at us, taken aback by our calm, steady approach.

It's a far cry from the panic they expected.

They stand in formation, watching us with hands raised to begin their assault if, when, we move in.

Lessiyara takes my hand as we march to the front of the line to stand next to Tivasta. Normally, we wouldn't garner such a position, but Lessiyara lowers her hood, letting long strands of white hair billow out alongside her cloak.

Vaikahlen hands drop. Some only a bit, while others hang at their sides. Jaws gape, mouths forming black holes in alabaster faces.

Berinasten pushes through the ranks with his face dull and lifeless.

But he stops in his tracks when he sees Lessiyara.

She squeezes my hand, squares her shoulders. I glance at her from the corner of my eyes and see her black horns. Short as they may be, they stand out starkly against her snow-white hair.

Her shoulders lift with a breath, and she and Sihetva drive the point home.

It swirls around her, sending her cloak and hair rippling. Light glows as if emanating from her.

Berinasten's face falls, mouth open and eyes wide.

Chapter Thirty Seven
Lessiyara

"If only I were stronger,
I'd be all that my darling needs.
If only I were stronger,
My darling would never weep."
- The half-remembered songs of Ma

He stares at me, gaping as Sihetva curls around me like a warm blanket without a single motion from me. He must see the remnants of my horns, but even if he didn't, it's obvious enough.

A fissure forms in his facade, and a trace of rage slips across his features, just barely visible at this distance.

But I see it in the way his hands curl at his sides, in the way his mouth closes too abruptly.

If we were closer, I bet I'd see a furrow in his brow.

My heart leaps at this small thing that's actually a huge thing. Sihetva and I have distracted them, thrown them off balance, something I never thought possible. I sigh, smiling in triumph even as he regains his composure.

Behind him, behind his ranks of Enlightened, Vahken and his Children of the Sword move out of the pines, flanking the statues I once walked amongst. Figures of white spin in place, dividing their attention between us and the enemy they never saw coming.

I fill my lungs, feel Sihetva coursing through the air I breathe.

Tivasta calls out, voice booming through the air, and we charge.

The Enlightened jolt, startled by our assault, but they regain themselves quickly. A life of discipline serves them well, but still, their shaky hands butcher the commands they shape for Sihetva.

Dirt explodes beneath our feet, but they've lost just enough control for Sihetva to rally its strength, to shield us and keep us aloft with well-timed gusts of wind, buffeting us, pushing us along, balancing us.

Spears launch, and arrows fly from the back of our ranks, and where they might otherwise be turned back on us in stolen breezes, they merely skew off target. They miss necks and eyes, hitting arms or legs instead.

Blood flows, pouring over stark white leathers and robes. Ragged tears reveal the silver metal below, glistening crimson, but the Enlightened make no sound. They limp or kneel, some shape Sihetva with one hand instead of two.

But they never stop.

A spear of ice shatters on leather armor nearby. But the one that follows immediately in its wake pierces the chest of a man running next to me, and he goes down with a guttural cry. A woman screams behind me, but I don't look to see why.

My heart races.

My blood roars through my veins.

Berinasten deserts his ranks, head bent low as he moves for me. I raise my shield, charging full force with my sword at the ready.

Sihetva rides in my wake, buzzing, burning, seething. The air crackles with its presence, and together we fly forward.

Until he captures Sihetva.

The ground beneath me swallows my feet and my momentum carries me, drops me. My sword flies free, sticking in the dirt, hilt up, and my face smashes into the earth.

Sihetva moves around me, fighting to free itself from Berinasten's grip, but he's regained himself. His hands twist, and the earth flips, spinning me in its grasp.

On all sides, the battle rages. Ronan's sword splits a man in two, slicing right beneath the chest piece. He cleaves an arm from another Enlightened. Red soaks into clean white armor, spills across the lush green earth.

I claw my arm free of the dirt, grasping for my sword with my heart in my throat. My fingers close around the hilt, and I jerk, trying to free it.

The air burns around me, hot with Sihetva's rage. But Berinasten's hands clench, forcing Sihetva to coil the earth tighter around my kicking feet.

Hand over hand, Berinasten drags the earth, drags me to him, and I grip my sword tighter, pull it with me. Dirt catches in my clothes, slipping under the neck of my shirt until I come to a stop at his feet. Roots twine around my arms, pinning them above my head, rendering my sword useless.

He looms over me, twisting his hands this way and that, bending Sihetva to steal the air from my lungs.

I gasp, throat collapsing, but adrenaline flows through me. I wrench my arm free of the dirt, sweat beading on my forehead with the effort. Dirt and tufts of grass spray across me. Roots still cling to me, twined around my arm, but I swing my sword, catching his leg.

Dark blood spills, and satisfaction burns through me.

He stumbles, grip loosening, and Sihetva seizes its chance. My earthen restraints explode outward, showering the battlefield with roots and dirt.

I press my advantage, screaming my fury as all the beatings of my past flash through my mind. Surging to my feet, I slash at him, catching his chest piece. A small gash appears on the white cover, but it doesn't pierce the metal beneath.

I swing again, pushing him back, cutting his other leg.

Blood spills.

Another hoarse scream rips through my throat, and I hear my mother, screaming as she died, echoing in my mind.

I lunge, plunging the sword forward, but Berinasten drives his hands to one side, gripping Sihetva and pushing my blade wide with a gust of wind. My momentum takes me, sending me skidding, and the ground reaches for me yet again.

It turns me over, dragging my hair through the blood of my fellows. Roots coil around my arms and legs, twist over my neck, wrapping tight.

I gasp for air, twisting, kicking, and thrashing, all to no avail.

Chapter Thirty Eight
Ronan

"They call themselves Enlightened, but
they know only force."
- The half-remembered teachings of Da

The Enlightened advance, slowly coming to meet us as we charge. They drive between Lessiyara and I, splitting us up quickly, and she plunges forward, aiming for the man she once called Father.

My sword dents armor, slips between the pieces, slices bone, removes limbs. Blood sprays the battlefield. I claw my way through, cutting a path to her. My heart races, and my muscles stretch and pull as I lunge, parry, strike. All around me, men and women fall.

An Enlightened stares me down, lifeless blue eyes piercing me. His fingers move in complicated patterns, and the air freezes around me. A burst of panic shoots through my veins because I know what comes next. I swing, aiming to take off his hands, but he moves just a little too quickly.

Two ice spears crystallize before me, flying forward. One shatters on my arm, weakening Sihetva's protection within the leather. The second follows instantly, piercing my upper arm. I grit my teeth, barely suppressing a scream.

Another set of spears slams into my thigh, shattering and then punching through, and I can't hold in the agony this time. I growl, driving forward, bashing my shield into the Enlightened's alabaster face. Blood gushes from his nose, and I slam the shield edge into the mess. His face collapses beneath my attack, spurting crimson.

I step back, fighting not to limp, testing my arm. Rivulets of blood stream downward, soaking my clothes beneath my armor, beneath the farmer's clothes I wear over it all. Sweat rolls down my back, but I have no time to rest, no time to gather myself or assess my injuries.

Another Enlightened pulls the dirt up over my feet. I throw my sword, grunting at the pain in my arm. The blade hits hard, plunges into his chest, knocking him back, and the dirt stops writhing.

I rip my boots free, wincing at the pain in my leg. My head rings with the clash of swords, the screams of my Sword Siblings. Blood soaks the ground, and bodies lie broken, more ours than theirs.

Turning in place, I search for Lessiyara, hating how easily we got separated, but two Enlightened close in on me, cutting off my search.

Chapter Thirty Nine
Lessiyara

"Sihetva can be your greatest friend, your confidante.
Share your life with it whenever you can."
- The half-remembered teachings of Da

All around me, Enlightened bend Sihetva to their will, forcing it to slaughter Children of the Sword.

Ronan cries out, and I seek him. My eyes bulge out of their sockets when I find him, standing amidst blood and battle. A spear of ice sticks through his arm, another from his thigh.

Tears prick at my eyes, and I buck, gasping, desperate.

Berinasten comes into view, looming over me. He sneers, finally showing the monster he truly is, and grips his hands tighter. My earthen prison contracts, squeezing the life from me.

Darkness closes in around me, and Father starts to fade.

Sihetva, please...

Take my offering.

It burns around me, and even now, I feel its hesitation to risk my life.

I'm already dying. Please...

I offer my body up, yet again.

And this time, Sihetva flows through me.

My veins burn, and a scream rips through me. Lightning blooms on my skin, arcing and scorching the roots that bind me until they fall away. The air crackles and rumbles, and the hairs rise on the back of my neck.

Fury boils my veins, curling my hands into fists. I rise to my feet, body burning with living lightning.

And I don't bother with my sword.

I lunge at Berinasten, knocking him to the ground. Energy flows through me, flows outward into the world. It singes every fiber of my being, but I grit my teeth against the pain, relishing the result.

All around, Sihetva moves free, striking Enlightened down with bolts of lightning and water drawn from the air just to fill their lungs.

It takes them down, left and right.

But it lets me have Berinasten, knows how much I need this.

I straddle him, gripping his face with sparking palms. He screams, writhing beneath me, and I savor his agony.

I ask Sihetva to pull the earth over his arms, to wrap vines over his throat, and it obliges happily. The energy around me buzzes, singing with anticipation as Berinasten thrashes.

I place a hand on his chest piece and lean forward, peering into a face of seared flesh scarred with snaking lines.

He holds my gaze, blue eyes wide.

"Ma and Da deserved better. *I* deserved better." The words come out a hiss, forced through teeth gritted against pain.

Sihetva burns brighter, and the lightning on my hand grows. His leathers burst into flames and burn away. The metal beneath crackles and glows as the lightning sings through it. His flesh sizzles and cracks and pops.

He cries out once more, but the sound comes out hoarse, ragged with smoke that pours from cracked lips.

I strike his chest, and when I lift my hands, Sihetva drives a spike of stone upward. His metal chest piece, already weakened, ruptures outward. Blood gushes from the wound, pouring out around the stone, and my heart races.

I stare at him, eyes as lifeless as ever.

Sihetva releases the lightning from my skin, but my veins still burn. Its energy moves through me, tearing me open, burning me from the inside out.

My eyes flutter, and my arms hang heavy at my sides. Darkness closes in, and I topple sideways.

"Lessiyara!" Ronan cries, somewhere far away.

And the world fades to black.

Chapter Forty
Ronan

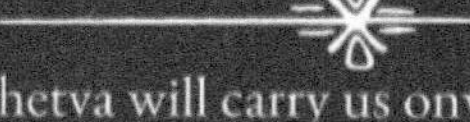

"Sihetva will carry us onward, keep us close, even if we part."
- The half-remembered teachings of Da

A stone spike rises from the earth to impale the man advancing on me, and my heart plummets. The ice spears evaporate, leaving small holes in my arm and leg.

But there's only one way that could happen, only one way Sihetva could freely aid us.

My veins run cold, and fear slices through me.

"No... Please, don't do it," I beg.

But it's already too late.

Sihetva swirls in the air around us, wild and free. It burns the armor from Enlightened, strikes them down with spears and spikes. It sends lightning crackling through them, wrenches the air from them in great, visible gusts.

It has its revenge, its freedom, and they fall all around me.

I turn, searching the battlefield for Lessiyara, peering over fallen Enlightened and bloodied Children of the Sword. My mouth goes dry when I see her, and my legs wobble beneath me.

Living lightning ripples over her, Sihetva's purest form, and she straddles Berinasten. The man lies limp, chest broken open with a stone spike, body a charred heap. The snaking roots of lightning line his burnt skin and smoking clothes.

It recedes from her, leaving her untouched, but I know the pain that comes from letting Sihetva run through you unbridled.

I take off at a sprint, leaping over bodies. Panic pushes the pain in my leg from my mind, and I surge toward her.

Her eyes flutter, and her arms fall limp at her sides. That beautiful blue gaze deserts us all as her eyes fall shut, and she topples sideways to lie beside Berinasten.

"Lessiyara!" I scream, closing the final distance between us.

My sword and shield fall to the ground somewhere along the way, forgotten and abandoned. I skid to a stop, dropping to her side on the bloodstained earth. My heart sticks in my throat, and my eyes prick with the promise of tears.

I lean over her, pull her into my arms. She lolls in my embrace, limp and barely breathing. Blood speckles her face, soaks her hair. I touch her snow-white cheek, and her skin nearly burns me.

My lungs falter.

"Lessiyara," I choke. "Please, wake up."

Dark lashes fan over her cheeks, unmoving. Bowing over her, I press my forehead to hers, begging Sihetva to help her, to bring her back.

"Please," I whisper, voice hoarse as tears fall free.

I rock her back and forth, and she rolls in my arms, mouth hanging open. My stomach twists at the sight, so I touch her neck, holding her steady.

A gentle hand touches my back, and a few whispered words crash over me. I shake them off, heart splitting open as I cradle Lessiyara to my chest. Her breasts still rise with shallow breaths, and I gulp back a sob.

"Ronan," the voice comes again, more insistent.

A hand comes into view, touches Lessiyara's neck, and I tear my eyes from her slack face. Tivasta kneels before me, eyes pinched with worry.

"She's still with us," she says. "We have to get her to a healer."

I nod, swallowing, trying to force back the lump in my throat.

Pushing myself to my feet, I lift her easily, cringing at the way her arms flop. I wince as pain bursts through my arm, and I nearly drop her. But I reposition her in my grip, holding her tight.

Her head lolls as I run to the healer's house, and my leg screams with agony. But I grit my teeth, pushing through it to save her.

Tivasta follows, choking back sobs the whole way. She falls behind, unable to keep up, but I know where I'm going, having spent far too much time there myself this last year.

The village blurs around me, and my heart races, drowning out the sounds of my footfalls. In the distance, the air fills with the sounds of villagers celebrating news of the end of battle, news of Berinasten's death. Bitterness swirls in my stomach.

They have no idea what it cost.

I careen around a corner, spraying small rocks from the path as I lope to Vilashi's house. The small cottage waits, just ahead, and my breath catches with relief as I draw near.

The door swings open, and she waves me in. The permanent lines which crease her face carve themselves deeper.

I turn, careful not to hit Lessiyara's head on the door frame.

"You know where to go," Vilashi says, voice creaking.

I move through her home to the little room in the back, passing the hearth and countless bundles of herbs hung from the eaves. Leaning my weight onto my good leg, I settle Lessiyara on the bed reserved for incapacitated patients, wiping blood-soaked hair from her face.

Panic grips me, and my heart stutters as I check for a wound that might have coated her so thoroughly. When I find none, I lean over her, cupping her cheeks and weeping with relief.

It must be Berinasten's blood.

Vilashi clears her throat beside me, and I straighten, moving aside to allow her room to work. I explain what happened, words tumbling from my lips, but Vilashi shushes me.

"I know, my dear," she says. Her gray bun bobs as she shakes her head lightly, offering up a sympathetic smile that stops my heart in its tracks. "I can feel the ways Sihetva moves within the body, remember?"

I nod. "I know, I just… What can I do?"

"Fetch me a bowl of water," she says, amber-brown eyes softening. "Heat it by the fire while I gather some herbs."

I rush from the room, casting a single glance back at Lessiyara as I go. Tivasta meets me in the doorway, finally catching up, and her face falls when she takes me in.

***

Vilashi brews tonics and teas, coaxing them into Lessiyara one after another with Sihetva's help to keep her from choking. I watch, transfixed, handing her anything she needs. Tivasta comes and goes, checking in as often as she can while handling the ripples our battle sent through our people.

But Lessiyara doesn't wake, doesn't move of her own will.

Only Sihetva's gentle manipulations of her throat as Vilashi pours another tonic. Only the ragged, halting rise of her chest as she rasps in another breath.

"How long was I like this?" I ask.

"Three days," Vilashi says. Exhaustion hangs on her words, heavy and sad. Then, guessing my motive for asking, she says, "But she's worse than you were."

My heart falters. "So, it'll take longer for her to wake?" I say, voice cracking even at a whisper.

Vilashi doesn't answer immediately, and my stomach drops. Panic churns within me, and Sihetva swirls in fractured, uneven currents in the air around us.

Finally, Vilashi says, "She…" Her voice breaks, and she closes her eyes for a beat before continuing. "The lightning did little to her body that our eyes can see. But inside, she suffered."

The room grows cold, and I feel Sihetva shifting in fear.

"I'll do everything I can, but it may be a while if she wakes."

My blood runs cold at that 'if,' and I reach for Lessiyara's hand, gripping it tight. The color drains from the world as I stare at her lifeless face, every bit the mask she used to slip on to hide.

A sob breaks through me, and I shudder.

***

Coren comes to call as night falls, settling my freshly cleaned sword and shield in a corner. Her stomach sticks out, still carefully shielding her baby from the world. Her husband deposits Lessiyara's weapons there as well, leaning them against mine.

I trace the lines of them with my gaze, wishing they'd been more effective if only to have avoided this.

Coren drags a chair into Lessiyara's room when Vilashi administers a tonic that must run its course for the night. She pushes the chair against the backs of my legs, saying, "Please, sit so Vilashi can tend to you."

I shake my head, but Coren stares me down. "Vilashi *just said* Lessiyara's care is done for the moment. I wouldn't have said anything otherwise. Now, sit."

She pushes the chair against my legs again, and pain bursts through my thigh, radiating from the hole in my flesh. I suck in a breath as I crumple into the chair, smacking my bicep on the armrest.

My teeth grind together, and I mutter, "Thanks."

"You're welcome," she says, voice far too bright. She gentles, adding, "And sorry."

In the other room, her husband clatters pots and pans, making something on the hearth. Vilashi kneels before me, knees popping and grinding. I wince for her, but she barely acknowledges it, making me wonder what tincture she's brewed for herself.

Her shears sparkle in the candlelight as she cuts the fabric of my trousers, exposing a circular hole in my thigh, perfectly edged and dark with dried blood. She nods slowly, inspecting the wound, then cuts at my sleeve, widening the tear left behind by the spear. Another perfectly round hole, this one all the way through.

"They missed the bone," she says, rising and putting the shears away. "You're lucky on that account. You would've felt a chill for months if they'd struck just a finger's width over."

I grimace at the thought.

She sorts through tinctures and salves, clinking jars and canisters together at the hutch in the corner. "Where did I put that…" she mutters.

I lean back in my chair, closing my eyes against the pain that seems worse now that I've seen the wounds and acknowledged their existence. I take deep breaths, half-tempted to focus on the pain just to forget my worries over Lessiyara's survival, even if only for a moment.

"Here it is," Vilashi says. "Now, I'd ask if you want to go to another room, a room that isn't already full of blood, but I don't see it happening."

I shake my head, opening my eyes to watch her settle a stool next to me. She lays jars, linen, and a candle on another stool. Pulling a cloth from her shoulder, she pours liquid from one of the jars onto the linen, filling the room with the pungent aroma of some astringent or other. My nose scrunches at the stench of it.

She dabs the cloth at the tender skin around the wound on my thigh, cleaning the dried blood away, and pain radiates through me at even that gentle pressure. I clench my hands into fists, wincing as my injured arm protests the movement.

Vilashi takes the jar in hand, cradling the cloth underneath the wound with one hand and pouring the astringent over my thigh. I hiss out a breath, gripping the armrest with my good arm, nails digging into the wood.

But the burn is short-lived.

I pull a deep, shuddering breath into lungs that have seen far too much abuse today.

With a new rag, she cleans my arm, and I nearly break the chair as my hand squeezes the armrest. "Damn it all," I hiss, voice tight, when the astringent pours over and through my wound.

Vilashi sits up, considering me. Her dark eyes narrow as they rake over me. She nods slowly, then rises to go to the hutch again.

"Coren, would you come here please?"

My sister rises from the floor near me, where I'd completely forgotten she sat, blinded by the agony of my injuries.

"Would you take a leaf out of that canister for me? I'd rather not touch it with blood on my hands," Vilashi says.

I listen as Coren does as the healer bids, retrieving a leaf here, a flower there. The jars and canisters bump together, tinkling melodically, and I close my eyes. Exhaustion settles over me, and I wish for sleep.

But my nerves wind tighter with every breath, and my eyes only stay closed for a few heartbeats before snapping open to check on Lessiyara.

The grating of stone on stone draws my gaze, and I turn to find my sister grinding ingredients together with a mortar and pestle. Under Vilashi's tutelage, she mixes the paste into a cup of water, then carries it over to me.

"You should drink this," Vilashi says. "It'll induce sleep. You need it to recover, yes, but it'll also make the stitches more tolerable." Her lips curve up in a wry smile as she adds, "For both of us."

I chuckle, but my eyes stray to Lessiyara.

Can I take the rest I'm offered?

"She's stable for now," Vilashi says. "If anything changes, I'll wake you."

I lean forward, cupping Lessiyara's face with one hand.

She doesn't move.

My insides churn, and I close my eyes, blowing out a breath. I press a kiss to her forehead, then rise on shaky legs, letting Vilashi lead me to the next room. My horns brush bundles of herbs along the way, leaving them swaying in my wake.

I settle on the edge of the bed in the corner, then take the cup Coren offers with a soft smile. The sweet liquid goes down smooth, and I lay back, waiting for darkness to claim me.

***

I wake to Coren singing softly in the chair by my bed. She stops when I sit up, setting her stitching aside.

Groaning, I rub a hand over my face, then eye the stitches on my leg and arm. "I'm glad Vilashi did these," I say. "If you'd done it, they'd heal in zig-zags somehow."

She scowls, but light dances in her eyes. "I'm so glad you're awake…" she teases.

But her light tone and the smile that follow do nothing to spare me the onslaught of memories, the rending feeling in my chest. The sight of Lessiyara, broken and covered in Berinasten's blood, eyes closed to the world, washes over me, and I cradle my head in my hands.

An empty future spreads out before me, reaches for me.

I could've had a family.

A life.

Berinasten's gone, and I finally have someone I want to build a life with, but...

My throat closes over a sob.

Coren rubs my back in slow circles. I crumple forward, wincing at the pain in my arm, in my leg, but the pain inside is so much worse. My shoulders shake as I sob, harder than Lessiyara would ever believe. My lungs heave, and my heart tears into pieces.

"Sh…" Coren whispers.

The bed sags beneath her weight as she sits beside me. She wraps her arms around me, pulling me close, and I lean against her as well as I can with her belly in the way. The baby shifts, and her stomach ripples against me.

But even that doesn't warm my heart.

My mind fills with the child I may never have, the child Lessiyara may never have, and another sob bursts from me.

"Come," Coren says. "You should see her. She's a little better than she was last night."

I lift my head to peer at my sister, unable to believe it. Hope sparks within me.

She must see it because she says, "She isn't completely better. But her breaths sound less painful."

I close my eyes, hating the sight of a world so cruel, the thought of a life so tortured.

After all she's suffered already, she shouldn't suffer more.

Sihetva hangs heavy and still in the air around us, stagnant in its repentance. But I know as well as it does that Lessiyara had no other chance at life. From what my Sword Siblings said when they visited last night, Berinasten would've killed her.

Coren hands me a crutch to keep the weight off my bad leg, then leads me to Lessiyara's room. I sink into the chair by her bed, taking up her hand and letting the crutch lean against the wall.

Her chest rises with slow breaths, drawn out far too long, but they don't rasp, don't grate through her lips.

A gust of air rushes from me, and my shoulders fall.

Throughout the day, Coren administers salves to my wounds, and Vilashi stops in frequently to coerce more tonics into Lessiyara. Each time, Sihetva wraps around her in silent apology, warming Lessiyara and smoothing her hair with gentle breezes.

And my heart cracks, just a bit more.

When Vilashi leaves once more to help the other healers with wounded Children of the Sword, Coren sits with me, telling me of the plans for the baby.

She only leaves me briefly when her husband comes to visit, and their whispers carry from the next room.

He cleans the battlefield of bodies, delivering news to families.

And I certainly don't envy him the task.

***

Tivasta sits by Lessiyara's bedside with me, holding her hand as the sun sets. I recline in the corner at Lessiyara's head. My arm rests on the bed beside her, fingers combing through her hair.

"Vahken and I have assembled a group to go up the mountain," Tivasta says. "To broker peace with the remaining Vaikahlen people on the terms that they do not enslave Sihetva at any point in the future."

I nod, barely paying attention to her words. She mentions taking Vahken for ease of navigation, since he can sense Sihetva as Lessiyara does, then goes on to list the people accompanying them, but my mind drifts.

Coren comes in, and Tivasta offers up her seat. "Sit, please."

I lean my head back against the wall, rolling it to the side. My eyes trace Lessiyara's features. Thick black lashes fan out over her alabaster cheeks. I brush a strand of snow-white hair from her forehead, tucking it behind her ear.

Movement draws my attention. A flutter of eyelashes. A subtle shift of her eyes beneath her lids.

I sit up, leaning in. My heart hammers, and I hold my breath, waiting, begging, for her to wake.

Her eyes roam under her lids, and I whisper, "Lessiyara? I'm here. Please, come back to me."

Sihetva stirs in the air around us, fawning over her, smoothing her clothes with gentle breezes.

Her lips part, but no sound emerges. Her eyes sweep side to side beneath her lids, but never open.

"Lessiyara?" I whisper, voice breaking.

She goes still, exhaling softly, smoothly.

I drop my head to rest beside hers, and my tears soak into the pillow. Tivasta rubs my back, but her breath hitches right alongside mine.

***

Two days pass, and despite Vilashi's assurances that her condition is improving, Lessiyara doesn't move. I wait, brushing Lessiyara's hair, helping care for her when Vilashi isn't cleaning or treating my wounds.

Sihetva mourns, chilling the air, but I can't be sure if it mourns out of regret or for Lessiyara's coming death. My heart twists at the thought, and I lean over her, smoothing her hair.

"Come," Vilashi whispers. "Her tonics need time to work, and I need to change your dressings."

"Can you do that here?" I plead.

But as she's said every time I've asked, she says, "There isn't room."

And there isn't.

The little table is full of tonic bottles and jars of salves that Vilashi applies to Lessiyara's hands at what seem to be random intervals. Vilashi's stool sits next to Lessiyara's bed, as does my chair, and the only other space in the room is occupied by the hutch full of healing herbs and equipment.

I sigh, pushing myself to my feet. The crutch slips under my arm easily, and I limp to the next room with my heart in my throat.

***

Coren rouses me as the sun's first light peeks in through the shutters. "Vilashi wants to dress your wounds," she says.

I groan, pulling my blanket up over my head. "Can't it wait? At least until the light is full."

Truth be told, I don't care about the light, don't care how early it is. I'm just not ready to stomach another day of staring at Lessiyara's unmoving form.

"She said it had to be now," Coren says, voice full of confusion and apology.

With a sigh, I sit up and ease myself off the bed. Nodding, I tell Coren to send her in.

Vilashi works quickly, spreading a numbing salve over the wounds before poking and prodding to check their progress. She slathers some poultice or other over the stitches, then wraps clean linen around my arm and leg.

"Alright, now come on," she says, voice urgent.

And finally, I look at her.

My heart leaps into my throat as worry constricts my chest.

But Vilashi wears a smile.

She hands me my crutch, leading me to Lessiyara's room with hurried steps, paying no mind to the bundles of herbs her horns set to swinging from the rafters.

My palms sweat, and a tiny ember of hope burns within me.

Is today the day?

Please, let her wake.

I swallow nervously, but when Vilashi steps aside to take up residence in the corner, Lessiyara looks the same.

The air rushes out of me, and my shoulders droop.

"Sit," Vilashi says, pulling the chair out for me.

I take my seat, leaning my crutch against the wall. My hand finds Lessiyara's, thumb moving slowly over her soft skin.

Her fingers tighten around mine.

My heart lodges itself in my throat, and I hold my breath, terrified to move, to speak, to breathe, lest I take the air she needs to wake.

Her eyes flutter open, showing brilliant blue to the world for the first time in far too long.

Tears prick at the corners of my eyes, sliding down over my cheeks. A sob bursts from me, and I lean forward, careful not to jostle her hand.

"Lessiyara?" I breathe, voice breaking.

She turns her head, wincing at the pain I remember all too well from my time as a funnel. But when she meets my gaze, she smiles, eyes dancing with the early morning light.

Chapter Forty One
Lessiyara

"Free of the snows and coldest eyes,
Free of worry, the sun does shine"
- The half-remembered songs of Ma

My body burns, and every movement sends searing pain through me. But when Vilashi bids me sip another tonic, I drink whatever she gives me.

My eyes dart to Ronan with every other heartbeat, unwilling to tear themselves away from him for long. He holds my hand gently, keeping it steady, and I wonder how fresh the memories of this pain are for him.

I take a deep breath as Vilashi holds a hand to my back and stifle the scream that begs to rip through my throat at the pain of even breathing.

But I'm alive.

Tears trickle over my cheeks, and though my body protests, I grip Ronan's hand a little tighter.

Tivasta rushes in, sobbing as she closes the distance. A smile plays on her lips, and she moves to throw her arms around me.

I brace myself.

"Careful," Vilashi warns. "She's still in a great deal of pain."

I blow out a slow, controlled breath, thankful for her insight. "It's okay," I whisper, voice strained by the agony of moving my throat, my tongue, my lips.

Gently, Tivasta leans over me, wrapping her arms around me as if I may break, and it feels like I just might.

But I lift my arm, pressing my free hand gently to her back, gritting my teeth and sucking a breath through them.

Her dark hair tickles my cheek, stinging me with even such a slight touch, and her tears fall on my shoulder. She shakes as she sobs, and I cringe as my entire body comes alive with pain. My torso strains to balance me, and every involuntary movement sends lightning sparking through my veins.

But I don't care.

I hug my aunt. I squeeze Ronan's hand. I even smile at Coren, my maybe someday sister.

Because even though it hurts, I'm alive.

***

The moon fills before I'm moved from Vilashi's house. It wanes before I can slip from the bed I share with Ronan. My legs cry out, wobbling beneath me, and he steadies me with a gentle touch.

"Are you sure?" he asks. "Another few days might be best."

"I'm sure."

"Do you want me to carry you?" he asks.

I shake my head. "You need to rest your arm and your leg."

"You need to rest more than that," he says, teasing. But I see the concern that lines his eyes.

"I know," I say. "But I need to do this."

He nods and follows me out of his house, *our* house. Agonizingly slow, we hobble through the village. People smile at us as we pass, and several offer to help us along our way.

But I don't want anyone else there when we reach our destination.

Only Ronan.

They seem to understand when we tell them where we're limping off to and give us the space I need.

The grass cradles my feet as we cross between fields, and the graveyard gardens come into view. I pick my way between patches of flowers, lovingly attended, until I find my parents.

Ma's flowers bloom, feathery petals open to the gentle early spring sun. Da's buds are just beginning to grow in size, dark crimson petals still closed up tight.

Ronan offers me a hand.

Moving slowly, I grit my teeth against the pain and kneel at their grave. My body burns, and the echoes of lightning sweep through me. But my knees hit the soft earth. I go still, controlling my breaths and letting the pain ease.

A single tear slips out, but I resist the urge to blink, to wipe it away, knowing the movement will only bring more agony.

Ronan releases my hand, and I slowly lower it to the earth. I gasp as the pain burns through me, but even that movement, that sharp breath, twists a knife in my chest.

But I have something to say, something to tell my parents.

"He's gone," I whisper. "Thank you for loving me while you could."

Sihetva moves gently through the leaves, tucking my hair behind my ear, so I don't have to move.

And I whisper, "Thank you," to my oldest friend.

Epilogue
Lessiyara

"Weep not, my child, for we may always
light a flame for our lost loves."
- The wise words of Tivasta

Ronan opens the door, and Tivasta breezes in. I smile up at her from my chair near the hearth. Suppressing a groan, I scoot forward.

But Ronan rushes back to my side, letting Tivasta close the door. He slips an arm around my waist, helping me up.

"You don't have to get up," Tivasta says. "I can set them up."

But I need to do this.

I shake my head, sending ripples of pain through my body.

"So stubborn, darling niece," Tivasta says, voice teasing.

But she knows why I rise.

She pushes a dark braid back over her shoulders, then tugs off her backpack. From it, she retrieves a few linen-wrapped packages.

She unwraps two candles and offers them to me. Ronan reaches out, taking them to spare me the pain of moving,, and settles them on the mantle next to his.

Two more linen-wrapped packages come out, but Ronan doesn't rush to take these. They fall into my hands, shockingly light. With a deep breath, I unwrap the linen, wincing with each movement.

Tiny wooden figurines of Ma and Da rest in my palm, delicate and beautiful. I stare at the intricate details, blinking away tears.

Ma's gentle smile peeks out, tentative yet warm. Da's eyes crinkle with mirth, and his braids flow behind him, frozen in an unseen wind.

"They're perfect…" I whisper.

"They match mine," Tivasta says, voice thick with emotion.

My lungs hitch, and I smooth a finger over them. Blowing out a breath, I step up to the mantle. My arms shake as I reach up, settling them next to their candles.

Kneeling, Ronan holds a twig into the fire until the end catches, then hands it to me. With a deep breath, I hold it up, lighting the flames of my parents' candles for the first time.

How many times has Tivasta lit candles for them?

How many times should I have done so?

I close my eyes, head falling forward. Because I should've thought of them more, should've had candles to light each time.

My heart skips a beat, and Ronan wraps his arms around me. Reaching out for Tivasta, I take her hand.

Sihetva swirls around me, warm and comforting.

And then I feel them. I hear the echoes of my mother's song in the wind, see the glow of my father's eyes in the fire.

A lump forms in my throat, but I greet my parents, held safely in Sihetva's embrace.

Thank you!

For buying this book. For reading it all the way through.

If you liked it, please leave a review on Amazon, Goodreads, Barnes & Noble, your blog... Anywhere, really. Reviews are the lifeblood of authors, helping books get noticed in the almighty eyes of search engine algorithms. Even if only a few words, a review is incredibly helpful.

And if you're eager to stay up to date on the latest dark fiction by Elexis Bell, sign up for her newsletter here:

http://eepurl.com/gnTZwf

Other Books by this Author

Literary Fantasy Novels

Soul Bearer

The Gem of Meruna

A Heart of Salt & Silver

Allmother Rising

A Blessed Darkness

Literary Thriller Novellas

Annabelle

Things Left Unsaid

Literary Post-Apocalyptic Novel

World for the Broken

About the Author

Elexis Bell is a quiet nerd with too many hobbies, including everything from gaming to shower-singing and even archery, weather permitting. She specializes in sarcasm and writing stories that make people feel. She's made a home for herself with her husband and a small army of cats.

She writes dark, gritty stories, sprinkling gut-wrenching emotions over high fantasy romance, thrillers, post-apocalyptic romance, and science fiction.

For further information, follow her on Instagram, Twitter, or Facebook, or check out her blog on her website. There, you can sign up for her newsletter to stay up to date on all future book releases, giveaways, and ongoing projects.

www.elexisbell.com

www.ingramcontent.com/pod-product-compliance
Lightning Source LLC
Chambersburg PA
CBHW030606310726
48979CB00003B/587

* 9 7 8 1 9 5 1 3 3 5 2 2 9 *